the River Knows

By Jayne Ann Krentz
writing as Amanda Quick

Second Sight
Lie by Moonlight
Wait Until Midnight
The Paid Companion
Late for the Wedding
Don't Look Back
Slightly Shady
Wicked Widow
I Thee Wed
With This Ring
Affair
Mischief
Mystique
Mistress
Deception
Desire
Dangerous
Reckless
Ravished
Rendezvous
Scandal
Surrender
Seduction

Other titles
by Jayne Ann Krentz

White Lies
All Night Long
Falling Awake
Truth or Dare
Light in Shadow
Summer in Eclipse Bay
Smoke in Mirrors
Dawn in Eclipse Bay
Lost & Found
Eclipse Bay
Soft Focus
Eye of the Beholder
Flash
Sharp Edges
Deep Waters
Absolutely, Positively
Trust Me
Grand Passion
Hidden Talents
Wildest Hearts
Family Man
Perfect Partners
Sweet Fortune
Silver Linings
The Golden Chance

By Jayne Ann Krentz
writing as Jayne Castle

Ghost Hunter
After Glow
Harmony
After Dark
Amaryllis
Zinnia
Orchid

the River Knows

AMANDA QUICK

DOUBLEDAY LARGE PRINT HOME LIBRARY EDITION

G. P. PUTNAM'S SONS
New York

This Large Print Edition, prepared especially for Doubleday Large Print Home Library, contains the complete, unabridged text of the original Publisher's Edition.

PUTNAM

G. P. PUTNAM'S SONS
Publishers Since 1838
Published by the Penguin Group
Penguin Group (USA) Inc., 375 Hudson Street, New York, New York 10014, USA • Penguin Group (Canada), 90 Eglinton Avenue East, Suite 700, Toronto, Ontario M4P 2Y3, Canada (a division of Pearson Penguin Canada Inc.) • Penguin Books Ltd, 80 Strand, London WC2R 0RL, England • Penguin Ireland, 25 St Stephen's Green, Dublin 2, Ireland (a division of Penguin Books Ltd) • Penguin Group (Australia), 250 Camberwell Road, Camberwell, Victoria 3124, Australia (a division of Pearson Australia Group Pty Ltd) • Penguin Books India Pvt Ltd, 11 Community Centre, Panchsheel Park, New Delhi–110 017, India • Penguin Group (NZ), 67 Apollo Drive, Mairangi Bay, Auckland 1311, New Zealand (a division of Pearson New Zealand Ltd) • Penguin Books (South Africa) (Pty) Ltd, 24 Sturdee Avenue, Rosebank, Johannesburg 2196, South Africa

Penguin Books Ltd, Registered Offices:
80 Strand, London WC2R 0RL, England

Published simultaneously in Canada

ISBN 978-0-7394-8172-1

Printed in the United States of America

This is a work of fiction. Names, characters, places, and incidents either are the product of the author's imagination or are used fictitiously, and any resemblance to actual persons, living or dead, businesses, companies, events, or locales is entirely coincidental.

While the author has made every effort to provide telephone numbers and Internet addresses at the time of publication, neither the publisher nor the author assumes any responsibility for errors, or for changes that occur after publication. Further, the publisher does not have any control over and does not assume any responsibility for author or third-party websites or their content.

This Large Print Book carries the Seal of Approval of N.A.V.H.

This one is for Susan Elizabeth Phillips: great writer and a member of the sisterhood. Here's to friendship.

the River Knows

PROLOGUE

Late in the reign of Queen Victoria . . .

She did not dare turn up any of the lamps for fear that some passerby would notice the light and remember it later when the police came around asking questions. The fog was thickening outside in the lane, but there was still enough moonlight slanting through the window to illuminate the tiny parlor, not that she needed the cold silver light. She knew the cozy rooms above the shop as well as she knew her own name. This small space had been her home for nearly two years.

She crouched in front of the heavy trunk in the corner and tried to insert the key into the lock. The task proved incredibly difficult because her hands were shaking so terribly.

She forced herself to take a deep breath in a futile attempt to slow her pounding heart. After three fumbling tries she finally got the trunk open. The squeaks of the hinges sounded like small screams in the deathly silence.

She reached inside and took out the two leather-bound volumes she had stored there. Rising, she carried the books back across the room and placed them in the little suitcase. There were dozens more books downstairs in the shop, several of which would have fetched nice prices, but these two were far and away the most valuable.

She had to limit the number of books she took with her; books were heavy. Even if she could have carried several more it would have been unwise to do so. A large quantity of valuable volumes missing from the shelves downstairs might arouse suspicion.

For similar reasons she had packed only a minimal amount of clothing. It would not do for the police to discover that a supposed suicide had taken most of her wardrobe with her into the river.

She closed the bulging suitcase. Thank heavens she had not sold the two volumes. There had certainly been times during the past two years when she could have used the money, but she had been unable to bring herself to let go of the books her father had treasured the most. They were all she had left, not only of him, but of her mother who had died four years earlier.

Her father had never really recovered from the loss of his beloved wife. No one had been greatly surprised when he put a pistol to his head following a devastating financial loss. The creditors had taken the comfortable house and most of its contents. Mercifully, they had deemed the vast and distinguished library of little value.

When she had found herself facing the customary career choices available to women in her position—a miserable life as a paid companion or a governess—she had used the books to do the unthinkable and, in Society's opinion, the unforgivable: She had gone into trade.

In the eyes of the Polite World, it was as though she had magically ceased to exist. Not that she had ever been acquainted with anyone from that world. The Barclay family had never moved in Society.

Her knowledge of book collecting and collectors, garnered from her father, had made it possible to begin turning a small profit after only a few months in business. In the two years that the shop had been open she had succeeded in establishing herself as a small but successful dealer of rare books.

Her new life, with its sensible wardrobe, journals of accounts, and extensive business correspondence, was a long way from the comfortable, genteel world in which she had been raised, but she had discovered that owning and operating her own shop was deeply satisfying. There was a great deal to be said for having control over one's finances. In addition, as a shopkeeper she had at long last been freed from many of the stultifying rules and restrictions that Society placed on well-bred single ladies. There was no denying that she had gone down in the world, but the experience had allowed her to take command of her own destiny in a way that had never before been possible.

Less than an hour ago, however, the dream of a bright, independent new future that she had begun to fashion for herself had been destroyed. She was now in the midst of a nightmare. She had no choice but to flee into the shadows, taking only a handful of personal items, the day's income from book sales, and the two precious books.

She must disappear—she understood that quite clearly—but she had to ensure that no one would feel compelled to search for her. Her feverish inspiration came from a report in the press that she had read a few days earlier.

. . . For the second time in less than a week the Polite World mourns the shocking loss of a socially prominent lady. Sadly, the river has claimed another victim.

Mrs. Victoria Hastings, said to be overcome by one of her recurrent bouts of despondency, threw herself off a bridge into the cold, merciless depths of the Thames. The body has not yet been recovered. Authorities speculate that it was either washed out to sea or else became tangled in some sunken wreckage. Her devoted husband, Elwin Hastings, is reported to be distraught with grief.

Readers will recall that less than a week ago, Miss Fiona Risby, the fiancée of Mr. Anthony Stalbridge, also cast her-

self into the river. Her body, however, was recovered . . .

Two ladies who moved in the Polite World had thrown themselves into the river in the same week. In addition, each year desperate and depressed women from far less exalted stations sought the same escape. No one would think it peculiar when it was discovered that an unimportant bookshop owner had committed suicide in a similar fashion.

She wrote the suicide note with trembling fingers, concentrating hard to find the right words, *convincing* words.

. . . I despair. I cannot live with the knowledge of what I have done this night, nor can I face a future that offers only the humiliation of a public trial and the hangman's noose. Better by far the ultimate oblivion of the river . . .

She signed her name and put the note on the small table where she had been in the habit of taking her solitary meals. She anchored the piece of paper with a small bust of Shakespeare. It wouldn't do to have it fall to the floor and perhaps go unnoticed by the police.

She put on her cloak and took one last look around the sitting room. She had been content here. True, the loneliness was sometimes hard to bear, especially at night, but one became accustomed to it. She had been thinking of getting a dog for companionship.

She turned away and picked up the heavy suitcase. Once again she hesitated. There were two hats hanging on hooks in the wall: a summer bonnet and a large-brimmed, feather-trimmed affair that she wore when she went out walking. It struck her that it might be a very good thing—a very *convincing* thing—if the feathered hat turned up floating near a bridge, perhaps snagged on a rock or a bit of drifting wood. She seized the hat and clapped it on her head.

Her gaze went to the curtain that concealed the bedroom. Another shudder slammed through her at the thought of what lay on the other side.

Clutching the suitcase, she hurried downstairs and into the back room. She opened the door and stepped outside into the dark alley. There was no reason to bother with a key. The lock had been shattered less than an hour ago when the intruder had forced his way inside.

She went cautiously along the alley, trusting to her memory of the narrow passage behind the row of shops.

With luck it would be a few days before anyone started to wonder why Barclay's Bookshop had remained closed for an extended period of time. But sooner or later someone—her landlord, most likely—would become alarmed. Mr. Jenkins would pound on the door for a time. Eventually he would grow angry. He would take one of the keys from the ring that he always carried and open up the shop, demanding the rent.

That was when the body in the upstairs room would be discovered. Shortly thereafter, the police would begin their search for the woman who had murdered Lord Gavin, one of the wealthiest, most distinguished gentlemen in the Polite World.

She fled into the night.

1

One year and two months later . . .

The mysterious widow had vanished again.

Anthony Stalbridge prowled slowly along the shadowy hallway, watching for a crack of telltale light beneath a door. All of the rooms appeared to be unoccupied, but he knew she had to be somewhere in the vicinity. A few minutes ago he had caught a glimpse of her disappearing up the dark flight of servants' stairs.

He had given her a little time before following her up the cramped staircase. When he emerged on the bedroom floor, however, Mrs. Bryce was nowhere in sight.

The muffled strains of a waltz and the dull roar of champagne-inspired conversation emanated from the ballroom. The ground floor of the Hastings mansion was ablaze with lights and crowded with elegantly attired guests, but up here there was only the dim glow of an occasional wall sconce and an ominous silence.

The house was a large one, but the only occupants were Elwin Hastings; his very new, very rich, very young bride; and the staff. The servants slept below stairs. That meant that most of the bedrooms on this floor would be empty.

Vacant bedrooms at a large party sometimes proved tempting to guests in search of a location suitable for an illicit tryst. Had Mrs. Bryce come up here to meet a man? For some obscure reason he did not care to contemplate that possibility too closely. Not that he had any claim on her. They had shared a few dances and some cautious, excruciatingly polite conversation at various social affairs this past week. That was the extent of their formal association. But his intuition—not to mention every masculine instinct he possessed—had warned him that in reality they were engaged in a reckless fencing match. It was a match he had no intention of losing.

Since their first meeting, Louisa Bryce had

done her best to discourage his attentions, verbally at least. That was not entirely unexpected, of course, given the old scandal linked to his name. What intrigued him was that she seemed to go out of her way to put off every other man in the room at every party she attended.

He was a man of the world. He knew that there were some women who were not attracted to men in a sexual manner, but, on the few occasions when he had coaxed Louisa out onto the dance floor and into his arms, he had been convinced that she was as sensually aware of him as he was of her. The waltz was an excellent test for that sort of thing. Then, again, perhaps he was deluding himself for the oldest reason in the world: He wanted her.

She could not know that her scholarly gold-rimmed spectacles, unfashionable gowns, and earnest, painfully dull conversation only served to fascinate him. The studious, boring veneer was so manifestly fraudulent. He had to admit, however, that it appeared to be quite effective on the rest of Society. Her name was not connected to that of any gentleman. He had made a point of confirming that fact, discreetly, of course.

As far as he could tell, Louisa was not involved in an intimate liaison with a man.

The lady was most certainly a mystery, and one of the most mysterious things about her was her stealthy curiosity concerning their host tonight, Elwin Hastings, and the gentlemen involved in Hastings's new investment consortium.

A door opened at the far end of the hall. He moved into the deep shadow of a small alcove and awaited developments.

Louisa emerged from the room. He could not see her features clearly in the gloom, but he recognized the uninspired maroon gown with its unfashionably small bustle. He also knew the proud tilt of her chin and the graceful set of her shoulders.

In spite of the decidedly indiscreet situation, or perhaps because of it, a hot thrill of desire tightened his lower body. He watched her coming toward him out of the shadows and remembered how she had felt in his arms when he had danced with her a short time ago. She had done her best, as usual, to appear prim and boring, but no amount of stilted conversation could disguise the wary intelligence and intriguing challenge in those amber eyes. Nor could any amount of dull chatter detract from the feel of her elegant spine beneath his palm. He wondered if she realized that the harder she tried to discourage him, the more he felt compelled to discover her secrets.

She hurried along the hall, oblivious of his presence, going back toward the servants' stairs. The light from a wall sconce gleamed briefly on the rims of her spectacles. He was debating whether or not to step out into her path and confront her or continue to follow her when a rough voice rumbled from the top of the servants' stairs.

"Who goes there?" a man asked sharply.

It was a demand, not a question, and it was not delivered in the polite, deferential tone of a servant.

Quinby. One of the two guards who accompanied Hastings everywhere lately.

Anthony reached out an arm, seized Louisa as she went past him, and dragged her to a halt.

She turned toward him, mouth opened on a small shriek of startled surprise. Her eyes were very wide. He clamped his free palm over her lips.

"Hush," he said into her ear. "Trust me."

He pulled her tightly to him and kissed her hard enough to enforce silence.

She resisted tensely for a couple of seconds. He deliberately deepened the kiss, demanding a response. Abruptly, she stopped fighting him. In that searing moment of intimate contact something as highly charged and as electrifying as a lightning bolt flashed between them. He knew she was aware of the sensation. He could feel her sudden, shocked reaction. It had nothing to do with the approach of the guard.

Quinby's heavy footsteps sounded in the hall. Anthony swore silently. He wanted nothing more than to continue kissing Louisa. He longed to drag her into the nearest bedroom, put her down on a bed, strip away the spectacles and the plain gown . . .

"What are you two doing up here?" Quinby demanded.

Anthony raised his head. He did not have to pretend a show of reluctance and irritation. Louisa stepped back, frowning as though she, too, was vexed by the interruption. He noticed that behind the lenses of her spectacles her eyes seemed a little unfocused and that she was breathing quickly.

"It seems we have company, my dear," he said evenly.

Quinby was almost upon them. Big and broad-shouldered, he was dressed in a dark overcoat. One of the pockets of the coat sagged with the weight of the object inside. A large, expensive-looking gold-and-onyx ring flashed on one hand.

Louisa rounded on the guard. Anthony sensed that she was unnerved, but she covered her reaction quite admirably by opening her fan with an irritated snap.

"I do not believe we have been introduced," she said in a voice that could have frozen a furnace. Although she was a good deal shorter, she somehow managed to look down her nose at Quinby. "Who are you to accost us?"

"No offense, ma'am," Quinby said, his hard eyes on Anthony, "but no guests are allowed on this floor. I'll see you both back downstairs."

"We do not require an escort," Anthony said coolly. "We know the way."

"Indeed," Louisa said. "We most certainly do."

She collected a handful of her skirts and

made to sweep past Quinby. He reached out and caught her elbow.

She gasped, as though shocked to the core. "How dare you?"

"Beggin' your pardon, ma'am, but before you go, I'm obliged to ask what you were about up here," he said.

She glowered through the lenses of her spectacles. "Take your hand off me immediately, or I shall see to it that Mr. Hastings is informed about this incident."

"He'll be informed about it in any event." Quinby was clearly unruffled by the threat. "It's my job to tell him when this kind of thing happens."

"What kind of thing, for heaven's sake?" she shot back. "Whatever are you implying?"

Anthony looked at Quinby. "Remove your hand from the lady's arm."

Quinby's eyes narrowed. He did not like taking orders, Anthony thought.

"At once," Anthony added very softly.

Quinby released Louisa.

"I'll be needing an answer to my question," he growled, his attention still fixed on Anthony. "Why did you come up here?"

The question was clearly aimed at him,

Anthony realized. Quinby was no longer concerned about Louisa.

Anthony captured Louisa's elbow in a proprietary manner, a lover's manner. "I should have thought the answer is obvious. The lady and I came up here to find some privacy."

He could tell that Louisa was not thrilled with the implications of that explanation, but she clearly knew that she had no alternative other than to follow his lead. To her credit, she did not miss a beat.

"Evidently we shall have to go elsewhere, sir," she said.

"So it appears," Anthony agreed.

He tightened his grip on her elbow, turned her around, and started toward the main staircase.

"Now, see here," Quinby said behind them. "I don't know what you two are about, but—"

"Precisely," Anthony said over his shoulder. "You have no idea at all what my very good friend and I are doing up here, and that is the way it will remain."

"I was hired to keep an eye on things around the mansion," Quinby announced, pursuing them down the hall.

"I understand," Anthony said. "However, the lady and I were unaware that the upper floors of the house were forbidden territory. We certainly saw no signs to that effect."

"Of course there aren't any signs," Quinby growled. "Folks like Mr. Hastings don't go around posting signs in fancy houses like this one."

"Then you can hardly blame us for wandering up here when we concluded that we desired to get away from the crowd downstairs," Anthony said pleasantly.

"Hold on," Quinby said.

Anthony ignored him. "I believe my carriage will provide the seclusion that we are looking for," he said to Louisa in a voice that was loud enough to carry back to Quinby.

She slid him an uncertain look, but mercifully she kept her mouth shut.

They started down the staircase. Quinby stopped at the top. Anthony could feel the guard's eyes boring into his back.

"We'll have to leave now," he said very quietly to Louisa. "If we don't, he will be even more suspicious."

"I came here with Lady Ashton," Louisa said uneasily. Her voice was equally low. "I cannot simply disappear; she'll be frantic."

"I'm sure one of the footmen will be happy to convey a message to her informing her that you left with me."

She stiffened. "I cannot do that, sir."

"I don't see why not. The night is young, and we have so much to talk about, do we not?"

"I do not know what you mean. I appreciate your timely intervention back there in the hall, but it was not at all necessary. I could have handled that man. Now I really must insist—"

"I'm afraid I am the one who must insist. You have aroused my curiosity, you see. I will not be able to rest tonight until I obtain some answers."

She gave him another quick, suspicious look. He smiled, letting her see his resolve. Her expression tightened, but she did not argue further. She was too busy plotting her escape, he thought, timing it, no doubt, to coincide with their arrival back in the ballroom, where the presence of the crowd would discourage a scene.

"You will have to forget any notion you might have of abandoning me, Mrs. Bryce," he said. "One way or another you will allow me to take you home this evening."

"You cannot force me to get into your carriage."

"I wouldn't dream of using force. Not when calm reason will very likely work just as well."

"What is the nature of this calm reason?"

"Why don't we start with the observation that you and I appear to have a mutual interest in our host's private affairs."

He felt her take in a quick, startled breath. "I have no idea what you are talking about."

"That was Hastings's bedroom you emerged from a few minutes ago."

"How do you know that?" she said. "You are guessing."

"I rarely guess, Mrs. Bryce. Not when I have the facts before me. I know that was Hastings's bedroom because I obtained a floor plan of the house yesterday."

"Good heavens, sir." Sudden comprehension and something that looked a lot like unmitigated relief brightened her face. "You are a professional burglar. I had began to suspect as much."

A proper, well-bred lady would have been horrified, he reflected. Louisa did not seem the least bit put off by the notion of being escorted by a member of the criminal class.

Instead, she was clearly intrigued. *Delighted* would not be too strong a word. He had been right: She was a most unusual female.

"You can hardly expect me to confirm your suspicions," he said. "The next thing I know you'll be summoning the police and having me arrested."

To his astonishment, she laughed. The sound captivated him.

"Not at all, sir," she assured him with an airy wave of her fan. "It is nothing to me if you make your living by stealing from the likes of Elwin Hastings. I must say, this news does explain a few things, however."

It occurred to him that the conversation was veering off in a rather bizarre direction.

"What do you mean?" he asked.

"I will admit that ever since I met you at the Hammond ball I have been quite curious about you, sir."

"Should I be flattered or alarmed?"

She did not answer that question. Instead, she smiled, looking as satisfied and smug as a small cat curled in front of the fire.

"I thought from the first that there was something decidedly mysterious about you," she said.

"What was your clue?"

"Why, you asked for an introduction and actually danced with me, of course." She flicked her fan open and closed in a small gesture that implied she had proved her point.

"What is so odd about that?"

"Gentlemen never care to make my acquaintance, let alone take me out onto the floor. When you danced with me again at the Wellsworth reception I realized immediately that you were perpetrating some clandestine scheme."

"I see."

"I assumed, of course, that you were using me as a cover to conceal your interest in some other lady." She paused delicately. "A married woman, perhaps."

"You have obviously spent a great deal of time and energy thinking about me in the past few days."

As much time as he had spent contemplating her, he thought. He found that satisfying.

"You were a puzzle," she said simply. "Naturally I felt the need to find an answer. I must say, this is a most fortuitous turn of events."

They arrived in the front hall before Anthony could come up with a response to that statement. A footman in old-fashioned blue-and-silver livery, a powdered wig on his head, stepped forward.

"Mrs. Bryce's cloak, please," Anthony said. "You may summon my carriage and then inform Lady Ashton that the lady has left with me."

"Yes, sir." The footman hurried away.

Louisa made no further protest. Anthony got the impression that she was as eager to be away now as he was. Apparently the idea of setting off into the night with a professional thief did not worry her overmuch. He was not sure how to take that.

The footman returned with a dull maroon cloak that matched the dull maroon gown. Anthony took it from him and arranged it around Louisa's shoulders. The small act of gallantry would send a message that would not go unnoticed. If Hastings questioned him later, the footman could say in all honesty that Mrs. Bryce and Mr. Stalbridge appeared to be on very intimate terms.

The carriage appeared at the foot of the steps. Louisa allowed herself to be handed up inside. Anthony followed before she could change her mind.

He sat down across from her and closed the door. The dark confines of the cab enveloped them. In the intimate space he was intensely aware of Louisa's delicate scent, a mix of some flowery cologne and woman. He was half-aroused, he realized. He had to force himself to concentrate on the business at hand.

"Now, then, Mrs. Bryce," he said, "where were we?"

"I believe you were about to tell me something of the nature of your unusual profession." She reached into her muff and withdrew a pencil and a notepad. "Would you mind turning up the lamps? I want to take notes."

2

There was an acute silence.

Louisa looked up. Anthony was gazing at her, dumbfounded. She gave him what she hoped was an encouraging smile.

"Don't worry," she said, opening the small, leather-bound notebook that she carried everywhere. "I don't intend to steal your trade secrets."

"Just as well because I don't plan to reveal them to you," he said dryly. "Put the notebook away, Mrs. Bryce."

A little chill feathered her nerves. It was the same shiver of alarm she had experienced when Lady Ashton had introduced him to her earlier in the week at the Hammond affair. His name had rung a very loud, clanging bell of warning, but she had assured herself that being asked to dance by the man whose fiancée was one of the two women who had drowned in the river a little over a year ago was sheer coincidence, not the Dread Hand of Fate. The social world, after all, was a relatively small realm. Nevertheless, when she saw him in the hall outside Hastings's bedroom tonight she almost panicked. He could not know it, but the truth was, encountering him there had given her far more of a jolt than she had got from meeting up with the guard.

She was certain she could have dealt with Quinby. After all these months in Society the image she and Lady Ashton had worked so carefully to establish had been generally accepted. She was Louisa Bryce, the unimportant, unfashionable, excessively dull relative from the country whom Lady Ashton had kindly taken in as a companion. There was no reason for Quinby to be overly suspicious of her.

Anthony's unexpected appearance in that hall, however, had shaken her nerve. This time there could be no denying that something more than coincidence was at work.

She had known intuitively from their first

meeting that the air of ennui and jaded disinterest that Anthony projected was an illusion. For that reason she had been very cautious around him. Perhaps it was for that very same reason he had fascinated her from the start.

The realization that he was very likely a professional jewel thief not only reassured her, it had given her a brilliant idea. At least it had seemed brilliant at the time. She was starting to have doubts. Perhaps it was not inspiration that had struck her a few minutes ago. In hindsight, it might have been foolhardy desperation.

She realized that he was watching her with a mixture of amused irritation and relentless determination.

"If you insist," she said, keeping her tone polite and trying not to show her disappointment. "No notes."

Reluctantly, she returned the notebook and pencil to the small pocket inside her muff.

He had made no move to turn up the interior lamps as she had requested, so his features remained carved in shadows. But she had danced with him several times in the past week. His enigmatic eyes and the implacable planes and angles of his face had been imprinted on all of her senses. When her gloved fingertips had rested ever so lightly on his shoulder during the waltz she had been vividly aware of the strength in the sleek muscles beneath his expensively tailored coat.

Dancing with Anthony was like dancing with a particularly well-dressed, well-mannered wolf: The experience was both dangerous and exhilarating. Kissing him a few minutes ago had been a thousand times more exciting and, no doubt, a thousand times more hazardous. She would never forget that shocking, thrilling embrace in the hall outside Hastings's bedroom, she thought.

There was an aura of cool self-mastery about Anthony, a steely edge that simultaneously attracted her and commanded her wary respect. She had heard that he had spent a great deal of time journeying to far-off lands before returning to England four years ago. She had a feeling that his experiences abroad had taught him to see beneath the surface in ways that others in Society did not.

The Stalbridge family was considered by

one and all to be heavily populated by eccentrics. For the most part they ignored Society. The Stalbridges, however, had become quite wealthy in recent years, and the family's bloodlines were impeccable. Given those crucial factors, Lady Ashton had explained, Society could not ignore the Stalbridges. Anthony and the other members of his family were routinely included on every guest list, although they rarely accepted invitations.

Any hostess who succeeded in attracting a Stalbridge to a social affair was widely considered to have achieved a great coup. The new Mrs. Hastings was no doubt very proud of having lured Anthony to the first ball she had given as a married woman.

Satisfied now that the notebook and pencil had vanished, Anthony lounged against the seat and contemplated Louisa with faintly narrowed eyes.

"What were you doing in Hastings's bedroom?" he asked.

The conversation was not going as she had intended. She had planned to take charge right from the start, but somehow he had seized control and was interrogating her. There was nothing she could do now but brazen it out.

"I opened that door quite by accident," she replied.

"I trust you will not be offended when I tell you that I do not believe a single word of that extremely flimsy story, and I doubt if the man who stopped us would have, either."

"I had a perfectly sound story prepared to give that odious creature," she shot back without stopping to consider her words. "If you had not interfered, I would have told him that I was merely looking for a room in which I could repair a tear in my gown."

"I don't think he would have found that story any more believable than I do." Anthony stretched out his legs and folded his arms across his chest. "By the way, the name of that odious creature, as you call him, is Quinby. He is a hired guard. Hastings recently employed two of them. Both carry revolvers."

She caught her breath. "Good heavens, sir. Are you telling me that Mr. Quinby was *armed*?"

"The gun was in the pocket of his coat. I expect he also carries a knife. In my experience, men who grow up on the streets are usually quite comfortable with them."

"I see." She swallowed hard, absorbing the information. "Did you acquire that experience in the course of your travels abroad?"

"You have, indeed, made some inquiries about me. I'm honored to have captured your attention to such a degree."

She flushed. "Yes, well, as I said, your peculiar interest in me made me curious."

"I do not consider my interest in you at all peculiar. Trust me when I tell you that you are nothing short of fascinating, Mrs. Bryce. And in answer to your question, yes, I did spend some time in places where men commonly go about armed, and I learned a great deal." He paused for emphasis. "I know men like Quinby when I see them."

She was not at all certain what to make of the nothing short of fascinating remark, so she decided to ignore it.

"Well, that certainly explains a few things about Mr. Quinby," she said briskly. "I did wonder why he felt he had the right to confront us in such a rude manner. I realized he was not an ordinary servant in the household."

"No," Anthony agreed. "Lesson Number One, Mrs. Bryce: The next time you see a man in a coat that bulges somewhat oddly, pay attention."

"I will most certainly do so. Thank you for the tip, sir."

"Damnation. I am wasting my time trying to frighten you, aren't I?"

"I assure you, I am quite capable of being frightened, Mr. Stalbridge, but in my opinion, there is no substitute for facts regardless of the subject. Obviously, the more one learns about the criminal classes, the better equipped one is to protect oneself. Since you are clearly an expert, I am very grateful for any information you choose to provide."

"I must give some thought to my tutorial fees."

"What an excellent notion, sir," she said, enthusiasm rekindling. "I am quite willing to pay for instruction in such matters. I would find it extremely useful."

He looked out the window into the night as though seeking answers from some metaphysical source. "Serves me right. I should have known better than to go down that path."

"I beg your pardon?"

"Never mind, Mrs. Bryce. I am talking to myself. You have driven me to it."

She tapped a gloved forefinger on the cushion. Now that the initial shock of learning that she had been accosted by an armed man was fading, curiosity and excitement sparked. Why did Elwin Hastings feel the need to hire a pair of guards? It was a most intriguing question. Another question followed quickly on the heels of that one.

She looked at Anthony. "How did you learn that Hastings had hired private guards and that they are armed?"

Anthony pulled his attention away from the street scene. "Let's just say that I pay close attention to Hastings's affairs."

"Obviously. Well, what's done is done. We must move on."

He seemed amused. "Is that all the thanks I'm going to get for rescuing you?"

She smiled knowingly. "Let us have a bit of honesty here, sir. It was quite convenient for you to make yourself known at that particular moment, was it not?"

"What do you mean?"

"While I had an excellent excuse, we both know it would have been considerably more difficult for you to explain your reason for being in the hall. In fact, it seems to me that *you* should be thanking *me* for rescuing you from what would have been an extremely awkward situation."

She sat back, satisfied that she had turned the tables on him with that bit of logic.

"Remind me to show my gratitude later," he said. "To return to the subject at hand, I can think of only two reasons why someone would sneak upstairs during a ball. The first and most obvious is to engage in a tryst. Tell me, did you go upstairs to meet Hastings?"

Startled, she could only stare at him in utter horror for a few seconds. Then she shuddered. "*No*. As if I would ever form a liaison with a man of his vile nature."

Anthony stilled. "What do you know of him?"

"Among other things, he is a recently wed husband who insults his wife behind her back by patronizing a notorious brothel."

"How the devil did you discover that?" Anthony said, sounding genuinely intrigued.

She almost laughed. "It never ceases to astonish me that men are always so shocked when they discover that women are not as naïve as they assume. We have our sources of gossip, sir, just as you do."

"I do not doubt that for a moment. Tell me, if you do not approve of Hastings's morals, why did you accept an invitation to the ball this evening?"

She hesitated, not ready to confide in him. His aggressive questioning was causing her to have serious second thoughts about the wisdom of seeking his assistance.

"Lady Ashton wished to attend," she said smoothly. "She asked me to accompany her."

Anthony gave that a moment's consideration and then shook his head once. "I'm afraid that version of events lacks the ring of truth."

The cool accusation sparked her anger. "That is unfortunate, because it is the only version that exists."

"If you did not go upstairs with the purpose of meeting Hastings, then I must conclude that you went into his bedroom with the intention of taking something."

She froze. "I do not see why I should answer your questions when you have failed to answer any of mine."

"Forgive me. Once I set out to satisfy my curiosity, I tend to become obsessive."

"What a coincidence. So do I."

"What were you looking for in Hastings's bedroom?" he said very softly.

Her mouth went dry. Leaving the ball with him had, indeed, been a very bad idea. She could see that quite plainly now.

"I have no idea what you are talking about, sir," she said.

"You will save both of us a great deal of time and energy if you simply answer the question."

She raised her chin. "Surely you do not expect me to respond to personal inquiries about my activities. We are barely acquainted, sir."

"After tonight, the Polite World will assume otherwise."

His words sent a searing chill through her. He was right. Gossip spread swiftly in Society. While it was safe to say that no one cared much about her, Anthony was a different matter entirely. Wealthy, single gentlemen with excellent bloodlines were always of great interest in elevated circles.

In addition, there was the notoriety that still swirled around him due to his fiancée's suicide. Tomorrow there would most certainly be talk, she thought.

"The gossip will pass quickly," she said. "Sooner or later you will dance with some other lady, and everyone will forget about me again."

"You sound quite eager to be rid of me. I am crushed."

"I am not some silly young girl fresh out of the schoolroom. We both know that you have no personal interest in me. You have been using me for some purpose of your own this past week."

"Is that what you think?"

"Yes, of course." She stomped quite ruthlessly on the little spark of wistful hope that had been flickering somewhere inside her. "Kindly credit me with some intelligence, sir. There is no other reason why you would have directed your attentions toward me. I must admit I have been wondering what you were about, but I believe that my questions have been answered tonight."

"Indeed? And what is that answer?"

"In light of your career as a gentleman-thief, you obviously have your reasons for wanting to attend certain social affairs. It is equally obvious that you find it useful to distract people so that no one notices when you go about your business. For the past week you've found Lady Ashton's poor relation from the country well suited to that purpose, haven't you?"

"You think I have been using you as camouflage for my criminal pursuits?" he asked, reluctantly fascinated.

She spread her gloved hands wide. "I believe magicians refer to it as misdirection. If people think that the jaded Mr. Stalbridge is amusing himself by seducing a country widow, they will not wonder what else he might be doing."

"Damnation," he said, not without admiration. "You really do believe that I am in the habit of helping myself to other people's valuables."

"It is the only explanation that makes sense in light of the facts." She cleared her throat. "May I assume that your evening career explains how the Stalbridge fortunes came to be revived in recent years? Lady Ashton told me that four years ago, before you returned to England, your family was rumored to be flirting with bankruptcy."

"You think I restored the family finances by taking up a career as a jewel thief?"

"You will admit it is a viable hypothesis."

"Based on the fact that I asked you to dance on a handful of occasions this past week? No, Mrs. Bryce, I will not allow that it is a reasonable assumption. Your evidence is far too weak."

"Oh, there is a bit more to it than the dances, sir," she said coolly.

He did not move. "How much more?"

"I saw you slip away from Lady Hammond's ballroom the other night. I assumed you had an assignation in the garden, but you went up the back stairs instead."

"Good Lord, you followed me?"

"Only as far as the foot of the stairs," she assured him. "I felt that, under the circumstances, I had a right to know what you were about."

"Circumstances? Damn it to hell, woman, all I did was dance with you a few times."

"Yes, and I knew there had to be a reason for that," she said. "As you, yourself, pointed out, there is a limited number of explanations for why a person would sneak up a flight of servants' stairs during a social affair. Until tonight I had assumed you were in the habit of meeting your lover in that manner, but this evening I began to suspect that you were more likely a thief."

"You take my breath away, Mrs. Bryce."

She doubted that was a compliment. So much for trying to prod him into telling her the truth. He obviously was not going to confess to being a burglar. Fair enough. She certainly wasn't about to confide her secrets to him, either, even if he did have an alarming effect on her pulse.

"Given your profession, Mr. Stalbridge, you are hardly in a position to question my activities, let alone criticize."

"Mrs. Bryce, this conversation is far and away the most riveting one I have had in years. I will, however, be blunt. I do not know what you intended tonight, but I must tell you that you took a grave risk going into Elwin Hastings's bedroom. You obviously have no conception of the enormity of the danger involved."

The grim certainty in his words gave her pause.

"Surely I was in no serious jeopardy of anything other than having to face a few moments of mild embarrassment," she said.

"If you believe that, then I must tell you that you do not know as much about Hastings as you seem to think you do."

"I will allow that you may know considerably more about him." She paused and then gave him an encouraging smile. "Perhaps you would be good enough to enlighten me?"

His expression hardened. "Pay attention, Mrs. Bryce. If Hastings had cause to suspect that you might be a threat to him, you would be in great jeopardy."

She stopped smiling. "Surely you are not implying that he might go so far as to murder me simply because he learned that I accidentally opened his bedroom door."

"Yes, Mrs. Bryce, that is exactly what I am implying."

She drew a sharp breath. "Really, sir, that is preposterous. He is certainly not a nice man, but he is a gentleman. I doubt very much that he would stoop so low as to murder a lady who had done him no grave harm."

Anthony sat forward abruptly, making her gasp in surprise. He captured her wrists in his hands and leaned in close.

"Heed me well, Mrs. Bryce. If I am correct in my conclusions about Elwin Hastings, he has already committed murder twice."

Horror reverberated through her. "Good heavens, sir. Are you certain?"

"I have no proof yet, but, yes, I am certain."

"I suppose I must take your word for it," she said slowly. "You no doubt have better connections in the criminal classes than I do, and therefore you are better informed about such matters."

"Do I detect a note of envy?"

"Well, I must admit, I would find detailed information about the criminal underworld extremely useful from time to time."

"Just what line are you in, Mrs. Bryce?" he asked very gently.

Another chill trickled down her spine. She was fiercely aware of the strength in his fingers. He wasn't hurting her, but she was most definitely a captive. It took a great deal of effort to keep her voice calm and even.

"Never fear, sir, I am not your competition," she assured him. "I have no interest in Hastings's jewels."

"Then what the devil did you hope to find in his room?"

She hesitated a moment longer and then made her decision. He already knew that she had been in the room, and he had not betrayed her to the guard. It was clear that he was no friend of Elwin Hastings, and, although he appeared to be a gentleman, he was a self-confessed professional thief, a species not known for its scruples. It was not as though she had a great many options here. Anthony was an unusual gentleman; not at all like other men. He just might consider helping her, if only because he might find the challenge intriguing.

"I was hoping to find proof that Hastings has a financial interest in a certain brothel," she said. "A place called Phoenix House."

She held her breath.

Anthony regarded her, evidently bereft of speech, for a very long moment. He released her wrists, but he continued to lean forward, resting his forearms on his thighs. He linked his fingers loosely together between his knees and regarded her as though she were a peculiar specimen in a strange zoo.

"You seek evidence that Hastings invested money in a brothel?" he asked, as though wanting to be quite clear on the subject.

She gripped her muff very tightly. “Yes.”

“Do you mind if I ask why?”

“Yes, I do mind. It is none of your affair, sir.”

He nodded. “No, I suppose it isn’t. What made you think that this proof might be in Hastings’s bedroom?”

“I managed to slip into his library earlier and go through his desk drawers. They were not even locked. I found nothing useful. The bedroom was the only other place I could think of to search.”

“You went through his desk looking for documents related to his financial affairs.” Anthony seemed beyond astonishment now. He merely shook his head. “Of all the idiotic, reckless, foolhardy—”

“I did not ask your opinion, sir,” she said, stiffening. “In any event, it was not that foolhardy. No one was about. The servants are all busy this evening.”

“It is a miracle you were not caught by one of the guards.”

“Yes, well, I was not aware of them at the time,” she admitted ruefully.

“A serious oversight.”

"Indeed," she admitted. She straightened her shoulders. "As I was saying, the bedroom was the only other place I could think of to search."

"I assume that you did not find the proof that you were seeking?"

"No, unfortunately." She sighed. "I went through all of the drawers in the wardrobe, and I searched beneath the bed. There is a small writing desk near the window. The drawer was unlocked, but there was nothing inside. I could not think of any place else to look. There was no sign of a safe."

"That is because it is hidden in the floor."

She widened her eyes. "You know that for a fact?"

"Yes. It is an Apollo Patented Safe, by the way, the most secure strongbox available on the market."

"I am most impressed, sir. You must, indeed, be very good at your work. You obviously do a great deal of research on your, uh, subjects. I did not even think to look for the safe in the floor."

"It is just as well. If you had remained in that room a moment longer, the guard would probably have discovered you inside."

"Even if I had found the safe, it wouldn't have done me any good. I regret to say that, although I can manage simple locks with a hairpin, I have had no experience opening safes."

"I am amazed to hear that there are some limits to your resources, Mrs. Bryce."

Stung, she clasped her hands tightly together. "There is no call for sarcasm, sir."

"If it makes you feel any better, to my knowledge no one has ever managed to finesse the lock of an Apollo. Occasionally safecrackers have resorted to explosive devices to get into one, because thus far that's been the only successful method."

"Then how did you plan to open Hastings's safe, sir? Because it is clear that was your intention tonight."

"Forgive me, I should have said that *almost* no one has ever managed to finesse the lock. There is one exception."

Her spirits soared. "You?"

"Yes."

She braced herself. "In that case and

given that we have come this far, I have a proposition for you."

"Stop right there, Mrs. Bryce." He held up a hand, palm out. "Do not say another word."

"I was merely wondering if your professional services might be for hire," she said quickly.

He did not move. "You wish to employ me to break into Hastings's safe?"

"Precisely. I failed in my mission tonight, but you are obviously an expert in such matters." She waved one hand to indicate his elegant evening clothes and the handsome, well-sprung carriage in which they rode. "Clearly, you have done very well for yourself in the past few years. I realize that you do not need to take on clients. But as you plan to open Hastings's safe anyway, I would be extremely appreciative if you would have a little look around while you are at it. I'd be interested in any paperwork relating to a brothel. I will make it worth your while."

"Mrs. Bryce, I do not take commissions for this sort of thing."

"I understand." She gave him her brightest, most encouraging smile. "But surely an intelligent businessman such as yourself would not turn down an offer of compensation from a grateful person."

He said nothing at all for an extended length of time.

"Well, sir?" she prompted.

"You are an extraordinary female, Mrs. Bryce."

"You are very much out of the ordinary, yourself, sir. I cannot imagine that there are a great many jewel thieves who move in Polite Circles."

That remark appeared to amuse him. "You'd be surprised, madam. Statistically speaking, I'm sure it is safe to say that those who move in elevated circles are no more honest than people who move in other spheres."

"On that we are agreed, sir," she said, "but the difference between the two groups is that the highfliers are far less likely to pay for their crimes than are those in the lower classes."

He cocked a brow. "You sound quite cynical, Mrs. Bryce."

"I do not have any illusions about the wealthy and the powerful, sir. I know all too well the damage they can cause and how easy it is for them to escape justice. But I do not think this is the time to debate such matters, do you?"

"No," he said. "We do appear to have more pressing problems."

"You no doubt intend to go back to Hastings's mansion later to finish your project. All I ask is that when you open his safe you look around for any documents dealing with Phoenix House. I will be quite happy to reimburse you for your trouble."

"Assuming I do not get shot dead in the process."

"Yes, well, I'm certain you are a very competent burglar, sir. After all, you have survived until now."

"I appreciate your faith in my professional abilities."

Hope surged through her. "Well? Will you agree to take the commission?"

"Why not?" he said, evidently resigned. "It's not as though I have anything more interesting to do this evening."

"Excellent." She gave him another bright smile. "I'll wait for you in this carriage."

"No, you will not, madam. I will take you home first. We will discuss the results of my efforts tomorrow."

"You do not appear to grasp a pertinent fact here, sir. I am paying you to do this job tonight. As your employer, I must insist on staying close by until you have finished the venture."

"In other words, you do not entirely trust me."

"My apologies, sir. I mean no offense. It is just that I have never had occasion to hire a professional thief. I would prefer to keep the arrangements as businesslike as possible." She hesitated as another thought occurred. "By the way, how much do you charge for this sort of thing?"

His eyes tightened dangerously. "Rest assured, I will give that question close consideration, Mrs. Bryce."

3

A businesslike arrangement. How in blazes had it come to this? He was about to crack Elwin Hastings's safe while his new accomplice—make that client—waited for him in a closed carriage in a nearby lane. His already complicated life had developed a few new and decidedly convoluted twists tonight.

For the second time that evening Anthony studied the shadowed hallway outside Hastings's bedchamber. The guard was gone. There was no indication that anyone else was lurking up here. He checked the alcove where he had hidden a short time earlier. It was empty.

Getting back inside the mansion had been simple enough. He had pulled on the long overcoat and low-crowned hat that he had brought along for the purpose. Louisa had watched closely, clearly intrigued by the sartorial transformation.

"If I am seen at a distance, it is unlikely that I will be recognized," he explained.

"You look quite menacing in that coat and hat, sir. It is amazing how it affects your appearance. I vow, you could easily pass for a member of the criminal class."

"The idea is to look like a respectable tradesman."

"Oh. Sorry."

He had scaled the garden wall without incident, although he had been forced to crouch behind a hedge when the second guard, Royce, made what appeared to be a routine patrol of the grounds.

Guided by the floor plan he had studied that afternoon and what he had seen of the house earlier, he had no trouble locating the servants' entrance. The back stairs that led to the upper floors were still clear. The harried staff was occupied on the ground floor dealing with the behind-the-scenes demands generated by a houseful of guests.

Satisfied that he had the hall to himself, he opened the door of Hastings's bedroom. Inside he stood quietly for a moment, allowing himself to absorb the feel of the moonlit room. He had been studying Hastings for over a year. He knew a great deal about his quarry.

He raised the corner of the carpet and found the safe exactly where it was supposed to be. He did not need to strike a light to see what he was doing. When one opened an Apollo Patented Safe in a clandestine manner, one did it by touch, not sight.

He got the strongbox open very quickly. The small set of safecracking tools he had brought with him had been specially commissioned from one of the finest craftsmen in Birmingham. The implements were more delicate and more sensitive than a surgeon's scalpels.

The interior of the Apollo was as dark as a small cave. He reached inside, pulled out all of the items, and placed them on the carpet in a shaft of bright moonlight. There were four velvet pouches of the sort used to hold jewelry, a number of business documents, five leather-bound journals, and an envelope containing three letters.

He flipped through the journals. Four were

written by people other than Hastings or his wife. The fifth was a record of payments received from individuals who were identified only by initials. The letters in the envelope were signed by a young lady.

He tucked the journals, letters, and business papers into pockets on the inside of his overcoat. Turning to the jewelry pouches, he unlaced each in turn. The first three contained an assortment of bracelets, earrings, and necklaces fashioned of diamonds, pearls, and colored gems. All of the pieces were in the modern style. They had no doubt belonged to the first Mrs. Hastings. She had been much admired for her sense of fashion. He picked up the fourth sack and poured the contents into the palm of his hand. Moonlight glinted on an emerald-and-diamond necklace set in gold. The design was old-fashioned and very familiar.

A savage exhilaration roared through him. He had anticipated finding some answers tonight. He had not allowed himself to hope that he would be this fortunate.

He put the necklace back into the pouch, retied the cord, and placed the little sack in a pocket.

He tossed the other three sacks back into the safe, closed the door and locked it. Next he repositioned the carpet. There was no telling how soon Hastings would check the contents of his Apollo, but when he did, he was sure to get a well-deserved jolt of alarm. No ordinary thief would leave most of the jewelry behind. When Hastings realized precisely what items had been taken, he would know that someone was hunting him. With luck he would start to sweat.

Anthony went to the door and listened intently.

Outside in the hall a floorboard squeaked. The first creak was followed by another, closer this time. Someone was coming down the hall toward the bedroom. One of the guards, most likely. Would he open the door of his employer's bedroom or was that forbidden territory? There was no way to know how thorough Quinby or Royce would be, but from what Anthony knew of Hastings's temperament, it did not seem likely that he would authorize either man to prowl through his private sanctuary.

Voices sounded out in the hall. A man whispered something in soft, urgent tones.

A woman responded, her voice equally low and eager.

Hastings had evidently brought one of the female guests up to his bedroom while his young bride was dutifully dealing with the crowd downstairs. The action certainly confirmed Louisa's already low opinion of his character. But the sensibilities of the very new Mrs. Hastings were not his primary concern at the moment. He had to get out of the room.

There were two alternatives: the window and the connecting door to Mrs. Hastings's bedroom. He chose the latter. If he went out onto the ledge he might not be able to find another unlocked window to crawl back through.

His hand was on the knob of the adjoining bedroom door when he heard the outer door of that room open. He stilled, listening as the couple entered.

"This is so damned risky, Lilly."

"Hastings and his guests have all had far too much champagne tonight. No one will notice that you and I have slipped away for a short time. In any event surely this is no more reckless than the way we used to

meet before I was forced into this ghastly marriage."

"But if anyone discovers us—"

"Darling, I have been so desperate for you. The past few weeks have been a nightmare. Hold me."

There was a rustle of heavy skirts and some passionate-sounding moans.

"Oh, God, Lilly. You cannot know what it has been like for me. I lie awake every night thinking of you in Hastings's bed. The image is driving me slowly mad."

"Do not torment yourself, my love. He was unable to consummate our marriage on our wedding night, and he has not come to me since."

"Hastings is impotent?"

"He says it is my fault. He claims I do not understand his special needs. I believe he goes elsewhere to satisfy those needs, and I am truly grateful, believe me."

"So am I."

Anthony released the knob and went back across the room to the door that opened onto the hall. He let himself out into the shadowed corridor and descended the rear stairs.

4

She did not realize how tense she had become waiting for Anthony to return until the carriage door opened abruptly. She nearly yelped in surprise when he vaulted up inside the darkened cab.

"Didn't mean to startle you, Mrs. Bryce."

He pushed open the trapdoor.

"Arden Square, Ned."

"Aye, sir."

The vehicle rumbled forward. Anthony dropped down onto the seat across from her.

She knew at once that something had happened. A hot, seething energy emanated from him. She felt as though she was sharing the carriage with a panther that had just scented prey.

"What kept you?" she said a good deal more sharply than she had intended. "I've been worried. You were gone for a very long time."

"Twenty minutes at most. Most of that time was spent in the garden, waiting for an opportunity to gain access to the house."

"Time does not pass quickly when one is waiting in a closed, unlit carriage." She peered at him, trying to make out his features. "Are you all right? Was there a problem?"

"Thank you for your concern. I am quite well, thank you. The only problem, such as it was, proved to be quite minor."

"You sound in remarkably good spirits for a man who has just risked his neck. Do you enjoy your work, sir?"

He gave the question some thought and then shrugged. "The exercise does seem to have elevated my mood. What of yourself, madam? Do you derive a bit of a thrill from creeping about in other people's bedrooms?"

"No, I do not," she said tightly. She raised her chin. "And there is no need to make it sound as though I am in the habit of doing that sort of thing."

"I see. You only flit through strange bedrooms when the fancy strikes, is that it? When was the first time you invaded someone's bedroom?" he asked.

A shiver of warning slithered down her spine.

You've said enough, she thought. In spite of his assistance this evening, the plain fact is you do not know this man. You cannot take the risk of revealing your secrets to him.

"Never mind," she said. "Tell me what you found. Did you get the safe open?"

"Certainly." He turned up one of the lamps, reached into the voluminous coat and brought out a handful of papers. "These were all that were inside the safe."

She stared at him, astonished. "You took all of his personal papers?"

"Yes. There wasn't time to sort through them to find the specific papers you wanted so I grabbed the lot."

"Good grief." What had she expected? He was a thief, after all. "I, uh, just wanted to know if there were any papers relating to the brothel inside the safe. I didn't actually intend—" She broke off. "Never mind."

"Here." He handed the papers to her. "See if you can find what you're looking for in that bunch."

Gingerly she took the papers and held them up to the light.

"They all appear to be business-related," she said, rifling through them. "Most deal with his new investment scheme. I don't see any relating to—" She stopped when she caught sight of a familiar address. Excitement stirred her pulse. "Ah, here we are. This one mentions the property at Number Twenty-two Winslow Lane."

She read through the document quickly and then looked up. "You have found the very document I was looking for, sir. According to this, Hastings recently invested a large sum of money in Phoenix House."

"Nothing like a satisfied client, I always say." He took several small, leather-bound books out of various pockets. "May I hope for repeat business?"

She ignored the teasing and examined the small books. "What have you got there?"

"I'm not sure yet. I took them because

most of them did not appear to belong to Hastings or his wife."

He handed a volume to her and opened one of the others to examine it.

"This is a private journal," Louisa said. She paused when she saw the name inscribed on one of the pages. "Good heavens, you're right. It cannot possibly belong to Hastings. According to this, it is the diary of Miss Sara Brindle. She is set to marry Lord Mallenby at the end of the month. How on earth did it end up in Hastings's safe?"

"An excellent question." He held up the book he had been perusing. "This journal belongs to a young lady named Julia Montrose."

"I've met her. She was recently engaged to Richard Plumstead. It is considered a spectacular match. Plumstead is in line for his father's title." She frowned. "This is all quite bizarre. Why would Hastings have these diaries?"

"I can think of one very good reason off hand."

She took a quick breath. "Do you think that he is blackmailing those people?"

"I doubt if young Julia or Sara has sufficient income of her own to pay blackmail. They likely receive only quarterly allowances. If Hastings is extorting money from anyone, it would be from someone else in the family. In the case of Julia, it would have to be her great-grandmother, Lady Penfield. She still controls the fortune in that family." Anthony paused. "She is quite elderly and not in good health."

"Lady Ashton said something about Sara Brindle's elderly aunt having control of Sara's inheritance."

Anthony opened the last of the small volumes. "This, I suspect, will prove to be a record of extortion payments."

"We must return those items to their rightful owners immediately," Louisa said.

"I agree. But some discretion will be required."

"Yes, of course. We cannot reveal our own identities." She paused. "What of the business papers?"

"Those I will keep," Anthony said coolly.

"But they belong to Hastings. It is one thing to take the blackmail items, but I think we should restore the papers to the safe."

He looked at her, his eyes pitiless in the soft light. "The bastard is not only a blackmailer, he is also a cold-blooded murderer. I feel under no obligation to return anything to him."

She felt everything inside her turn to ice. "That is the second time you have said you believe him to be a murderer. Do you have any evidence?"

"I didn't until tonight."

He withdrew a black velvet pouch, opened it, and turned it upside down. She watched a cascade of gold and blazing gems spill into his fingers.

"Good heavens," she whispered. "It must be worth a fortune."

"It is. And it also proves that Hastings is guilty of murder."

"I don't understand. You took that from his safe tonight?"

"Yes."

She stared at the glittering pool, stunned in spite of herself. "You really *are* a jewel thief."

"This necklace belonged to a woman named Fiona Risby."

She jerked her gaze back up to his grim face. "Your fiancée? The woman who threw herself off a bridge?"

"I was never completely convinced that Fiona committed suicide. Finding this necklace in Hastings's safe proves I was right. He killed her."

"You're certain that is her necklace?"

He poured the necklace back into the pouch. "Yes. It is quite distinctive. A family heirloom. Fiona wore it the night she died."

"What are you going to do? Now that you have taken it from Hastings's safe, it is no longer evidence against him because it is not in his possession." She paused delicately. "I hesitate to point this out, sir, but if the police discover that you have the necklace they might well consider you a suspect."

"I couldn't leave it behind in the safe; it would never be found there. Hastings would never allow the police to search his mansion."

"I see what you mean. But what are you going to do with it?"

"I'm not sure yet," he admitted. "But by the time I call on you tomorrow, I hope to have a plan."

"You are going to visit me in Arden Square tomorrow?" she asked, suddenly cautious.

"Of course." Anthony's smile was dangerously enigmatic. "I have yet to collect my fee for this night's work."

5

Anthony let himself into the darkened town house. There was no one around to open the door. His small staff knew that they were not expected to wait up for him.

He went into the library and tossed the heavy overcoat across the back of a chair. He peeled off his evening coat, unknotted his black tie, and loosened the stiff collar of his shirt.

He set the items that he had removed from the safe on a table next to a reading chair and splashed some brandy into a glass. After taking a long swallow of the brandy, he lowered himself into the chair. Picking up some of the business papers, he began to read.

Twenty minutes later he had no doubt about what he was looking at. The papers were confirmation of the rumors he had been hearing in his clubs. Elwin Hastings was masterminding another investment consortium. There was nothing surprising in that. Hastings had been involved in a number of financial ventures over the past few years. What was strikingly unusual about this particular scheme was the identity of one of the participants.

He finished the brandy, rose, and poured himself another. It was late, but he was in no hurry to go to bed. He knew that when he finally did sleep he would likely dream of Fiona Risby. He would not see the young, beautiful, vibrant woman she had been in life; rather he would see her as she appeared after they pulled her out of the river, dead eyes filled with accusation.

He took the necklace out of the velvet pouch and studied it. One of the two questions that had been driving him for the past year and two months had been answered with ringing finality as far as he was concerned. Fiona had not committed suicide. Hastings had murdered her.

But the second question still remained. He

needed to know why Fiona had been killed. Above all he had to discover if he was responsible for forcing her into the dangerous situation that had resulted in her death.

He drank some more brandy. A plan began to take shape in his mind.

Some time later he went upstairs to bed. To his amazement it was not the image of Fiona's body that disturbed his sleep; it was Louisa Bryce's face he saw. She looked at him through the invisible veil of her spectacles, watchful and mysterious. In his dreams he chased her through an endless maze of corridors knowing that he could not stop until he had unlocked her secrets.

6

The nightmare began the way it always did . . .

A muffled thud reverberates down below. The sound comes from the rear of the shop. The new lock that she installed last week has just been forced.

She is suddenly cold from head to toe, paralyzed by fear. Her heart is pounding. Panic roils her stomach. Icy perspiration dampens her nightgown. She is clutching the quilt as though it were a shield.

Iron hinges squeak. The door is opening. The monster is inside the shop.

He has come for her. For the past month

she has lived with a growing dread. Tonight her worst fears have come true.

She must move. She cannot stay here in bed like a terrified child waiting for the demon to find her.

The bottom step creaks beneath the weight of a heavy, booted foot. There is no attempt at stealth. He wants her to know he is coming for her.

She must get out of bed this instant or there is no hope. Screaming will do no good. There is no one in the room next door to hear her. She is not even certain that she could call for help. The frightening paralysis has affected her voice as well as the rest of her body.

She forces herself to concentrate on the desperate plan that she concocted a few days ago. The act of focusing her mind on something other than raw fear gives her strength.

Employing every ounce of will she possesses, she pushes aside the covers and gets to her feet. The floor is very cold. Somehow that helps to steady her nerves.

Another step creaks. He is midway up the stairs now. Not hurrying. Taking his time.

"I warned you, Joanna." His voice is filled

with a chilling lust. "Did you really think you could defy me? You are nothing but a foolish little shopkeeper. A nobody who must be taught her place in the world."

With the next step his voice sharpens, rage surfacing. "You should have been grateful that a gentleman of my rank was willing to give you so much as a second glance. Grateful, do you hear me, you stupid bitch? You should have begged me to take you."

The bedroom has no door. There is only a heavy curtain to block the intruder's path. It is closed.

She realizes that the window is uncovered and that she is silhouetted against the slant of light cast by the fog-drenched moon. Hastily she draws the drapes, plunging the small room into inky darkness.

She knows this cramped space well. The monster has never seen it, though. With luck, he will fumble about when he moves into the deep shadows, allowing her an opportunity to escape through the doorway behind him.

He is in the sitting room now, coming toward the curtained bedroom. She can hear the soft thud of his boots on the thin carpet.

"Women like you need to be taught their place. I'm going to show you what happens to females who don't display the proper degree of respect for their betters."

She picks up the heavy poker that she had placed on the floor beside the bed. The length of iron is heavy. She holds it with both hands and prays.

There is a faint scraping sound on the other side of the curtain. At the edges of the hanging fabric a wavering glow appears. The monster has struck a light.

So much for her plan to temporarily blind him with the darkness of the bedroom. Her nerve nearly fails. The hilt of the poker suddenly feels slippery in her fingers. She flattens herself against the wall beside the curtained doorway.

"It's time, Joanna. You have kept me waiting long enough. Now you will pay for your insolence."

The curtain opens abruptly. The beast's face is illuminated by the light he holds. His handsome features are twisted into a mask of demonic desire.

The flame dances evilly on the edge of the knife he grips in one hand.

He moves into the room and starts toward the bed . . .

Louisa came awake suddenly, breathless with fear. Her nightgown was damp from perspiration.

Had she cried out this time? She hoped not. She did not want to alarm Emma again. In recent months the nightmares had been far less frequent. She had even begun to hope that they were behind her forever.

She should have known better.

She shoved aside the covers and began to pace the room, trying to work off the unnatural energy that caused her heart to pound and made breathing difficult.

After a while she calmed somewhat. She went to the window and looked out, searching the shadows for the prostitute in black.

The streetwalker was not in the park tonight. Perhaps she had come earlier in the evening. More likely the poor creature had given up trying to attract a client and gone back to wherever it was that she slept. Arden Square was a quiet, extremely respectable neighborhood. This was not one of the places where men came in search of prostitutes.

She had noticed the woman in black for the first time a few nights ago. The stranger had worn a black velvet cloak and a black veiled hat that concealed her features, a widow who had most likely been forced onto the streets by the death of her husband. It was a common enough story. She had stood in the deep shadows of a tree for a time, evidently waiting for some gentleman seeking the services of a prostitute to come by in a carriage.

Perhaps she had abandoned this neighborhood and moved to another street. Or perhaps the widow had given up all hope and cast herself into the river like so many other desperate females had done.

The world was so cruel to women in the prostitute's situation, Louisa thought. Ladies driven into acute poverty by the death of a husband had very few alternatives. On the one hand Society condemned them, but at the same time it made it almost impossible for them to find respectable employment.

I was so lucky, Louisa thought. There but for the grace of God . . .

Filled with sadness and a deep sense of outrage, she left the window, went to the desk, and turned up the lamp. She knew she would not sleep now. She might as well take another look at the notes she had made earlier.

She opened her little journal and began to read, but after a while she closed the notebook. She could not concentrate. For some reason all she could think about was the way it had felt to be held in Anthony's arms, crushed against his chest while he kissed her.

When she finally went back to bed, she took the memory with her and hugged it close as a talisman against the nightmare.

7

The following morning dawned crisp and sunny. She dressed in a thin chemise, drawers, and a single petticoat. There were many who would have been horrified by the minimal amount of undergarments, to say nothing of the lack of a corset. Fashionable women often wore as much as fourteen pounds of underclothes beneath their even heavier gowns. But she and Emma were both staunch advocates of the rational dress movement, which held that ladies should wear no more than seven pounds of underwear. As for corsets, the movement had wisely declared them to be injurious to women's health.

The dark blue gown she chose was also

designed in accordance with the commonsense principles of the movement. The bodice was snug-fitting in the current style, but it lacked stays and was only lightly laced. The bustle was small and minimally padded for shape. The skirts contained considerably less fabric than was normally found in more stylish, elaborately draped gowns.

The reduced amount of material in the skirts was a crucial factor: By reducing the overall weight of the dress, it made walking much easier. The voluminous folds of the majority of fashionable gowns combined with the many layers of petticoats worn underneath made it impossible for a woman to take an invigorating stroll in the park. She was reduced to slow, mincing steps. If she tried to move at a brisker pace, her legs became hopelessly entangled in her skirts.

Louisa picked up the small notebook lying on the bedside table and went down the hall to the stairs. Emma's door, she noticed, was still closed.

In the kitchen she found the housekeeper, Mrs. Galt, with her husband, Hugh, and her niece, Bess. Hugh, a burly man in his mid-forties, took care of the garden and Emma's beloved conservatory. Bess served as the maid-of-all-work. The three were having their tea when Louisa walked into the room. They all rose quickly.

"Good morning," Louisa said. "I just came for a cup of tea."

"Good morning, ma'am." Mrs. Galt smiled. "You're up early. Would you like some toast to go with your tea?"

"That would be lovely."

"I'll bring a tray into the study in a moment." Mrs. Galt turned to the stove and picked up the kettle.

"I'll go see to the fire, ma'am." Bess bobbed a quick curtsy and hurried down the hall.

"Thank you," Louisa said.

She gave Mr. and Mrs. Galt another smile and started down the hall to the study.

She had not gone far when she heard the low murmur of Mrs. Galt's voice behind her.

"Well, now, I'm surprised to see her up and about at this hour. She came in very late last night. She cannot have got much sleep, and that's a fact."

"Sleep's the least of it, if you ask me." Mr. Galt's voice was a soft rumble. "It's that business of coming home in a gentleman's carriage that makes one wonder. First time *that*'s happened since we came to work here."

"Hush, now," Mrs. Galt said quickly. "We've known from the start that this is an odd household. It was no secret that Lady Ashton is a noted eccentric, but the wages are excellent. Don't you dare do or say anything that might cause all of us to lose our posts."

Louisa sighed and continued down the hall. It wasn't easy keeping secrets around servants. One had to constantly bear in mind that there were always other people in the house aside from herself and Emma.

Not that Mr. Galt had spoken anything less than the truth. She *had* come home quite late last night, and she could not deny that arriving back here at Number Twelve in a carriage other than the one in which she had departed was certainly a first. So was being walked to the door by a gentleman.

In the study she found a cheery blaze crackling on the hearth.

"There you are, ma'am," Bess said, getting to her feet. "It will be nice and cozy in here soon enough."

"Thank you," Louisa said.

"Here's your tea, ma'am," Mrs. Galt said from the doorway. She set a tray on a table. "Let it steep a bit."

"I will," Louisa promised. She needed her tea to be strong this morning. There was a great deal of thinking to be done.

She waited until she was alone before she sat on the chair behind her desk. Clasping her hands on the blotter, she surveyed the small room. The bookshelves were gradually filling up with volumes, among them a wide assortment of sensation novels. She had developed a passion for them in the past year because they generally featured stories of illicit love affairs. It had become clear to her that, given her secret past, an illicit love affair was the only sort she could ever hope to have.

Each new book increased her sense of security. It was as if every addition to her small library was a brick in the fortress wall that she was constructing around herself.

But the reality was that she would never be truly safe. Emma had done her best to make her feel welcome, but the small flame of hope that burned within her, refusing to be entirely extinguished, was enveloped in an icy dread. She felt this same gloom almost every morning when she woke up, and it was usually the last sensation she experienced every night before she went to sleep.

The emotion had a depressing effect on her spirits at times. Even on the sunniest days, the knowledge that someday she might be discovered and arrested on a charge of murder was always there, hanging over her head like an ominous thundercloud.

Meeting Emma had been a stroke of the most incredible good fortune. But she was only too well aware that the new life she had found for herself could be destroyed in an instant if her dark secret were ever revealed to the world.

Don't think about the past or the future and, most of all, don't think about Anthony Stalbridge. Concentrate on your work.

Her new career as a secret correspondent for the *Flying Intelligencer* was the one bright star in her life. It provided distraction from the melancholia and fear and gave her a strong sense of motivation and purpose. She had determined to dedicate her life to journalism.

She opened the leather-bound notebook she had brought downstairs. In her short career as a reporter she had learned the value of keeping good notes. For the sake of speed and out of concern that her notebook might be found and read by one of the servants or some other prying eye, she used a private code. She was always careful to spell out proper names, however. It would not do to get those wrong.

She picked up a pen and went to work, reviewing and elaborating on the brief, cryptic notes she had made.

There seemed to be little doubt that Hastings was engaged in blackmail, a criminal enterprise that meant he was even more vile than she had first thought. Unfortunately, she could see no way to expose him without also exposing the identities of his victims, which would not be right.

Of course, there was still the evidence linking him to Phoenix House, she reminded herself. The papers Anthony had retrieved from the safe confirmed Hastings's involvement as an investor in the brothel. That news alone would be sensational enough to satisfy Mr. Spraggett, the publisher of the *Flying Intelligencer*. Spraggett prided himself on presenting only the most lurid and riveting news to the reading public. The announcement that a high-flying gentleman in Society was part owner of a whorehouse would sell a lot of newspapers.

But what if Anthony was right about Hastings also being a murderer? Now there was a piece of journalism that would send shock waves through the Polite World, not to mention the rest of the country. Her pulse kicked up at the prospect of bringing a killer to justice.

An hour later familiar, brisk footsteps sounded in the hall, then a short, forceful knock on the library door.

"Come in, Emma," she called.

The door opened. Emma, Lady Ashton, strode into the room. Emma never simply walked or strolled; she was a strider. A large, no-nonsense woman fashioned like a Grecian statue, she possessed a unique view of the world.

Today she wore a comfortably styled bronze gown. Her silver-gray hair was knotted in a tight twist at the back of her head. At sixty-three she was still a handsome woman. She was also an extremely formidable one. After losing her husband at an early age, Emma had defied convention and set out to see the world. When she eventually returned to England, her wealth, combined with her breeding and social connections, had enabled her to resume her natural place in the Polite World.

A little over a year ago she had consulted with an agency that supplied paid companions and governesses. Emma planned to write her memoirs. She wanted to employ a *lady of good character and sound education who possessed modern opinions* to assist her in the project.

She had gone through half a dozen ladies of *good character and sound education* who claimed to possess modern opinions before, in absolute desperation, the agency had sent over their newest applicant. Louisa and Emma had hit it off from their very first meeting.

"We shall put it about that you are a distant relative," Emma decreed over tea. "That way you will be treated with more respect than if it were known that you were my paid companion and secretary."

By the time Emma discovered that Louisa met only two of the three requirements that had been stipulated to the agency she was quite prepared to overlook the missing qualifications.

Louisa would never forget Emma's verdict. It had come in the wake of a particularly bad nightmare, one that had left Louisa shattered and vulnerable. When Emma had offered comfort, Louisa had broken down, weeping, and related what happened the night she brained Lord Gavin with a poker.

The need to confide her dreadful secret to her friend had been overwhelming. She knew Emma well enough by then to be aware that her benefactress was unlikely to call the police. Emma did hold extremely modern opinions, after all. She had believed Louisa's version of events. Nevertheless, who wanted a murderess living in their household?

After Louisa poured out her secret and apologized for the deception, she braced herself for dismissal. Instead, Emma had patted her on the shoulder and said, "Never mind, dear. The value of a good character is vastly overrated in my opinion."

* * *

"Good morning, Louisa." Emma crossed the study to warm herself in front of the fire. "You're up rather early, considering that you did not get home until quite late last night. I didn't even hear you come in."

Louisa put down her pen. "I didn't want to wake you."

Emma moved to stand in front of the desk. Her blue eyes sparkled with curiosity. "My, my. Anthony Stalbridge. When I got your message from the footman, you could have toppled me with a feather."

"I seriously doubt that. Nothing could topple you, Emma."

"Of all the gentlemen you might have run off with last night, Stalbridge strikes me as far and away the most intriguing of the lot."

Louisa flushed. "It wasn't what you think, Emma. Mr. Stalbridge and I encountered each other under somewhat unusual circumstances."

"The best sort, I always say."

"I found him waiting for me in the hall outside Hastings's bedroom."

Emma's eyes widened. "Good heavens."

"He came to the rescue when one of Hastings's hired guards attempted to question me."

"Hastings employs *guards*?"

"Yes."

"How very odd."

"He has good reason. It transpires that he is not just an investor in a brothel. It appears that he is also a blackmailer who has been extorting money from some very distinguished families."

Emma stared at her, shocked. "Never say so."

"There is worse to come. Mr. Stalbridge believes that Hastings murdered his fiancée, Fiona Risby. He suspects that Hastings also killed his own wife."

Emma sat down abruptly and gripped the arms of the chair.

"Tell me everything, dear," she said. "Right from the start."

Louisa gave her a quick summary of events.

Emma listened intently and then sat back. "This is astonishing. Absolutely stunning. And here I thought you'd set off for a romantic tryst. I was so *happy* for you, dear. I admit I was somewhat concerned because the man in question was Anthony Stalbridge. Nevertheless, I thought it was a good sign that you were starting to emerge from your shell."

"I have told you on numerous occasions that I have no plans to emerge from my shell. At least not in the sense that you mean."

"Rubbish. You just haven't found the right man." Emma frowned. "But enough of that. What is your opinion of this business about Hastings being a murderer?"

Louisa drummed her fingers on the desk. "To be honest, I do not know what to think. There is no doubt that Hastings has a financial interest in Phoenix House, and it seems clear that he is also a blackmailer, but I am not at all certain that we can leap to the conclusion that he murdered Fiona Risby."

"I agree. Her death was, by all accounts, a suicide." Emma considered briefly. "But there is that necklace Stalbridge found in Hastings's safe. Emeralds and diamonds set in gold, you say?"

"Yes. It looked quite valuable. At this point, however, I have only Mr. Stalbridge's word that it belonged to Fiona. Even if that proves to be true, it no longer constitutes proof of Hastings's guilt now that it has been removed from the safe."

Emma gave a ladylike snort. "Stalbridge was right about one thing: Leaving it in the safe would have served no purpose. If Hastings really is guilty of murder, he is hardly likely to allow the police to search his house."

"And even if it were found in the house, I've no doubt that Hastings would be able to provide some explanation. He could always claim that the necklace belonged to his first wife, who had admired the Risby necklace and had ordered an exact copy from a jeweler."

"Not that Victoria Hastings would have worn a copy of anyone else's jewelry," Emma said dryly. "She was a lady who set the fashion. She did not follow it."

"I recall that you mentioned she was noted for her sense of style."

"Yes. She was a very beautiful woman."

Louisa quickly opened her notebook to the pages labeled VH. At the start of the investigation into Hastings's business affairs she had asked Emma for some background information on Hastings and his first wife. She had also interviewed the lady's maid who had worked for Victoria Hastings.

There were not many notes on Victoria. At

the time she had not considered the first Mrs. Hastings important, but in hindsight a couple of phrases took on new meaning.

She ran her finger down a page of her own cryptic handwriting and paused.

"You mentioned that she was one of the few women you had met who knew how to swim," she said.

"She was the *only* woman I ever met, aside from myself, who knew how to swim," Emma stated. "It is not a skill that many females ever learn."

"That would seem to lend credence to Mr. Stalbridge's theory that she may have been murdered. Why would a woman who could swim choose to jump off a bridge as a means of suicide?"

"Any woman, skilled swimmer or not, who leaped into the river fully clothed would likely drown," Emma pointed out. "A fashionable lady often wears nearly forty pounds of clothing. The sheer weight of her skirts and corsets would draw her down to the bottom as surely as if she were chained to a boulder."

Louisa shuddered. "True." She consulted her notes again. "You said you did not know her well."

"No. I don't believe she had any family connections of her own to speak of. I met her occasionally at various social affairs, but that was the extent of our acquaintance."

"Her maid told me that Hastings was in the habit of discussing his business affairs with her. It is rather uncommon for a husband to do that. He must have admired her intelligence."

Emma nodded. "She seemed to me to be a very shrewd woman. I can well imagine that she had a head for financial matters."

Louisa closed the notebook again and leaned back in her chair. "There is something that worries me about Mr. Stalbridge."

Emma raised her brows. "I am pleased to see that your intuition is functioning well. Tell me, what is it that alarms you? Aside from the fact that he knows how to break into a safe, of course." She paused for emphasis. "I trust you do realize that is a rather unusual talent for a gentleman?"

"I admit that skill does raise a few questions, but what concerns me the most is that he appears to be obsessed with the notion that Fiona Risby did not commit suicide. I got the impression last night that he would go to any lengths to prove that she was murdered."

Emma gave a small shrug. "I expect it is because he would like to clear his own name."

Louisa stopped drumming her fingers. "What on earth are you talking about?"

"You were not moving in Society last year at the time of Fiona's death. You did not hear the rumors that circulated."

"What sort of rumors?"

"There was gossip to the effect that Mr. Stalbridge was about to end his engagement to Miss Risby at the time. Some said that the prospect of facing the humiliation of being jilted was what drove Miss Risby to take her own life."

Louisa shuddered. "Any woman who is rejected by her fiancé certainly finds herself in a dreadful situation as far as Society is concerned. But would she resort to suicide?"

"It wouldn't be the first time. A jilted woman becomes something of a pariah in the Polite World. There are those who would have expected her to retire from Society altogether, as though she were a widow in the first year of mourning."

"Was she from a wealthy family?" Louisa

asked. She told herself it was the journalist in her that was interested in the answer. She had no *personal* curiosity about the woman Anthony had chosen for his bride.

"Yes, indeed," Emma said. "The Risby fortune is quite substantial. The fact that Fiona was an heiress would certainly have gone some distance toward easing her plight. There were bound to be other suitors. Also, she was very lovely. A charming young lady, indeed. I'm sure her father could have found another eligible gentleman for her. Nevertheless, the experience of being cast aside by Stalbridge would have caused enormous distress for her and her family."

"I see."

Of course Fiona Risby had been rich, beautiful, and charming. What else? Louisa picked up a pen and did a little staccato on the desktop.

"The marriage was considered an excellent match," Emma continued. "Both families were exceedingly pleased. The Stalbridges and the Risbys have been close friends for years. Their estates in the North march side by side."

"I see," Louisa repeated. She realized she was tapping the pen tip with such force now that she was leaving little marks on the blotter. She made herself put the writing instrument down.

"I should mention that there were other rumors last year," Emma continued somberly. "Rumors that were far worse than those concerning a broken engagement."

Shocked, Louisa straightened. She did not take her eyes off Emma's face. "Surely no one suggested that Mr. Stalbridge actually murdered Fiona Risby."

"I'm sorry to say that there was some speculation to that effect."

"*What?* Why would he do such a thing? What possible motive could he have had?"

Emma looked at her very directly. "There was talk that Mr. Stalbridge discovered Fiona in the arms of another man."

A little shiver went through Louisa. "Surely *you* didn't believe he murdered her?"

"My dear, if there is one thing that I learned in the course of my travels, it is that any man or woman, regardless of social background or degree of civilization, may be driven to murder under certain circumstances." Emma met her eyes in a very somber look. "The only question is which circumstances will motivate a particular individual."

Louisa swallowed hard. "I cannot quarrel with you regarding that conclusion."

Emma's face softened. "My apologies. I never meant—"

"There is no need to apologize. You are right, Emma. Nevertheless, I think it is safe to say that Mr. Stalbridge did not murder Fiona Risby."

"What makes you so sure of that?" Emma sounded genuinely curious.

"Surely if he had killed her he would not be searching for the real murderer."

"It has been a little over a year since he lost his fiancée," Emma said quietly. "Mr. Stalbridge is no doubt in the market for a new one, but the old gossip will likely complicate the business. Under normal circumstances, he could look for a bride among the most distinguished families in Society. As I told you, the Stalbridges can claim a very distinguished lineage, and now that their fortunes have been repaired they hold an unassailable position in Society. However—"

Emma stopped and gave a tiny shrug.

Louisa got a sinking feeling in the pit of her stomach. “I understand what you are saying. Many of the best families will surely hesitate before marrying off a daughter to a gentleman who is rumored to have murdered a woman.”

“Even if they don’t believe that gossip, they will be quite hesitant to allow a daughter to become engaged to a gentleman who is said to have jilted his first fiancée. What if he does it again? Concerned parents will be wary of subjecting a daughter to that sort of social humiliation.”

“In other words, whether he is guilty of jilting Fiona or of killing her, he has a strong incentive to make it appear that she was murdered by someone else,” Louisa concluded.

“He would need persuasive evidence, but if he succeeds, Society will conclude that he is innocent. He would then be free to marry any of the wealthy heiresses who will no doubt be cast before him by their extremely enthusiastic parents.”

8

Elwin Hastings looked across the desk at his bride of two months. He knew himself to be the envy of many men. Dressed in a fashionable green gown, her honey-brown hair piled high in an elaborate coiffure that required the attentions of a hairdresser every morning, Lilly was nothing short of beautiful.

It was all he could do not to pick up the heavy crystal vase on his desk and hurl it at her silly, brainless head.

"Next time you will show me the guest list before you instruct Crompton to send out the invitations," he commanded. "Is that understood?"

"Yes, of course." Lilly clamped her hands

together very tightly in her lap. Resentment flared in her eyes. "But you told me that Crompton knew who was to be invited to the ball. You said your secretary is aware of precisely how things are to be done in this household when it comes to social affairs and that I am to leave everything in his hands."

"I will speak with Crompton immediately and inform him that Anthony Stalbridge is to be removed from all future guest lists," Elwin said.

"I don't understand why you are so angry that he attended our ball. Mr. Stalbridge is from a very prominent family. He is the nephew of the Earl of Oakbrook. Indeed, there is even speculation that he might someday come into the title because the old earl has never remarried and there is no heir."

"Like everyone else in that family, Oakbrook is a devoted eccentric." Elwin controlled his rage with an effort. "Everyone knows that all the old earl cares about these days is his archaeological research. I am well aware of Stalbridge's bloodlines, Lilly. I repeat, from now on, he is not welcome in this house."

Lilly burst into tears. "I thought everything went so well last night."

The tears were more than he could tolerate. He pushed himself to his feet. "That will be all, Lilly."

She jumped up from the chair, cheeks flushed with anger. "I do not comprehend why you are in such a temper today. Did Mr. Stalbridge do something to annoy you last night? I heard he left early with Lady Ashton's relative from the country. I forget her name."

He ground his teeth. Disaster had struck last night, but he was not about to inform the stupid girl of that unpleasant fact. "My reasons for not wanting Stalbridge in this house are none of your concern."

"That's what you tell me every time I ask you what is wrong. You've been in an absolutely vile mood since our wedding day. It is as if you have turned into a different person. When you asked Grandfather for my hand you were all that was charming and polite. Now everything I say or do is wrong in your opinion. I vow, I do not know how to please you."

"Leave me, Lilly. I have business to attend to."

She whirled and rushed to the door, her eagerness to escape plain.

The feeling was mutual, Elwin thought, watching the door close behind her. She was everything he had believed that he wanted in a second wife: young, beautiful, and, most important, an heiress. True, her grandfather had made his fortune in trade, but after a couple of generations had passed one could overlook that sort of family background as long as there was enough money involved.

Nevertheless, Lilly's empty-headed chatter and her obsession with gossip and clothes were driving him mad. On top of everything else, she was useless in bed. Unlike Victoria, she had no intuitive understanding of his special needs.

There were certainly times when he missed Victoria, he reflected. Fortunately, there was an establishment in Winslow Lane where his particular requirements were understood and catered to in the most satisfactory fashion.

He would give a great deal to be rid of his new wife, but he could not afford to dispense with her just yet. On their wedding day he had discovered to his horror that he had not obtained control of Lilly's entire inheritance. Her grandfather, the clever bastard, had tied up the remainder of her fortune in such a way that it was doled out in annual stipends.

For all intents and purposes, Elwin thought bitterly, he was being forced to live on an *allowance*. Furthermore, if anything untoward were to happen to Lilly the yearly payments would be stopped immediately.

It was demeaning. Humiliating. An outright insult. This was what came of allowing men like Lilly's grandfather to buy their way into Society. Bloody hell. If it weren't for the damned money, he would never have even considered a woman with Lilly's background as a potential bride.

This was the second time he'd been forced to marry well beneath his station. First Victoria and now Lilly. *And all because of money.*

It wasn't right that a man of his breeding should be forced to stoop so low. A white-hot rage seared through him. He suddenly realized his hand had closed around a heavy silver paperweight. He hurled it against the wall. It struck the blue velvet drapes with a soft thud and tumbled onto the carpet.

He had needed money very badly this past

year. Things had started to go wrong almost at once after Victoria died. It was certainly fortunate for him that Society did not condemn a man to three years of mourning as it did widows. Widowers were expected to remarry, the sooner the better. Although he'd had no particular desire to acquire another wife, it had not taken him long to realize that a financially sound marriage was his only hope of remaining solvent.

In the months following Victoria's plunge into the river he had suffered several serious financial reverses. The death of Phillip Grantley two weeks ago had come as a devastating shock. Among other things, he had depended on Grantley to collect the blackmail money in an anonymous, untraceable manner. The blackmail scheme was the only one of his business arrangements that had continued to work properly after Victoria's demise.

More crucially, it was Grantley who had concocted the plan for the new investment consortium that was his only hope of freeing himself from Lilly and her stingy grandfather.

Grantley's supposed suicide had panicked him for several reasons. The fear that one of the blackmail victims had discovered the identity of the agent who collected the payments and had taken lethal action had badly rattled his nerves. Victoria had insisted that they select victims who were wealthy, elderly, and frail. It was difficult to imagine any of them tracking Grantley down, let alone killing him, but the possibility that one of them had done just that could not be ignored. What if that same individual had also learned that he, Hastings, was the person behind the scheme? It was that fear that had caused him to hire the two guards.

Luckily, there had been no further indications that he was in danger. Indeed, in the past few days he had begun to believe that he had overreacted. Perhaps his suspicions and fears were groundless. Maybe Grantley really had taken his own life. It wouldn't be the end of the world, because the investment consortium was fully formed and ready to be launched.

He had even been thinking of dismissing Quinby and Royce, but the disaster last night had changed everything. The fear had returned to chew on his vitals. Much as he disliked having the guards constantly hovering, they were necessary for his peace of mind, if nothing else.

He consoled himself with the thought that when the profits from his new investment venture began to pour in he would at least be able to rid himself of his irritating bride. He wondered if the suicide of a second wife would raise too many eyebrows in the Polite World. Perhaps an accident this time. But first he had to deal with the current catastrophe.

He reached for one of the velvet bell pulls hanging on the wall behind his desk and yanked hard, twice. Quinby and Royce appeared immediately.

He looked at Quinby first. It had been evident from the outset that he was the more intelligent of the two guards. He was also the most dangerous and the most annoying.

"Tell me again what happened in the hall outside my bedroom last night, Quinby."

"I already gave you a full report, Mr. Hastings." Quinby raised one shoulder in a careless shrug. "Nothing more to add."

Elwin clamped down on another wave of rage. Quinby's attitude was infuriating. He was rarely overtly insolent or disrespectful, but the lack of deference for his betters was always there, just under the surface. It was obvious that he had been born into the lower classes. He did a remarkably good job of concealing the accents of the street, but they were there, nonetheless, in his speech. That gold-and-onyx ring on his finger was clearly expensive—a gentleman's ring—but the bastard worked for a crime lord. How did he dare to consider himself the equal of a true gentleman?

Royce, on the other hand, hulking and dim-witted, at least displayed proper respect for those born into a higher station.

If he had any choice in the matter he would dismiss Quinby in a heartbeat, Elwin thought. But that was the problem, of course. He did not have a choice. He required protection, and, according to Clement Corvus, Quinby was the best in that line. Elwin believed it. One look at Quinby's eyes told you that he was cold to the bone.

"Go through your tale again," Elwin ordered evenly.

"I was doing my usual rounds," Quinby said, sounding bored. "Keeping an eye on the interior of the house while Royce watched the gardens. I finished the top floor and went down the back staircase to the floor where the master bedrooms are located. There was a lady and a gentleman in the hall. They were kissing."

"Mrs. Bryce and Mr. Stalbridge."

"Yes, although I didn't learn their names until I talked to the footman."

The woman had definitely been Louisa Bryce, Elwin assured himself. Her identity had been confirmed by the servants who had seen her leave with Stalbridge. There was no mistaking Lady Ashton's unfashionable country relative. With her spectacles, unstylish gowns, and dull conversation, she was a perennial wallflower at every social event she attended. The only mystery about her was why Stalbridge had shown some interest in that direction.

Elwin leaned back in his chair, trying to think. This was another one of those occasions when he missed Victoria's shrewd insights. She had always been extremely clever when it came to comprehending what motivated men.

"Any idea how long Stalbridge might have been up there in that hall outside my bedroom?" he asked.

"Not more than a few minutes," Quinby said. "When I spoke with the servants a couple of them mentioned having seen him in the ballroom shortly before I found him upstairs."

"How long does it take to crack a safe?"

Quinby spread the fingers of one hand. "Depends on the expertise of the safecracker. Most of the professionals are fast. Very fast."

Royce cleared his throat. "Beggin' yer pardon, sir, but your strongbox is an Apollo Patented Safe."

"What of it?" Elwin demanded, forcing himself to hang on to his patience.

"They're known for being impossible to crack without the aid of an explosive device," Royce said. "And there weren't any used last night. Explosives, that is."

"Damn it, Stalbridge is not a professional safecracker." Elwin surged up out of his chair and started to pace the room. "He's a gentleman."

Quinby's mouth twisted in a derisive smile, but he did not offer a comment.

Elwin tensed. "What do you find so amusing, Quinby?"

"Just struck me that, although there seems to be an unwritten rule that says a member of the lower classes can't aspire to be a gentleman, there's no law that says a gentleman can't become a member of the criminal class."

Insolent bastard, Elwin thought, but he refused to allow himself to be drawn into a discussion of the niceties of social rank with a man who had come out of the gutters of London.

"My point," he said aloud, "is that Stalbridge has no reason to turn to burglary or safecracking. The family has become extremely wealthy in the past few years. And where in blazes would a gentleman learn the trade of safecracking?"

"Good point," Quinby said. "Probably not the sort of thing they teach at Oxford and Cambridge."

Elwin clamped his teeth together. He could not afford to let Quinby distract him. He had to keep his attention fixed on the problem at hand.

Royce cleared his throat again. "Beggin' yer pardon, sir."

Elwin sighed. "What is it now, Royce?"

"The name Stalbridge, sir," Royce said diffidently. "Would there be any connection to Mr. Marcus Stalbridge, the gentleman who designed the Apollo Patented Safe?"

Elwin felt as if he had been struck by lightning. He turned slowly, slack jawed.

"What's this?" he said tightly. "Marcus Stalbridge designed my safe?"

Quinby scowled. "What the devil are you talking about, Royce?"

Royce fidgeted nervously. "Got a cousin who knows a bit about the safecracking business."

"That would be Bert," Quinby said. "And the reason he knows something about the business is because he is a professional safecracker."

"Retired now," Royce said hastily.

"Get on with it," Elwin snapped.

"Yes, sir." Royce shifted uneasily on his big feet. "It's just that I've heard Bert talk about the subject. More than once he's told me that, generally speaking, the professionals avoid Apollos because in the end the only way inside is to blow a hole in them."

Elwin gripped the back of a reading chair. "What are you getting at, Royce?"

"Explosives create a lot of noise and draw attention, which is not what your average safecracker is after," Royce explained, assuming an instructive mien. "Especially if the safe happens to be located in a private house like this one, where there are usually a number of people on the premises."

"I am not interested in how one cracks a safe," Elwin said, spacing each word out with great care the way one does when conversing with an idiot. "Tell me more about Marcus Stalbridge."

Royce's head bobbed up and down several times. "Yes, sir. Well, the thing is, sir, Marcus Stalbridge is much admired by my cousin and certain of his, uh, colleagues on account of he holds the patent on the Apollo."

"Damnation." Elwin wanted to throw something at the nearest wall. "Anthony Stalbridge grew up in the household of a man who invented the most secure safe on the market, the very safe I happen to own. If anyone would know the secret of opening an Apollo, it would be him."

"Or his father," Royce pointed out helpfully.

"Bah. Marcus Stalbridge was not here last night. His son was."

"What of the woman, Mrs. Bryce?" Quinby asked.

"She's not important." Elwin waved that aside with a short, chopping movement of one hand. "A little nobody. Stalbridge must have used her for some purpose. Probably as camouflage to hide his real reason for being in that part of the house in the event he was discovered coming out of the bedroom."

"I don't think it's wise to jump to conclusions," Quinby said.

"Surely you are not going to suggest that Mrs. Bryce cracked that safe," Elwin snapped.

Quinby's shoulder rose in another one of his annoying shrugs. "Never pays to underestimate a woman."

"It strains credibility to the breaking point to think that dull female is a skilled safecracker," Elwin said, "but someone opened my safe last night. Whoever he was, he certainly knew what he was about. There was nothing to indicate that anyone had even been in my bedroom. If I had not opened the safe this morning I still wouldn't know that certain very valuable items were missing."

Quinby lounged against the corner of the desk with the insouciant ease of a man who felt as if he were in his own home. "Calm yourself, Mr. Hastings. We'll get this sorted out."

Another burst of rage flashed through Elwin. "Don't you dare patronize me, you criminal bastard. Remove yourself from that desk at once. I've had enough of your insolence. Who in bloody hell do you think you are?"

Quinby's jaw jerked. His eyes turned very, very cold. He rose slowly from the corner of the desk, uncoiling like a cobra.

A small, breathless whisper of dread swept through Elwin. He reminded himself that Quinby and Royce took orders from Clement Corvus and that Corvus had instructed them to guard him. Nevertheless, the fact remained that both men held their current positions in Corvus's organization precisely because they were capable of cold-blooded violence.

Royce's blunt features screwed up into an expression that was no doubt intended to express polite curiosity.

"Beggin' yer pardon, sir," he said. "As you just said, by all accounts, Mr. Stalbridge is a wealthy gentleman. Why would he want to break into your safe? He doesn't need your valuables."

That, of course, was the question here, Elwin thought. He released his death grip on the chair and forced himself to concentrate.

There was only one thing that connected Stalbridge and himself: the death of Fiona Risby. And that damned necklace was the only piece of jewelry that had been taken. Coincidence? What in blazes was going on here?

For a time after Fiona was pulled from the river rumors had circulated to the effect that Stalbridge was not convinced that she had committed suicide. But even if he did suspect that Fiona had been murdered, why did he care? By all accounts, he had been about to terminate the engagement, anyway. There was even gossip that he had found her in bed with another man. What possible interest could he have in avenging her? And why would he wait this long to act? And if Stalbridge was the thief, why did he also help himself to the extortion items and the business papers?

It was all so bloody bewildering. He felt hopelessly muddled and very, very uneasy. Something had gone badly wrong.

He stalked to the window and stood looking out into the garden. He wished he could discuss the problem with someone he could trust. He certainly did not intend to confide in Quinby and Royce. He was playing a dicey game with their employer at the moment. The last thing he wanted to do was make a slip that might get back to Clement Corvus.

In the old days he would have sought Victoria's advice. She had possessed an extraordinarily clever mind when it came to fitting together the pieces of this kind of puzzle, but Victoria was gone, and so was Grantley, the only other person he could consult. There was no one else he could trust.

He hesitated. There was always Thurlow, he thought. Victoria was the one who had chosen him as the seducer par excellence to compromise the various young ladies in their extortion scheme. Thurlow had his talents. He was, according to Victoria, one of the most handsome men in London. Certainly the innocent young women he had seduced had thought so.

Thurlow, however, was also a devout gambler. That was what had made him so useful, of course. He was regularly in need of money to clear his debts. But Victoria had never entirely trusted him. "A gambler's first loyalty is to the next game of cards," she had said.

Another uneasy thought arose. Thurlow knew about Grantley. Damnation, maybe it was Thurlow who had murdered Grantley. That appalling possibility sent another jolt of fear through him. Had Thurlow decided to go into the extortion business himself? Perhaps he had started out by getting rid of the middleman—Grantley—and then helped himself to the items in the safe, items that Thurlow, himself, had originally stolen from the young ladies. It seemed highly unlikely that Thurlow was skilled in the art of safecracking, but perhaps it was not altogether impossible. That still left the question of Stalbridge's role in the affair.

Elwin began to feel as if he were sinking into quicksand. It was all so damned complicated.

He swung around to face Quinby and Royce. "Here is the plan. First, you will both make certain that Stalbridge does not come anywhere near me or this house again. Is that understood?"

"Yes, sir," Royce said dutifully.

Quinby shrugged.

Elwin hesitated. He desperately wanted to order the guards to kill Stalbridge and

Thurlow as well, just to be safe, but that was not possible; they were Corvus's men. The crime lord was unlikely to agree to allow members of his organization to be used to murder two gentlemen.

Corvus was not overly troubled by scruples, but killing two respectable men, one of whom moved in Society, would be a dangerous business for a man in his position. That sort of violence would attract Scotland Yard's attention. Corvus had no reason to take that risk.

"Second," Elwin said, "I want to employ someone to keep a watch on a man named Thurlow, who lives in Halsey Street. I assume one of you is acquainted with the sort of person who can be hired to perform such a task?"

Quinby shrugged again.

Royce cleared his throat. "There's a man named Slip, who might be interested in that type of employment."

9

Shortly before two o'clock that afternoon brass clanged on brass with precision and absolute authority. Someone was on the doorstep, demanding and expecting admittance.

Louisa felt her pulse leap. She tried in vain to suppress the quickening of her senses and the tingle of excitement that made her stomach flutter. *Concentrate on the business at hand. Do not allow yourself to be distracted.*

Mrs. Galt hurried past the open door of the study, wiping her hands on her apron.

Emma appeared in the doorway. She was dressed in the old gown she used when she worked in the conservatory. Anticipation lit her eyes.

"I expect that will be your Mr. Stalbridge," she said.

"He is not *my* Mr. Stalbridge." Louisa put down her pen in a very deliberate way, trying to appear cool and composed. "But, yes, I imagine that will be him. He did say he would call this afternoon to collect his fee."

Emma gave a small ladylike snort of amusement. "As if a Stalbridge needs your money. I doubt very much that is why he is here."

The front door opened. A low, masculine voice emanated from the front hall. Louisa felt a shivery little thrill stir the fine hairs on the nape of her neck. *Calm yourself. This is a business arrangement, not a love affair.*

A moment later Mrs. Galt appeared, looking suitably impressed and not a little curious.

"There's a Mr. Stalbridge here to see you, Mrs. Bryce," she said. "Says he's expected."

Mrs. Galt had every reason to be interested, Louisa thought. Until now the only regular gentleman caller at Number Twelve Arden Square was Mr. Rossmarten, Emma's sixty-five-year-old admirer from the Garden

Society. The two shared a mutual passion for orchids. Having learned a great deal about Emma's adventurous past, Louisa was fairly certain the pair shared another sort of passion, as well. Discreetly, of course.

"Please show him in, Mrs. Galt," Louisa said, maintaining her composure with an act of will. "And then we will need a fresh tray of tea, if you don't mind."

"Yes, ma'am."

Mrs. Galt disappeared back toward the front hall. Masculine footsteps echoed.

Mrs. Galt reappeared in the doorway. "Mr. Stalbridge."

Something deep inside Louisa tightened at the sight of Anthony. Until now she had only seen him illuminated by the glittering lights of a ballroom or enveloped by the shadows of a darkened carriage. A part of her had wondered if the disturbing sensations she experienced in his presence would vanish in the light of day. But Anthony was as coolly elegant and just as excitingly dangerous in an expensively cut coat of dark gray wool and matching trousers as he was in his black-and-white evening attire. He wore a stylish striped four-in-hand tie, and his shirt featured the latest winged collar. His dark hair was brushed straight back from his high forehead. She liked the fact that he was clean shaven. Whiskers were currently quite fashionable for men, but she was not fond of the style.

He inclined his head with masculine grace.

"Ladies," he said politely.

Mrs. Galt vanished in the direction of the kitchen. There was a short silence. Anthony waited, looking amused.

Louisa finally became aware of the fact that Emma was making a small, urgent motion with one hand. It dawned on her that she was just sitting there, staring at Anthony. Embarrassed, she pulled herself together to make the introductions.

"Good morning, Mr. Stalbridge," she said hastily. "Please come in. I believe you are acquainted with Lady Ashton?"

"Of course." Anthony came forward and bent over Emma's hand. "A pleasure to see you again, madam."

"Mr. Stalbridge," Emma said in her customary crisp manner. "Do sit down, sir."

"Thank you."

He crossed the small space to take the remaining armchair. He looked at Louisa, eyebrows slightly raised in silent inquiry.

"It is quite all right, sir," she said. "I have explained the unusual circumstances of our association to Emma. You may speak freely in front of her."

Anthony regarded Emma with grave interest.

"You are involved in this business of proving that Hastings has a financial investment in a brothel?"

Emma smiled. "No. It is Louisa's project, but I am happy to assist her in any way I can."

"By obtaining invitations for her so that she may search the households of persons of interest?"

Emma was impressed. "How very clever of you, sir. That is, indeed, one of the ways I try to be of use."

Louisa cleared her throat delicately. "What did you conclude concerning the extortion evidence, Mr. Stalbridge?"

"I read the journals and letters. It appears that there are five people being blackmailed. As I suspected last night, it is not the young ladies who are paying the extortion money. In each case it is a wealthy, elderly female relative who also happens to be in rather frail health."

"Why are they paying blackmail?"

"Each of them is paying it to protect the reputation of a young female relative who was compromised."

"How dreadful." Louisa paused, frowning. "Was it Hastings who compromised them? I suppose, objectively speaking, he is not unhandsome, but I should have thought him a bit too old to appeal to very young ladies."

"That is one of the interesting aspects of the situation," Anthony said. "Each of the young women was compromised by a man who is variously described in their letters and journals as *a Greek God with golden hair*, *the most beautiful man on the face of the earth,* and *a knight in shining armor.* All agree he is in his late twenties."

"Hastings has dark hair going gray and is in his forties," Emma pointed out.

"So there is another man involved in the blackmail scheme," Louisa mused.

"Yes," Anthony said. "I will make arrangements immediately to return all of the items to their rightful owners anonymously and assure the victims that the blackmail is at an end. However, that avenue of inquiry is obviously closed to us."

"Of course," Louisa said. "We cannot risk exposing the identities of the victims."

"No." Anthony met her eyes. "Nor would they be likely to assist us in any event. Mrs. Bryce, I think it is time we discussed my fee for last night's services."

Louisa straightened. "Yes, of course. How much would you say that sort of thing is worth?"

"I do not want your money. What I want is information."

She tensed. "I beg your pardon?"

"I have come here today to lay my cards on the table. As payment for last night, I hope that you will see fit to do the same."

"What do you mean?"

"I explained that, thanks to the necklace I discovered in the safe, I have concluded beyond a shadow of a doubt that Elwin Hastings murdered Fiona Risby."

"Yes, you did say that," she agreed politely.

His smile was very cold. "I see you have some doubts."

"Forgive me for interrupting," Emma said evenly, "but it did occur to me to suggest to Louisa that perhaps you might have a *motive* for pointing the finger of blame at Elwin Hastings. That is not quite the same thing as proving that he killed her."

Anthony nodded once, comprehending immediately. "Yes, of course. You wonder if I am concerned that the old rumors will prevent me from shopping for a bride in certain circles. You concluded that perhaps I have set out to implicate another in the crime in order to clear my own name."

Louisa winced at the phrase *shopping for a bride*.

Emma's brows rose. "You will admit that it is a possibility that cannot be entirely dismissed."

Anthony met her eyes in a very direct fashion. "At this moment I can only offer you my word that is not the case. Last night I found the proof I needed to convince myself of what I have believed for some time."

"The necklace," Louisa said.

"Yes." He turned back to her. "To my mind it is all the evidence I require to be convinced that Elwin Hastings murdered Fiona, but I am left with another question, one for which I intend to get an answer."

"What is that?" Louisa asked.

"I'm very sure he killed her, but I have no notion *why*. There is simply nothing to connect Fiona Risby with Elwin Hastings other than the fact that they were both at the same ball on the night she disappeared."

"There must have been a large crowd at that ball," she pointed out. "How did you narrow the suspects down to Hastings?"

"There were several aspects of the situation that made me curious about him. The first was the death of his wife a few days later. I found the suicides of two women in Society, carried out in precisely the same manner less than a week apart, extremely coincidental, to say the least."

Louisa tapped her pen lightly against the blotter. "One may have inspired the other. A woman overwhelmed by melancholia who happened to read of another woman's suicide might decide to take the same path."

Emma frowned. "I admit that I did not know her well, but I must tell you that I was quite shocked to hear of Victoria's death last year. At the time I remember thinking that she did not seem at all the sort to take her own life."

"That was my impression of her, too," Anthony said. "I am even more convinced that Fiona would never have done such a thing."

The door opened again. Mrs. Galt set the tea tray on the table in front of Emma.

"I'll pour, Mrs. Galt," Emma said. "Thank you."

"Yes, ma'am."

No one spoke until Mrs. Galt was gone and the door was once again closed.

Louisa looked at Anthony. "You were saying that the coincidence of the two suicides caught your attention."

He lounged deeper into his chair and regarded her over steepled fingers. "There were actually three suicides that same month. The third was Joanna Barclay, the woman who killed Lord Gavin. You may recall the name. The murder created a great sensation in the press."

Louisa froze. Icy tendrils of fear uncoiled inside her. She was very careful not to look at Emma.

"Yes," she managed. "I believe I did hear something about that suicide."

It was all she could do to keep breathing normally. The old terror began to creep out of the deep shadows, where it was always lurking. *He could not possibly know who she was*. As far as the world was concerned Joanna Barclay was dead. Society had long since forgotten the sensation Lord Gavin's death had created.

But Lord Gavin had relatives. He had been married. There was a widow. Lady Gavin did not currently move in Society, of course, because she was still in mourning. Nevertheless, she was out there, somewhere. Perhaps Anthony was acquainted with her. Perhaps he had concluded there was some connection to the deaths of Fiona and Victoria. Perhaps he would feel it necessary to investigate the suicide of Joanna Barclay . . .

"Mrs. Bryce?"

She jumped at the sound of Anthony's voice. He was watching her with an unsettling, enigmatic expression.

"Sorry," she said quickly. "I was just thinking about what you said, sir."

Emma gave her a worried look. "Do you feel faint, dear?"

"No, not at all." Louisa forced her chaotic

fears back into the shadows. *Get hold of yourself. You're allowing your imagination to run wild. You must deal with this situation one step at a time.*

"Please continue with your explanation, sir," she said coolly. "What of the third suicide?"

He continued to regard her in silence for a few heartbeats. She did not like the calculating expression in his eyes. Eventually he inclined his head slightly, as though accepting her explanations.

"I made some inquiries into Miss Barclay's suicide," he said, "but I was forced to conclude that there was no connection to the deaths of Fiona or Victoria Hastings. Miss Barclay was a bookseller. She had nothing to do with the Polite World, and there was no indication that Hastings knew her in any capacity. She specialized in rare and expensive volumes. Her clientele consisted primarily of collectors. Hastings is not interested in books."

He had gone so far as to make inquiries. Cold perspiration dampened Louisa's chemise. In an effort to settle her nerves, she removed her spectacles and began to polish the lenses with a handkerchief.

"Hmm," she said, trying to appear thoughtful again.

"As I recall," Emma said, composed, as always, in a crisis, "the sensation press made it plain that there was no mystery whatsoever about Miss Barclay's death. She had a very strong motive for taking her own life. She must have known that she would be arrested for the murder of Lord Gavin. Obviously she could not bear the thought of the ordeal that was to come."

"Indeed." Anthony tapped his fingertips together once. "I was convinced to abandon that line of inquiry." He did not take his attention off Louisa. "But the suicides of both Fiona and Mrs. Hastings continued to make me uneasy. I made some more inquiries, this time into Elwin Hastings's business affairs."

Louisa abruptly stopped polishing her spectacles. Curiosity surfaced above her fear. She popped the spectacles back on her nose and peered at him. "Did you find anything that aroused your suspicions?"

"Unfortunately, no. Hastings was involved in one of his investment consortiums at the time of the deaths, but I could not see any possible link between Fiona and his financial affairs."

Louisa cleared her throat. "Forgive me for mentioning this, sir, but I must. Is there any possibility that Fiona and Mr. Hastings were intimately involved?"

"None whatsoever."

The denial was flat and unequivocal. It allowed for no argument.

"I see," she said. "Very well, then."

"I spoke with several people who saw Fiona and the Hastingses at the ball that night. Evidently Mr. and Mrs. Hastings had gone out into the gardens to take some fresh air. Fiona was also seen leaving the ballroom. She was alone, and she, too, went into the gardens."

Emma handed him a cup of tea. "There would have been a number of people out in the gardens that night."

"True." Anthony took the cup and saucer and set them on the table beside his chair. "In any event, the Hastingses were seen returning from the gardens some time later. They called for their carriage and left almost immediately."

"What of Miss Risby?" Louisa asked.

Anthony's jaw hardened. "She was never seen alive again."

"I don't understand. Are you saying no one noticed her come back into the ballroom?"

"Yes, Mrs. Bryce, that is what I am saying. She went out into the gardens alone and never returned. When she was pulled out of the water at dawn she was still in the gown that she had worn to the ball. The necklace was gone. It was assumed that it had fallen to the bottom of the river."

Emma stirred her tea with an absent air. "I hadn't heard those details."

"For obvious reasons, the Risbys were anxious to maintain as much privacy as possible," Anthony said.

"Go on," Louisa urged, fascinated now. "Were there any other clues that led you to link the deaths of the two women?"

"In the course of the autopsy it was discovered that Fiona had suffered a blow of some kind to her head. The authorities concluded that she had hit a rock or some other underwater obstacle when she jumped, but there are other possibilities."

Louisa stifled a small shiver. There were

indeed other ways one could sustain a blow to the head. A poker, for example, could create a most grievous wound, a killing wound.

She touched her tongue to her suddenly dry lips. “Is that all you found in the way of clues?”

“Yes,” he admitted. “In the end, I was forced to abandon my inquiries.”

“I don’t understand,” Louisa said. “If that is the case, what led you to take the risk of opening Hastings’s safe last night?”

“The supposed suicide two weeks ago of a man named Phillip Grantley,” Anthony said.

Louisa looked at Emma for clarification. Emma shook her head, indicating she was equally mystified. That meant that Grantley had not moved in Society.

Louisa turned back to Anthony. “Who was Phillip Grantley?”

“My informant told me that Grantley was well acquainted with Elwin Hastings. It appears that Grantley handled Hastings’s business affairs. Hastings happens to be in the midst of putting together another investment consortium, just as he was last year when Fiona and Mrs. Hastings died. I found the coincidences too intriguing to ignore."

Comprehension struck Louisa. She sat forward, excitement pulsing through her. "That is why you attended the same balls and receptions that I attended this past week. We were both seeking information on the other members of Hastings's investment consortium."

"Yes." He smiled faintly. "I noticed you when I found myself practically tripping over you in Lord Hammond's library."

She had just picked up her cup. Shocked, she set it down again with a loud clang of chine-on-china. "What are you talking about?"

"On the night of the Hammond ball you entered the library in what could only be described as a furtive manner about thirty seconds after I got there."

She stared at him, appalled. "You were already *inside* the library that night?"

"I sought shelter behind the draperies," he said. "It was a bit awkward. Can't recall the last time I was obliged to conceal myself in that fashion."

"Good heavens." Chastened, Louisa

slumped back in her chair. "You were actually there in the library when I searched it? I was so sure I had been unobserved."

"As you can imagine, my curiosity was aroused," Anthony said, watching her intently.

"Later that evening you requested an introduction," Emma observed.

That was the night he had first danced with her, Louisa thought wistfully. The night when she had allowed herself to dream a little.

"When I noticed you slip away to search Wellsworth's library a few evenings later," Anthony continued, his attention still on Louisa, "it became clear that we might well share a mutual interest in Hastings. Last night you confirmed my theory. I think the time has come to pool our resources."

"Hmm," Louisa said.

"Before we proceed," Anthony added deliberately, "I have a question of my own. Considering how much I have confided in you, I would appreciate an answer. In fact, I think it is fair to say that I deserve one."

She sat back in her chair. "You want to know why I am investigating Hastings's financial affairs."

"It seems a reasonable question under the circumstances."

Reasonable or not, she would have to answer it, she decided. If she did not, he would probably refuse to join forces. And it was clear to her now that that was the only way she would be able to pursue the investigation to its conclusion. The lure of reporting two murders in Society was irresistible.

"Very well, I will do so, sir, under one condition."

Emma pursed her lips. "Louisa, I am not at all certain this is a good idea."

"Forgive me," Louisa said gently, "but I feel I have no choice." She looked at Anthony. "Will you agree?"

"It depends on the condition," he said evenly.

"If you wish my assistance in this matter, you must agree to a partnership."

Anthony's eyes tightened a little at the corners. "You wish to become involved in an affair of murder, Mrs. Bryce?"

"I wish to help you investigate Mr. Hastings," she corrected evenly. "I am not yet convinced that you are right when you say that he is a murderer twice over. Nevertheless, you have made me sufficiently curious to want to inquire more deeply into the matter."

"Why the devil would you want to help pursue a killer? It is dangerous work."

"Yes," Emma put in swiftly. "Very dangerous work. Louisa, I really don't think you should go forward with this plan. You take enough risks as it is."

There was a short silence. Anthony switched his attention to Emma.

He had picked up the scent, Louisa thought. There would be no distracting him now.

"Very well, sir." She folded her hands together. "I will explain myself, but I must warn you that there really is no choice but to cooperate. If you do not, we will likely continue to find ourselves tripping over each other for the foreseeable future."

Anthony studied her. "Mrs. Bryce, are you so bored with Society that you seek to take grave risks to your person merely to amuse yourself?"

"I am going to tell you something that very few people know. Emma is one of those people. Another is the editor and publisher of the *Flying Intelligencer*."

"That rag? What in blazes can you possibly have to do with a disreputable paper that thrives on the most lurid sensations?"

She had expected that reaction, she reminded herself. Nevertheless, she was crushed and annoyed by his casual disdain.

"As it happens," she said coolly, "I am a correspondent for that disreputable rag."

Anthony went very still. It was, she reflected, the first time she had seen him stopped cold in his tracks. She tried to take some satisfaction from that turn of events. His opinion of her had no doubt plummeted to a very low point, but at least she had managed to startle him. She had the feeling that did not happen very often.

"You are a correspondent?" he repeated, his voice quite neutral.

"A *secret* correspondent," she clarified. "I write under the name I. M. Phantom."

"Well, it no doubt serves me right." He shook his head and then his mouth twitched a little.

She glowered. "You find my career amusing, sir?"

"Astonishing would be a better word." He

paused. "My sister would be thrilled to meet you."

Louisa brightened. "She reads my work?"

"Of course. But that is not the only reason why she would enjoy making your acquaintance. As it happens the two of you have a great deal in common."

"I don't understand. Is your sister also a correspondent?"

"No, but she is in a similar profession, one that, like yours, compels her to conceal her identity."

"What does she do?" Louisa asked eagerly. She had never encountered another woman who had also assumed a false identity.

"She writes plays under the name E. G. Harris."

"I know her work." Louisa was barely able to contain her excitement. "Her plays are staged at the Olympia Theater. The current one is *Night on Sutton Lane*. I went to see it last week. There are several thrilling sensations including the most astonishing scene of a ship sinking at sea."

"I'm aware of that."

"One believes the heroine must surely drown because she was involved in an illicit love affair, and everyone knows that illicit love affairs always come to bad ends in sensation dramas. Nevertheless, at the last minute a gentleman appears out of nowhere and saves her." Louisa sighed. "Unfortunately, he is not Nigel, the man whom she loved."

"As I recall, Nigel was already married," Anthony said.

"Yes, but he didn't know it, you see. He thought his wife was dead when she had actually been locked up in an asylum by her scheming brother."

"I assure you I have seen the play, Mrs. Bryce. There is no need to describe it."

She blushed, embarrassed. "Yes, of course."

Emma chuckled. "Louisa is a great fan of your sister's plays, sir."

"So I see." Anthony raised his brows. "It so happens that I have read some of your news reports, Mrs. Bryce."

"I'm surprised to hear you admit that you have read anything printed in the *Flying Intelligencer*." But a little thrill of pleasure went through her. He had read her work.

"The *Intelligencer* has two categories of readers," he said dryly. "Those who will admit to reading it and those who will not admit to reading it. That is especially true since I. M. Phantom's pieces began appearing. I offer you my sincere congratulations, Mrs. Bryce. You have managed to astound Society on a number of occasions with your revelations of scandal in high places."

She felt a sudden need to defend herself. "I am not interested in scandal solely because of the sensation it will cause. It is a desire to see justice prevail that motivates me, sir."

He cocked a quizzical brow. "Justice?"

"Too often people who move in elevated social circles abuse their positions of privilege and power. They take advantage of those who are weaker than themselves knowing full well that it is unlikely that they will pay for their crimes."

"I see. You feel called upon to mete out justice by exposing such people?"

"There is little else that can be done." She widened her hands. "Everyone knows that it is virtually impossible for Scotland Yard to conduct an investigation in the Polite World. All the doors are closed, and there is no way to open them. You said yourself, there was no chance that the police would ever be able to search Hastings's house."

"True. Nevertheless—"

"Thanks to Emma I find myself in a unique position," she continued. "I am able to circulate in some of the best social circles without calling attention to myself."

He glanced at Emma.

Emma poured more tea. "It has been interesting, I must say."

"I wish to make it plain that I pride myself on accuracy," Louisa said firmly. "I always investigate quite thoroughly before I write my reports. The last thing I want to do is cause pain or humiliation to an innocent person."

"Enough." Anthony raised a hand, palm out. "I do not doubt your zeal or your intentions, Mrs. Bryce."

She dared to relax slightly.

"I have been wondering how you came by your information," he continued. "Can I assume that, as a member of the press, you have informants?"

"Yes," she said, cautious again.

"I would like to know the name of the person who put you onto Hastings's trail."

She pondered that for a moment. Miranda Fawcett enjoyed her role as a behind-the-scenes source of secrets for a newspaper correspondent. She could no doubt be persuaded to aid Anthony in his investigation, provided she could be convinced to trust him.

"My informant might agree to assist you," she said, "but I make no guarantees."

Veiled anticipation leaped in Anthony's eyes. "I understand."

Louisa clasped her hands. "Let me make myself very clear, sir," she said coolly. "This conversation will end here and now if you do not agree to make me a full partner in this affair."

His eyes tightened dangerously at the corners. "I do not think that would be wise, Mrs. Bryce."

"I do not think that you have any choice, Mr. Stalbridge."

10

Ten minutes later he went down the steps of Number Twelve, crossed the street, and started through the small park in the center of the square. He was not in what anyone would term a pleasant mood.

Louisa was a correspondent for the *Flying Intelligencer*. That piece of information had come out of nowhere, blindsiding him. He had never heard of a female reporter, let alone one who did her work from inside exclusive circles.

Astounding as her career was, it did explain much of what had made him curious in recent days, including her secretive forays in the Wellsworth and Hammond households and her interest in Hastings. It also explained the unfashionable gowns, the spectacles, and the boring conversation at every social event she attended. Louisa had gone to great lengths to make certain that people did not take any notice of her. Like it or not, however, she was going to lose some of her precious anonymity now that her name was linked with his. He wondered how she would deal with that.

He walked through a stand of trees and found himself in a small clearing in the middle of the park. He passed two green wrought-iron benches and a statue of a nymph. On the far side of the greenery he crossed another street, turned a corner, and entered a narrow lane. When he emerged onto a busy street, he briefly considered and then discarded the notion of whistling for a hansom cab. He needed to work off some of the frustration Louisa's bargain had sparked.

He did not want her to be involved in this affair, but it seemed there was no other choice. She had made it clear that she would pursue the investigation of Hastings with or without his assistance. The only thing he could do now was keep an eye on her. That would probably not be easy, he decided.

11

"I know that it is highly unlikely that I can talk you out of this venture," Emma said. "Nevertheless, I feel I must try. There are so many risks involved."

Louisa got to her feet and went to the garden window. "I have taken risks before."

"Not like this. You have never investigated a murder."

"That is precisely why I cannot pass up this opportunity. A story about the shocking murders of two women in Society that can be tied to Elwin Hastings is simply too important to ignore. Men like Hastings rarely pay for their crimes. This is a chance to drag one to justice."

"Keep in mind that you do not know for

certain that Hastings murdered anyone. You have only Mr. Stalbridge's opinion of the facts to go on at this point. I told you, he may have his own reasons for wanting to fix blame on someone."

Louisa looked out into the garden. "I do not think that he is pursuing this investigation solely to clear his own name, Emma. Frankly, I do not believe that he gives a fig for Society's opinion of him. My intuition tells me that he is genuinely convinced that Hastings murdered Fiona. He is determined to obtain justice for her."

"Perhaps you want to attribute such noble motives to him because you would like to believe that the two of you have something in common," Emma said gently. "Both of you seeking justice, et cetera, et cetera."

"I suppose you may be right." Louisa turned around. "But either way, I am determined to see this through."

"Do not mistake me, dear, I have nothing but admiration for your work as a correspondent, but I fear that you are becoming reckless in your pursuit of justice in the Polite World."

"I appreciate your concern, and I promise you I will be careful."

Emma sighed. "It is your old anger and fear of Lord Gavin that drives you. The man is dead, but he haunts you still."

"I will not quarrel with you on that account. What happened last year is a nightmare that will be with me to the end of my days. Perhaps I have allowed it to push me into a risky business. At the same time, I cannot help feeling that I am doing what I was meant to do. My work as I. M. Phantom satisfies something in me that nothing else can equal."

"You are determined to go forward with this arrangement you have made with Anthony Stalbridge, aren't you?"

"I have no choice." Louisa gripped the edge of the windowsill. She fell silent for a moment. "He must have loved her very much, Emma."

12

Anthony went up the steps of the large house on Brackton Street. Dreading what lay ahead, he banged the gleaming brass knocker. Footsteps sounded in the hall. The door opened to reveal a tall, cadaverously thin, gray-haired man in a butler's suit.

"Mr. Stalbridge, sir. Do come in."

"Good afternoon, Shuttle." Anthony moved into the hall and tossed his hat onto the marble-topped side table. "All is well with you, I trust?"

"I am in excellent health, thank you, sir." Shuttle closed the door. "Your mother and sister are in the library. Your father, of course, is in his workshop."

"Thank you."

Anthony went along the hall and paused in the open doorway of the library, steeling himself for the assault. There was a large desk and an easel in the room, both positioned to catch the best light from the tall windows overlooking the extensive gardens. His mother, Georgiana, was at the easel, paintbrush in hand. The sun highlighted the silver in her dark hair. She was in her late fifties, tall and gracefully made. A paint-stained apron covered her gown. Clarice sat at the desk, poring over a stack of papers covered with her handwriting. Her latest script for the Olympia, no doubt. A cloud of red curls framed her elfin face and blue eyes.

"Good afternoon, ladies," he said from the door. "You both appear to be busy. I will not intrude." He took a step back. "I just stopped by to have a word with Father."

"Tony." Clarice looked up suddenly. "Come back here. Don't you dare try to leave without explaining yourself."

"Sorry," Anthony said, edging farther out into the hall. "I'm in somewhat of a hurry at the moment. Later, perhaps."

"No, not later," Georgiana declared. She set aside her brush. "Your grandmother was here not more than an hour ago and told us everything."

He swore under his breath. His grandmother, Lady Payne, was an indomitable woman who never failed to live up to her name. Her chief occupation in life, as far as he could tell, was to meddle in family affairs. At one time or another they had all suffered from her interference, but of late she had been focusing most of her attention on him.

To be fair, she was not alone. These days it seemed that everyone in the large clan was concentrating the full force of their no doubt well-intentioned attention on him. Fortunately, the only members of the extended Stalbridge family who were in town at the moment were his grandmother, mother, father, and sister.

Nevertheless, given the razor-sharp intelligence and forceful willpower that characterized virtually every leaf on the Stalbridge family tree, it was little wonder that he was doing his best these days to avoid even the four relations who did happen to be in London.

"Is it true?" Clarice demanded eagerly. "Did you really sweep a mysterious widow named Mrs. Bryce away from the Hastingses' ball last evening and carry her off into the night in your carriage?"

He loved his sister. She was several years younger, sharp of wit, compassionate by nature, and generally quite entertaining, but there was no denying that she had a flare for the dramatic, a side effect of her playwriting talents, no doubt.

"Mrs. Bryce and I did leave the ball together," he said, choosing his words with care. "However, we went down the steps and got into the carriage in an entirely normal manner. As I recall, there was no sweeping involved. Now, if you will excuse me, I will go find Father."

"Wait, you must tell us more about her," Georgiana insisted. "Who is she? What of her family background? What became of Mr. Bryce? Your grandmother did not have a great deal of information. The only facts she had were that Mrs. Bryce is a distant relation of Lady Ashton's and that she has absolutely no sense of style."

Anthony smiled at that. "The lack of details must have been extremely frustrating for her."

"Does she really wear her spectacles when she goes to a ball?" Clarice asked.

"Yes," Anthony said.

"Well?" Georgiana prompted. "What of her husband?"

"I do not know what became of Mr. Bryce," he admitted. "The important thing is that he is no longer around."

"Grandmother says Mrs. Bryce is out of mourning so he must have died at least three or four years ago," Clarice offered.

"One could make that assumption, yes," Anthony agreed.

"Your grandmother indicated that she does not appear to have any money in her own right," Georgiana observed. "Evidently Lady Ashton has taken her in out of the kindness of her heart."

"That seems to be the case," Anthony agreed. "Now, if you will excuse me—"

"What is she like?" Clarice asked.

Anthony gave that a few seconds of close contemplation.

"Unconventional," he said finally.

"In what way?" Clarice demanded. "We want details, Tony. This is the first woman you have shown any interest in since Fiona died. The least you can do is tell us a little about her."

"Among other things she admires your plays," he said.

"You told her that I write for the Olympia?" Clarice's eyes widened.

"I believe she was quite pleased that the heroine who had the illicit affair in *Night on Sutton Lane* did not drown at the end of the story even though she was not rescued by the man who had seduced her."

"I couldn't have Nigel rescue her," Clarice explained. "He was already married."

"I did try to explain that," Anthony said. With that, he made good his escape.

He climbed the stairs and went down the long hall to the large room at the back of the house. The architect had intended the space to serve as a master bedroom and sitting room, but it had functioned as his father's workshop for as long as he could remember.

The muffled clang of metal on metal reverberated through the upstairs hall. It was a familiar sound, one he remembered well from his childhood. He had spent countless hours in the workshop. When he had not been actively assisting his father with a project, he had wiled away a considerable amount of time playing with the unique clockwork and mechanical toys his father had created for him.

One thing about having an inventor for a parent, he thought, opening the door: Life had never been dull.

"Is that you, Clarice?" Marcus Stalbridge had his back to the door. He did not turn around. "I haven't finished work on your burning house project yet. Bit of a problem with the chemicals that create the smoke, I'm afraid. They produce far too much of the stuff. The audience won't be able to see the action on the stage."

Anthony closed the door, folded his arms, and propped one shoulder against the wall. "Clarice is planning to burn down a house?"

"Tony. About time you got here." Marcus put down a wrench and swung around. "I sent that message hours ago. Where the devil have you been?"

Dressed in a heavy leather apron, grease-stained shirt and trousers, and a pair of sturdy boots, his father could easily have been mistaken for a dockside worker or a carpenter, Anthony thought. He certainly did not present the typical image of an English gentleman descended from a long line of the same.

Marcus had been educated as an engineer. According to everyone who had known him in his youth, he had been inventing things since he was old enough to climb out of his cradle. He was in his sixties now, a big man with big, competent hands and aggressively modeled features. His green-and-gold eyes could be disconcertingly piercing and direct when he was consumed with the creation of one of his countless inventions. At other times he appeared vague and distracted. Everyone knew that expression well. It meant that Marcus was dreaming up a new device.

“My apologies, sir,” Anthony said. “I’ve been busy today, and then, when I arrived, I had some difficulty getting past that pair of inquisitors downstairs.”

Marcus wiped his hands on a rag. “Expect your mother and sister had a few questions for you. Your grandmother paid us a visit earlier.”

“I heard. Tell me about Clarice’s burning house.”

“It’s another one of her sensations. She says the competition is becoming quite fierce. Every theater in town is trying to outdo the others with dramatic scenes on stage. Ghosts, storms, runaway trains, rotating towers, and the like have all become quite common. She says fires never fail to dazzle audiences."

"It will be difficult to top the sinking ship in her latest production. It is so realistic the critics complained because they got damp."

"Bah." Marcus grimaced with disgust. "The critics always find something to complain about. The audiences love the show."

"Now she wants to burn down a house on stage?"

"Yes. The hero has to rescue a child trapped in the flames."

"I'm sure it will be thrilling."

Marcus pursed his lips. "Not as thrilling as Clarice had hoped, I'm afraid. It seems the owners of the Olympia got a trifle nervous when she told them she planned to use real flames on stage. But I've come up with an alternative that I think will work. It involves an array of fire-colored lights and a great deal of smoke."

"I shall look forward to it."

"Speaking of sensations, your grandmother told us that you and a widow named Mrs. Bryce managed to create a small one of your own last night. What happened? I thought you were deeply involved in your investigation of Hastings. Did you change your mind?"

"Don't look so pathetically hopeful. I'm afraid Mrs. Bryce is connected to my investigation."

"Devil take it." Marcus grimaced. "Should have guessed as much. When your mother and I and Clarice heard that you had taken a lady home from the ball, I suppose we leaped to the assumption that perhaps—"

"I had allowed myself to be distracted? I'm sorry to disappoint you."

Marcus leaned back against a workbench. "You can't blame us for worrying about you, Tony. You're obsessed with this business of proving that Hastings murdered Fiona. It's a dangerous business you're pursuing. If you had been caught prowling through Hastings's house—"

"I found Fiona's necklace last night," Anthony said quietly.

Marcus stared at him. "Bloody hell. Where?"

"It was in Hastings's safe."

Marcus exhaled heavily. Then his eyes narrowed. "Are you certain it's the Risby necklace?"

"Yes. He must have taken it off her after he killed her."

Marcus rubbed the back of his neck. "So you were right, after all."

"It certainly looks that way."

Marcus folded his arms, thinking. "But it makes no sense. Why would he do such a thing?" He squinted a little. "You don't think it's possible that he seduced her, do you? A lover's quarrel, perhaps?"

"No," Anthony said.

"You sound very certain. I know you were fond of Fiona, Tony—we all were—but don't let your old affection blind you to certain possibilities."

"Fiona was not intimately involved with Hastings."

Marcus did not look entirely satisfied, but he nodded, not arguing further.

"Very well, then," he said. "What of a motive? What possible reason could he have had for murdering an innocent young woman?"

"I don't know. That's one of the things I intend to find out."

"Give it up, Tony. Too much time has passed. You won't be able to prove anything now."

Anthony went to stand at one of the workbenches. He looked down at the array of tools arranged on the wooden surface. "Hastings has been blackmailing several wealthy old ladies for over two years."

"You're joking. Hastings? An extortionist?"

"I found the proof in the safe, along with the necklace. Unfortunately, like the necklace, it was useless. I will make arrangements to return the extortion evidence to the various victims anonymously, but for obvious reasons none of them can be expected to testify against him. In fact, I very much doubt that they even knew the identity of their blackmailer."

"Good Lord." Marcus grimaced in disgust. "The man's a villain, all right. But if you can't prove anything, what do you hope to do?"

"First things first." Anthony looked up from the tools. "My main objective at the moment is to discover why he murdered Fiona. That question has plagued me from the start of this affair."

"And just how in blazes will you manage that?"

"I'm certain there was no intimate connection between them. That leaves the possibility that Fiona somehow learned too much about his business affairs. Perhaps she discovered that he was a blackmailer."

Marcus thought about that. "You think he killed her to keep his secrets?"

"It would be a strong motive."

"Perhaps. But, again, how will you prove it after all this time?"

"I don't know." Anthony went to the steel safe that stood on one side of the room. He put a hand on the gleaming green surface and traced the decorative gold design with one finger. "Hastings's safe was, indeed, an Apollo, as you said. He had it installed in the floor of his bedroom, just as Carruthers told you. Thank you for getting the information for me."

Will Carruthers of the Carruthers Lock and Safe Company was an old friend of the family. He was the exclusive purveyor of the Apollo Patented Safe in London. Carruthers had sold the safe to Hastings. He had also overseen its installation.

Marcus's brows arched. "I take it you

haven't lost any of your safecracking skills?"

"I was a bit rusty, but I had it open inside of thirty seconds."

"Would have been fifteen in the old days." Marcus smiled reminiscently. "I'll never forget the many happy hours you spent picking locks in this workshop, testing out new devices for me." His white brows snapped together again. "Which reminds me, it's about time you provided me with some grandchildren. I need new assistants. You're never around anymore, and Clarice is always busy with her plays."

"Someday," Anthony promised. "When this other affair is concluded."

"Promises, promises." Marcus's expression sharpened. "What of Mrs. Bryce? Where does she fit into this?"

"It's complicated. Last night I encountered her just as she emerged from Hastings's bedroom."

Marcus's mouth opened, closed, and opened again. "His *bedroom*? Are you joking? What in blazes was she doing in there?"

"The same thing I had intended to do. She

went there to search his private possessions."

"Why?"

"She was looking for proof that Hastings invested funds in a brothel."

"She cracked the Apollo?"

"No. But after she made my acquaintance in the hallway outside the bedroom she hired me to do the job for her."

"She *hired* you?" Marcus was practically sputtering now.

"She mistook me for a jewel thief. As I said, it's somewhat complicated."

"Good Lord." Marcus scowled. "Who the devil *is* this Mrs. Bryce?"

"I am still working on the answer to that question. However, I have discovered that, among other things, she is a correspondent for the *Flying Intelligencer.*"

"I don't believe it. She writes for the sensation press?"

"Yes."

"But you despise the press because of how it handled Fiona's tragic death. I find it difficult to believe that you have formed an association with a journalist."

"It comes as something of a surprise to me, as well, sir. But, then, I have discovered that Mrs. Bryce has a way of keeping one off balance. While we're on the subject, I would appreciate it if you would keep Mrs. Bryce's career a deep, dark family secret. She goes to great lengths to conceal her identity."

Marcus's brows shot skyward. "Because she's a female?"

"In part, no doubt. But the primary reason she uses a pen name is because she conducts her journalistic investigations in the Polite World. Her career would come to an end rather quickly if her identity were to be revealed to Society."

"That's a fact." Marcus snorted. "Her name would be dropped from every guest list in town if word got out. She would never receive another invitation."

"Precisely."

Marcus stroked his chin thoughtfully. "This is astonishing. Absolutely astonishing."

"Do you recall the Bromley scandal?"

"I should think so. Talk about a sensation. Who would have imagined that pretentious, self-righteous prig, Lord Bromley, was making money off a ring of opium dens. When the news appeared in the *Flying Intelligencer*, Bromley was forced to leave the country on an extended tour of America. He hasn't dared return."

"Mrs. Bryce is the one who first reported that story and presented evidence to the public. She writes under the name I. M. Phantom."

"So she's Phantom." Marcus paused, frowning. "And now she's after Hastings. Well, well, well."

"I tried to talk her out of conducting the investigation, but she won't hear of it. I feel responsible for seeing to it that she doesn't come to any harm, so I have agreed to work with her on this venture. For the foreseeable future it will appear to the world that she and I have formed an intimate liaison."

"I see." Marcus looked shrewd. "And have you?"

"I assure you, our association is based entirely on business."

"According to your grandmother, everyone is saying that you have formed an intimate liaison with Mrs. Bryce."

"That is the point, sir. With luck, the gossip will serve as camouflage. If people, including Hastings, believe that Mrs. Bryce and I are involved in a liaison, they are less likely to guess what we are really about."

"An interesting theory," Marcus said without inflection.

"Unfortunately, it is the only one I've got. Good day, sir."

Anthony left and walked swiftly toward the staircase. He half-expected Clarice to be lurking in the front hall, but luck was with him. There was no one around downstairs. Nevertheless, he did not breathe easily until he was safely outside on the street.

Marcus waited until he heard the front door open and close. When he was certain that Anthony had departed, he took off the leather apron and went downstairs to the library.

Georgiana and Clarice were both drinking tea. They looked at him with expectant expressions.

"Did Tony tell you anything about his association with Mrs. Bryce, Papa?" Clarice asked.

"A little." Marcus took the cup of tea that Georgiana held out to him. "It is all quite amazing. Bizarre, in fact."

"Do you think he is serious about her,

dear?" Georgiana asked. "Or is she some passing fancy?"

"She's no passing fancy," Marcus said, absolutely certain of the conclusion. "Although I don't think Tony realizes that yet. He's still fixated on finding Fiona's killer."

"What do you think of Mrs. Bryce?" Georgiana asked.

"Difficult to say. Haven't even met the woman." Marcus drank some tea and lowered the cup. "But from what I've heard so far, I'd say she would fit rather well into this family."

13

Miranda Fawcett agreed to meet with them the following day. She received Louisa and Anthony in a grand drawing room that resembled the lobby of a luxurious theater. Red velvet curtains trimmed with gold cords framed the windows. The carpet was crimson, decorated with an elaborate flower motif. The sofa and chairs were gilded and covered in gold upholstery. A heavy crystal chandelier hung overhead.

Miranda, herself, was equally striking in a turquoise-blue tea gown and a vast amount of pearls. She wore an impressive crown of hair done in an intricate style that must have taken hours to prepare. Louisa was certain their hostess was wearing a wig. Very few women of Miranda's age—or any other age, for that matter—possessed such a great volume of hair. The rich brown color was equally suspicious.

"A pleasure to meet you, Mr. Stalbridge." Miranda sparkled up at Anthony as he inclined his head over her hand.

"The pleasure is all mine, Mrs. Fawcett." He straightened, smiling. "You are a legend, madam. But, then, you know that. No actress has ever been able to replace you on the stage. I was fortunate enough to see your last performance as Lady Macbeth."

Louisa nearly fell out of her chair. Anthony could certainly turn on the gallantry at will. Half an hour ago, when he had arrived in Arden Square to collect her for their appointment with Miranda, he had not seemed the least bit pleased at the prospect of meeting the retired actress. He had, in fact, been quite stunned to learn the identity of her informant.

"How the devil did you come to meet Miranda Fawcett?" he growled, following Louisa up into the carriage.

"I was able to do her a small favor shortly after I took up my career as a journalist," Louisa explained. "She was grateful."

"The woman must be nearing sixty."

"I believe so, yes."

Anthony leaned back against the seat and grew thoughtful. "In her day she was said to be the mistress of some of the most powerful men in the country."

"So Emma told me."

"There were rumors that she formed a long-term liaison with a man named Clement Corvus."

"I believe Miranda has mentioned his name on occasion."

"Louisa, the man is reputed to be a crime lord."

"Surely not, sir." She smiled serenely. "Had Mr. Corvus been a criminal he would have been arrested."

"From what I have heard, he is far too clever to get caught. He is always careful to keep himself at arm's length from the criminal activities from which he profits. They say he lives like a gentleman of wealth and means while running an underworld empire. On the street he is known as The Raven."

The authority that rang in his voice captured her attention. She regarded him with sudden curiosity.

"You seem to know a great deal about Mr. Corvus," she said.

Anthony hesitated. "He has been on my mind of late. I'll be frank. The fact that you have a connection with his former mistress makes me extremely uneasy."

"I do not believe that there is anything *former* about their relationship," Louisa said, amused. "I have the impression that they are still quite close. Miss Fawcett makes an excellent informant. I would not be surprised if much of the information she has given me came directly from The Raven."

"Why would he wish to assist a newspaper correspondent?"

She gave a tiny shrug. "Perhaps it amuses him. I know Miss Fawcett finds being my informant extremely entertaining."

"Just what sort of favor did you do for her?"

"It is a long story."

Watching Miranda glitter and glow now, Louisa felt a mix of amusement and admiration. At the height of her career, Miranda had been the most celebrated actress in England. She had also toured America to great acclaim. Although she had left the stage it was plain that she had lost none of her ability to charm an audience.

Miranda dimpled at Anthony. "You are very kind, sir. I must admit, sometimes I cannot believe that I have been out of the theater for so long. I miss it dreadfully. Real life can be so excruciatingly dull." She flashed a knowing smile at Louisa. "At least it was until I made the acquaintance of Mrs. Bryce. I vow, she has brought a new zest into my drab existence."

Anthony sat down in one of the gold chairs. "Mrs. Bryce does have a way of injecting a certain excitement into things."

Louisa shot him a repressive glare. He gave her a polite smile.

"Indeed, she does," Miranda said. She regarded Anthony with an expectant air. "She tells me that you are assisting her in one of her exciting little investigations, Mr. Stalbridge."

"I thought it would be amusing," Anthony said. "I, too, have found life a trifle dull of late."

Louisa raised her eyes to the ceiling.

Miranda gave a throaty chuckle. "Mrs. Bryce will soon rectify that problem for you."

"I have already noticed a marked change in the monotonous routine of my daily affairs," he assured her.

Hah, Louisa thought. Nothing about his life could possibly be routine, let alone monotonous.

"I can well imagine that," Miranda murmured. "One hears that after you returned from your extensive travels abroad a few years ago you immersed yourself in the business of managing your family's finances."

Startled, Louisa looked at Anthony for confirmation.

"It is dull work," he admitted. "Unfortunately, it became painfully clear that I was the only one in the family with a head for investments."

Miranda chuckled. "By all accounts you are, indeed, exceptionally skilled in that regard. One hears that you saved the entire Stalbridge clan from bankruptcy."

"Our fortunes have historically tended to fluctuate somewhat," he said politely.

Miranda winked. "Not since you took the helm. I trust your family is suitably grateful for your financial talents."

He smiled. "Very few members of my family pay any attention whatsoever to finances. They only notice if there is suddenly no money conveniently at hand."

Louisa felt the heat rush into her face. To think she'd once imagined that he had restored the family fortune via a career as a jewel thief.

She cleared her throat. "Thank you for seeing us, Miranda," she said in a businesslike manner. "It was very kind of you."

"Nonsense. I've been looking forward to it." Miranda smiled. "I do so enjoy our little conferences."

Anthony looked at her. "May I ask how you and Mrs. Bryce came to form your interesting association?"

"Hasn't she told you?" Miranda raised her brows. "The truth is, sir, I am very much in her debt. Several months ago she came to me because she discovered that I was about to invest a considerable sum of money in an investment scheme that was being concocted by two socially prominent gentlemen."

Anthony looked at Louisa.

"The California Mine Swindle," she said.

"Ah, yes." Anthony leaned back in his chair. "I remember it well. Grayson and Lord

Bartlett were the two men behind the swindle. In the wake of the reports in the press, they were forced to retire to their estates."

"The scheme was a complete fraud, of course," Miranda said coldly. "It was designed to take advantage of people like me. People who possess money but who do not move in Society."

"Yes," Anthony said quietly. "I know."

Miranda made a soft sound of disgust. "Grayson and Bartlett would never have dreamed of ruining any of their high-ranking acquaintances in the Polite World, but they did not hesitate to destroy those whom they felt were beneath them. I was not the only intended victim."

Louisa gripped her muff very tightly. "They laughed about it."

Anthony contemplated her with an enigmatic expression. "How did you come to learn of the scheme in time to warn Miss Fawcett?"

"It was a matter of the sheerest chance," she said. "Emma and I attended an art exhibition one evening. The hall was very warm. I stepped outside to get some fresh air, and I overheard part of a conversation that was taking place between Grayson and Lord Bartlett. I did not catch all the details, but it was enough to know that they were plotting some villainy involving Miss Fawcett."

"She came to me with the story," Miranda added. "As soon as I heard the names of the two men I realized immediately that they must have been discussing my investment. I couldn't understand what they were about. I have no head for that sort of thing, you see. So I mentioned it to a very good friend of mine who has an excellent brain for business. He grasped the implications at once and made some inquiries."

"Miranda contacted me to thank me and to tell me what her friend had uncovered," Louisa concluded. "I determined to inform the world about the swindle because there were a number of other victims. I made an appointment with the publisher and editor of the *Flying Intelligencer* and overnight I became I. M. Phantom."

"And I became one of I. M. Phantom's secret informants." Miranda twitched her skirts into even more perfect, graceful folds and regarded Anthony with an expectant expression. "Now, then, Louisa said in her message that you wish to ask me some questions."

"They are related to our investigation of Hastings," Anthony said. He spoke deliberately. "We found some evidence indicating that he pursued a career as a blackmailer."

Miranda made a soft, disgusted sound. "I have always considered blackmail one of the lowest of crimes."

"Most of the items we found were personal possessions of young ladies that contained rather passionate references to a handsome lover," Louisa said. "What we do not understand is how the items came into Hastings's hands."

Miranda nodded thoughtfully. "I don't suppose you can tell me the names of any of the victims?"

"No, I'm afraid not," Louisa said. "We feel an obligation to protect their identities."

"I quite understand," Miranda said. "I would like to help you, but I'm not entirely sure what you want from me."

Anthony looked at her. "You seem to know a fair amount about Hastings. You were able to tell Louisa the names of some of his business associates and that he might have a financial interest in a brothel."

"Yes," Miranda said. She winked at Louisa. "I, too, have my informant."

"We do not believe that Hastings put together the blackmail scheme on his own," Louisa said. "We know that he had at least one other employee, a man of business named Phillip Grantley, but Grantley put a pistol to his head two weeks ago."

"What we would like to know," Anthony said, "is whether Hastings has any other people working for him. Specifically a handsome, blond-haired man in his late twenties. We believe there is such a person and that he was the one who compromised the young ladies whose relatives were later blackmailed."

"Ah, yes, now I understand," Miranda said. "I do not know the answer offhand, but I will be happy to make inquiries. Will you give me a day or so?"

"Certainly," Louisa said. "Thank you so much. Mr. Stalbridge and I are very grateful."

"Nonsense." Miranda waved one hand in a graceful gesture. "You know I quite enjoy our little adventures."

"There is one more thing," Anthony said.

Miranda gave him an inquiring look. "Yes, Mr. Stalbridge?"

"Forgive me if I am being overly personal, but Louisa tells me that you and Clement Corvus are well acquainted."

Miranda's laugh was low and sultry. "Indeed, we are, sir. For more than twenty years now."

Anthony took an envelope out from an inside pocket of his coat. "In that case may I ask that you give him this with my compliments the next time you see him?"

14

Anthony handed Louisa up into the carriage. He had hired a cab for the afternoon rather than use his own vehicle. There was no need to advertise to the world that he and Louisa were calling on the retired actress.

When he sat down across from her, he realized that Louisa was fairly shimmering with suppressed curiosity. It occurred to him that no matter what her mood, he was fascinated by her. Whenever he was in her presence he was aware of a deeply sensual, mysteriously feminine energy that compelled all that was male in him. He felt drawn to her by invisible bonds. It had never been like this with any other woman.

"What was in that envelope?" she demanded.

He made himself pay attention to the question. "Some papers relating to the investment consortium that Hastings recently formed with Hammond and Wellsworth," he said.

"I don't understand. Why do you think Mr. Corvus would be interested?"

"Because according to those papers, he is the fourth investor in the consortium."

Her eyes widened. "Oh, my."

"But by far the more intriguing part is that it appears Hastings and the others are planning to cheat Corvus out of his fair share of the profits. Evidently they have concluded that if they keep certain facts about the venture from him, he will never realize that the slice of the pie he will eventually receive will be much smaller than that of the others."

"They assume that because Clement Corvus does not come from their world and cannot join their clubs he will never discover the truth. They are happy to take his money and then turn around and cheat him." She made a tight little fist with one hand. "That is so typical of that sort."

"Corvus is a crime lord, Louisa. Not a

saint. There is no need to feel sorry for him. He has cheated his fair share of people over the years and no doubt done a good deal worse."

"I suppose that is true." She turned her attention to the street scene beyond the carriage window. "It is the arrogance of Hastings and the others that I cannot bear. Men like that think nothing of crushing someone else, provided that person is of a lower class."

"Have you always been this concerned about the villains who move in Society?" he asked quietly.

She flinched a little, as if she had forgotten he was there until he spoke. When she turned back to him he saw wariness in her eyes. He sensed she regretted the small display of intensity.

"Forgive me," she said, keeping her voice very even. "I am aware that there are occasions when I become too emotional about my work."

He smiled. "I do not mind strong passions."

She blinked. "You don't?"

"No. In fact, I find them quite exhilarating at times."

She searched his face, bewildered. "I don't understand what you mean, sir."

"This is what I mean, Mrs. Bryce."

He leaned forward, cupped the back of her head with one hand, brought her face very close to his, and covered her mouth with his own.

She seemed stunned for a few seconds, but she did not try to pull away. He felt a shiver course through her. He tightened his grip. She put one gloved hand very delicately on his shoulder. Her lips parted slightly.

Everything inside him leaped with excitement. It was all he could do not to pull her down onto the seat, push up her skirts, and sink himself into her. That thought made him realize that the windows were uncovered. Without releasing Louisa he used one hand to yank down the blinds.

When the shadows of the closed cab enveloped them, he gripped her head with both hands, anchored her, and deliberately deepened the kiss. Her mouth was soft and infinitely inviting. He drank from the warm well she offered as though he had been deprived of water for months, maybe years.

He heard the tiniest of feminine moans.

The small sound enthralled him. He was thoroughly aroused now, hard and straining against his trousers. He lowered one hand to Louisa's breast, learning the shape of her through the fabric of the gown.

There was another little sound, a small gasp of surprise this time, and then her fingers tightened convulsively around his shoulders.

"Mr. Stalbridge," she got out in a choked voice.

"I know." He groaned and raised his head reluctantly. "This is hardly the time or place. My apologies, madam. I am aware that this is not the way this sort of thing is usually done. All I can say is that where you are concerned, nothing seems to occur in a predictable fashion."

She stared at him through fogged-up spectacles, her mouth open, cheeks flushed.

Amused, he removed her spectacles. She blinked and then frowned ever so slightly when he took out a freshly laundered handkerchief and proceeded to polish the lenses.

He handed the spectacles back to her.

"Thank you," she said, sounding breathless.

She put on the spectacles and suddenly became very busy adjusting her hat and straightening the skirts of her gown.

He watched her for a moment, enjoying the sight of her sitting there across from him, savoring the knowledge that she had responded to him. After a time he raised the blinds.

When Louisa eventually ran out of small chores she cleared her throat, sat back, and clasped her hands very tightly together.

"Well, then," she said, and then stopped.

"You didn't answer my question," he reminded her gently.

Her brows snapped together. "What question?"

"When did you develop your great passion for bringing the criminals of the Polite World to justice?"

"Oh. After I came to stay with Emma." She looked out the window. "Before that I took it for granted that there was nothing that could be done about such people."

"Did something happen to someone you care about?" he asked, probing carefully. "Something that inspired your desire to see justice rendered among those who move in Society?"

"It was nothing personal," she said smoothly. "Merely my observations of the world."

She was lying, he realized. Very interesting.

He smiled slightly. "One of these days I will have to introduce you to a friend of mine. He is a man who understands what it is to be driven by a passion for justice. The two of you will have much to talk about, I think."

She glanced at him, frowning slightly. "Who is he?"

"His name is Fowler. He is a detective in Scotland Yard."

An expression that could only have been horror flashed across her face. It was gone almost immediately, but not before it had made a forceful impression on him.

"You are personally acquainted with a *policeman*?" she asked tightly.

There was mystery upon mystery here. He folded his arms and lounged deeper into the corner of the carriage, his curiosity thoroughly aroused.

"Fowler was the man who investigated

Fiona's death," he explained. "He also dealt with the suicide of Victoria Hastings. Like me, he was convinced that there was a connection to Elwin Hastings, but he could find no way to prove it."

She was gripping her parasol so fiercely now, it was a wonder the handle did not snap. "Did this detective also investigate the third suicide that you mentioned? The one that took place that same month?"

"Joanna Barclay? Yes. He was obliged to look into it because he investigated the murder of Lord Gavin."

"I see."

She seemed to be having difficulty breathing.

"Are you feeling unwell?" he asked, abruptly concerned.

"No, I'm fine, thank you." She hesitated. "I was not aware that you were associated with someone from Scotland Yard."

"I do not advertise it to the world for obvious reasons. Fowler is equally cautious about keeping our connection quiet."

"I see. You must admit that it is somewhat unusual for a gentleman of your rank to have a close acquaintance with a policeman."

He shrugged. "Fowler and I share a mutual interest."

"Proving that Hastings murdered Fiona?"

"Yes."

"Can I assume that Mr. Fowler is the source of your information concerning Elwin Hastings?"

Anthony inclined his head. "He also supplied me with some background on Clement Corvus. Fowler has been most helpful."

She gave him a brittle little smile. "How nice for you."

15

A short time later Anthony escorted her to the front door of Number Twelve and bid her farewell.

"Send word to my address immediately if and when you hear from Miranda Fawcett," he said as Mrs. Galt opened the door.

"I will," she promised, desperately wanting to be rid of him.

He gave her a cool, assessing look and then stepped back. Nodding politely to Mrs. Galt, he went down the steps toward the waiting cab.

Louisa rushed into the hall, feeling as if a legion of demons were in pursuit. She practically hurled her bonnet and gloves to Mrs. Galt.

"Is Lady Ashton home?" she asked.

"Not yet, ma'am. She's due back from her Garden Society meeting very soon, though."

"I'll be in the study."

It was all she could do to walk, not run, down the hall. She went into the study and closed the door behind her. Clasping the knob behind her back with both hands, she sagged against the wooden panels.

She could not seem to catch her breath. It was as though she were wearing a steel corset. Her pulse was pounding. She wanted to flee, to hide, but there was nowhere to go.

She needed something for her nerves. Pushing herself away from the door, she crossed to the brandy table, yanked the stopper out of the decanter, and splashed a large amount of the contents into a glass. She swallowed too much the first time, sputtering wildly and choking a little. Gasping for air, she began to pace the room.

"Remain calm," she said. "He cannot know who you are. There is no way he will ever learn the truth."

Wonderful. Now she was talking to herself.

She took another swallow of brandy, a smaller sip this time, and went to the window. She looked out into the garden.

Inwardly she was reeling. Perfectly understandable, she assured herself. She had sustained one great shock followed by another. First there had been that devastating kiss. Then had come the equally devastating news that the man who had just thrilled her senses was personally acquainted with the detective who had investigated the murder of Lord Gavin.

She tried another sip of brandy. It was some time before her breathing returned to normal, but gradually the panic drained away.

It would be all right, she thought, setting the empty glass aside. She would have to be very careful, of course, but she was in no immediate danger of discovery. Clearly Anthony was consumed with his desire to avenge Fiona. As long as his attention was riveted entirely on achieving justice for the lady he had loved and lost he had no reason to become overly curious about the woman who was helping him in the project. Did he?

She tried to think logically. Unfortunately, the brandy rather muddled her brain. One thing was obvious, however. It would be best if there were no more kisses. It would be extremely foolish to become involved in an illicit affair with Anthony Stalbridge. No good could come of it. Illicit affairs always came to bad ends.

A sense of gloom replaced the nervy fear. She gripped the edge of the window, leaned her forehead against the glass panes, and closed her eyes. What would it be like to be loved the way Anthony had once loved his dear Fiona? She knew that she would never learn the answer to that question.

16

Daisy Spalding awoke to a sea of pain. The opium concoction she had taken last night had worn off, leaving her to the anguish of her bruised and battered body. She sat up cautiously on the narrow cot and took stock. She had survived another client, but only by the skin of her teeth. If one of the other customers had not heard the noise through the walls and come to investigate, she would have been dead this morning.

The client last night had been the most violent one yet. She had seen the madness in his eyes when he had tied the gag around her mouth and bound her hands behind her back. She had been terrified, but by then it was too late.

She had worked in the brothel for only a few weeks. She did not think she would last the month. After Andrew had died, the man to whom he had owed money told her that she could repay the debt by going to work in Phoenix House for a couple of months. She had considered the river for the first time then, but the creditor had persuaded her.

"Phoenix House is not like other brothels," he assured her. "All of the women who work there come from respectable backgrounds, just like you. They earn excellent money because they occupy a station far above that of the average streetwalker. They are *courtesans*, not street whores. Gentlemen are willing to pay well for the company of refined ladies."

But a whore is a whore, Daisy thought. She had been a fool to think the business would be different just because she had once been a lady.

Terrified of landing in the workhouse, she had accepted the offer. She did not discover until much later that when she went to work in Phoenix House, her husband's creditor had received a handsome fee from the proprietor, Madam Phoenix.

Madam Phoenix had explained to her that she was not pretty enough for the regular customers. The only opening was for a woman who was willing to take on the rough trade. Some of the gentlemen liked getting a bit violent, she explained. It aroused them, but no serious damage was done.

Daisy got to her feet, cringing, and looked at her reflection in the cracked mirror over the washstand. Her eyes were black and blue. Her jaw was badly swollen. She was afraid to examine the rest of her body.

This time the damage was serious. Next time it might well prove fatal. If she was doomed to die at the age of twenty-two, she preferred to take her own life. Damned if she would give that privilege to a gentleman who would likely have a climax if she expired because of his brutality.

In spite of her bleak determination to seek the ultimate escape, however, her will to live prevailed. She had heard whispers of an establishment in Swanton Lane where women of the street could go for a hot meal. Some said that the woman who ran the place could sometimes help a girl find respectable work under another name.

What did she have to lose? Daisy thought. But she would have to be very careful. Madam Phoenix was cold and utterly ruthless. It was whispered that she was responsible for the mysterious disappearance of the former madam. And the hard-eyed man she entertained in her private quarters looked even more dangerous.

Daisy shuddered. If Madam Phoenix discovered that one of her prostitutes had fled to the Swanton Lane establishment, there was no telling what she might do. She would consider it a very bad example for the rest of the women of Phoenix House.

17

The note from Miranda Fawcett arrived the following morning. Anthony was still at home when he got word from Louisa. He whistled for a cab and went to Arden Square immediately.

Anticipation and a disturbing heat flooded through him as the vehicle halted at the steps of Number Twelve. It dawned on him that the prowling excitement he was feeling had nothing to do with the coming interview with Miranda Fawcett. He was aroused at the prospect of seeing Louisa again, of sitting close to her in the carriage.

Damnation. What was happening to him? He could not recall the last time he had felt this way simply because he was about to take a ride with a lady.

Louisa was waiting for him in a black gown, black gloves, and a black net veil that concealed her features. He wondered if the clothes were left over from the death of her husband. The thought that Louisa had once loved another man irritated him for some reason. He pushed it aside.

He had to admit the gown and veil made an excellent disguise. Until now he had not realized how perfectly anonymous a widow in full mourning was on the street.

"Do you often find it necessary to go about incognito in the course of your work?" he asked, handing her up into the carriage.

"I have discovered that widow's weeds are quite useful on occasion," she said, settling onto the seat.

He sat down across from her. She looked at him through her veil, more invitingly mysterious than ever. He forced himself to concentrate on the matter at hand.

"What did you learn from Miss Fawcett?" he asked.

"There was only a name and an address in Halsey Street."

She handed him a piece of paper. He glanced down, reading quickly. "Benjamin Thurlow."

She crumpled the black netting up onto the brim of her black hat and looked at him. Her face was flushed. Behind the lenses of her spectacles her eyes were bright with excitement. He wondered if she looked that way when she was in the grip of passion or if it was only her work as a journalist that inspired such enthusiasm.

"Are you acquainted with this Mr. Thurlow?" she asked.

He reflected briefly and then shook his head. "No." He stood, raised the trap, and spoke to the driver. "Halsey Street, please."

"Aye, sir."

The vehicle rumbled forward into the fog.

"Clearly the next step is to interview him," Louisa declared. "But we must be subtle about it. We do not want to tip our hand."

"I understand, Mrs. Bryce," he said politely. "I will endeavor to be discreet. I feel certain that I can succeed by following the excellent example you set. I cannot tell you how much I appreciate the training in investigative work that you are so graciously providing me. I was certainly very fortunate to meet up with you. Who knows what grave mistakes I might have made had you not come along to set me straight in the fine art of making subtle inquiries."

She wrinkled her nose. "Forgive me. I should not have presumed to lecture you. I fear I am not accustomed to working with a partner."

"It appears we must both make adjustments."

"I suppose so."

He stretched out his legs and folded his arms. "You take your profession very seriously, don't you? It is not a lark or a game to you."

"Did you think it was?"

"It is difficult to imagine why a woman in your obviously comfortable situation would undertake a career as a journalist."

"I find it very satisfying."

"Yes, I can see that. Do you have informants other than Miranda Fawcett?"

"Oh, yes," she said. "Miranda is extremely helpful, of course, and, as you have seen, I also have the advantage of Emma's social connections and her knowledge of Society." She paused. "But from time to time I also rely on another source."

"Who is that?"

"Roberta Woods. She is dedicated to helping women who, for whatever reason, find themselves forced to make their living on the streets. She manages a little establishment in Swanton Lane where she serves meals to women who cannot afford them. She also directs those who want help to a place she calls The Agency."

"What does it do?"

"The people there give the women training on a new device called a typewriter. Have you heard of such machines?"

He smiled. "My father invented one. He is still working on improvements. He believes it will revolutionize many aspects of industry and business."

"He's right." Louisa suddenly glowed with enthusiasm. "It is a marvelous device. The people at The Agency say that there will soon be a typewriter in every business establishment in the country. Of course, that means that there is a growing need for people who are skilled in operating them."

"I see. The Agency supplies typists to employers."

"Yes. Because the skill is rare, many businesses are only too happy to hire trained women for such positions. The people at The Agency tell me that typewriters are opening up a whole new field of respectable employment for females. It is very exciting."

"I know that career opportunities for women are very limited."

"Few are ever entirely safe from the threat of finding themselves on the street. Even ladies from the most affluent levels of society turn up in Swanton Lane. Very often they are widows whose husbands left them penniless or in debt. They are forced to sell themselves to buy food and pay for their lodging."

"I can see that you take a great interest in Roberta Woods's soup kitchen. How did you learn about it?"

"After I came to live with Emma I took over the business of managing her charities for her. She has provided funding for Miss Woods's establishment for years. Miss Woods and I have become well acquainted. We share some mutual interests when it comes to exposing gentlemen in Society who take advantage of others."

He studied her. "What sort of information do you learn at that place?"

She smiled bleakly. "You would be

amazed by how much the women of the night know about the men in the Polite World."

"I have never given the matter much thought, but now that I do, I can see that prostitutes would be an excellent source of information."

She looked at him. "Swanton Lane was where I learned that Hastings became a frequent customer of Phoenix House several months ago. He now has a weekly appointment there. I am told that he never cancels it for any reason."

"Interesting."

Her brows came together. "Don't you find it odd that a gentleman would have a standing appointment at a brothel?"

"I'm afraid that it is not that unusual, Louisa."

"Oh."

He smiled. "If it matters, I can assure you that I do not have such an appointment."

She reddened. "I never meant to imply anything of the kind, sir."

He had embarrassed her enough, he thought. "Tell me more about the California Mine Swindle. I recall being impressed by the details that I. M. Phantom provided in the press. How did you learn so much?"

"As Miranda told you, I called upon her the day after I overheard the conversation. I did not really expect her to receive me, let alone trust my word. But to my surprise she not only invited me into her home, she listened to what I had to say. We came up with a plan."

"What was that?"

"Miranda is nothing if not an excellent actress. When the men contacted her to get her to sign the final papers she acted the part of a naïve female who was only too pleased to have an opportunity to be involved in an investment scheme with two such distinguished gentlemen. I hid behind a service door in the drawing room, listening to every word and making notes."

"What was your next step?" he asked, fascinated.

"I sent a cable to the editor of the newspaper in the town in California where the gold mine supposedly existed. He was kind enough to reply immediately, saying that there was no mine anywhere in the vicinity. He strongly suspected fraud and urged caution. He also said he would like the details for his paper."

"That was when you got the idea of becoming a correspondent?"

"Yes," she said. "I immediately made an appointment with the publisher and editor of the *Flying Intelligencer*. We met and discussed my offer to write a series of occasional news reports from inside Society, as it were, beginning with the notice of a swindle perpetrated by two very prominent gentlemen."

"I assume he leaped at the opportunity?"

"Mr. Spraggett did not hesitate for even a second," she said with a note of pride.

"That does not surprise me." He contemplated her for a moment longer. "If it is not too personal a question, may I ask what happened to Mr. Bryce?"

"Sadly, he was taken off by a fever shortly after we were wed."

Smoothly said, he noted, and with just the right touch of regret.

"My condolences, madam."

"Thank you. It has been a number of years now. The pain of the loss has receded." She pushed her spectacles higher on her nose and assumed a determined expression.

"We must consider how we are going to approach Mr. Thurlow."

"It would be best if you remained in the carriage while I talked to him."

"Absolutely not."

He nodded, accepting the inevitable.

"I had a feeling you would say that."

18

Halsey Street proved to be a small, cramped passage in a modest part of town. Drenched in fog, it seemed to exist in some separate, isolated world. Louisa studied the scene through the window of the cab. The neighborhood appeared deserted. There were no pedestrians and no traffic.

Anthony ordered the cab to halt, opened the door, vaulted down onto the pavement, and lowered the steps. Louisa adjusted her veil and allowed herself to be handed out of the vehicle.

"Be so good as to wait for us," Anthony instructed the driver.

"Aye, sir." The man settled back and took

a flask out of one of the pockets of his coat. "I'll be here when you're ready to leave."

Louisa walked with Anthony through the swirling mist to the front door of Thurlow's lodgings.

Anthony rapped sharply. There was no response.

"That is odd," Louisa said. "I can understand Mr. Thurlow being out, but one would think that there would be a housekeeper about."

Anthony studied the heavily draped windows with a speculative expression. "If there is a housekeeper, she may have gone shopping."

Something in his tone caught her attention. "What are you thinking, sir?"

"That we will obviously have to come back another time." He took her elbow and started toward the waiting cab. "Come along, Mrs. Bryce. I will take you home."

"Hah." She came to a halt, forcing him to stop, too. "Do not think you can fool me so easily, sir. You are plotting to get me out of the way so that you can return here to Halsey Street and break into Mr. Thurlow's lodgings to have a look around, are you not?"

"You wound me with your lack of trust, madam."

"I shall do more than wound you if you try to keep me out of this."

"If you think that I am going to allow you to break into Thurlow's rooms with me, you are delusional. I will not be responsible for your arrest on burglary charges."

Pointedly, she looked around the empty lane. "I see no sign of a constable anywhere in the vicinity. We are highly unlikely to be arrested if we are careful. No one will take any notice of us if we go in through the front door. If someone does happen to see us, he or she will simply assume that the occupant has let us inside."

"The front door is most likely locked, Mrs. Bryce."

"I'm certain that a person capable of breaking into an Apollo Patented Safe will have no great difficulty with a simple door lock. I will stand in front of you while you do your work. My skirts will conceal your actions."

"And if someone does question our presence inside the house?" he asked.

"We will tell them that we are friends of Mr.

Thurlow and had cause to be concerned about his health."

"Huh." He contemplated that for a few seconds. "Not bad. Not bad at all."

"We entered to assure ourselves that he was not ill," she continued blithely. "Who would contradict us?"

"Thurlow, himself, perhaps, if he happens to walk in on us while we are searching the premises?"

"He is hardly likely to summon a constable once we inform him that we are aware he is involved in an extortion scheme."

Anthony's teeth gleamed in a wolfish smile. "Mrs. Bryce, you and I do tend to think alike when it comes to certain matters."

"Indeed, sir." She smiled, aware of a keen sense of anticipation. "Now, if you would be so good as to go about your business?"

"This shouldn't take long." He put his hand on the knob and twisted experimentally. The door opened easily. "Not long at all."

Louisa frowned. "Mr. Thurlow must have neglected to lock the door when he left."

Anthony pushed the door open wider, revealing an empty hall. Louisa did not like the heavy silence that emanated from the interior of Thurlow's lodgings. She felt the hair stir on the nape of her neck.

Anthony glided into the shadowed opening. There was a predatory alertness about him that sent another little chill across her nerves. He, too, sensed that something was very wrong.

She followed him inside, raised her veil, and looked around.

Thurlow's lodgings were typical of those belonging to a man of modest means. She looked into the parlor, which was quite small and sparsely furnished. A hall led to the kitchen and a rear door that likely opened onto an alley. A narrow staircase ascended upward into deep shadow.

Anthony closed the door. "Is there anyone home?" he called in a voice that was pitched to carry to the upper floor. The reverberating silence seemed almost suffocating.

Louisa ran a fingertip along the top of the hall table. Her glove came away slightly smudged.

"He employs a housekeeper, but from the looks of things I would say that she does not come around every day."

"Which may explain why she is not here today," Anthony said.

He went into the parlor and opened the drawers in the desk. Removing a sheaf of papers he rifled through them quickly.

"Anything of interest?" she asked.

"Bills from his tailor and other tradesmen to whom he owed money." Anthony put the stack of papers back into the drawer and picked up a small notebook. He flipped through the pages. "Miss Fawcett was right. Thurlow is, indeed, an inveterate gambler."

"What have you got there?" She tried to peer over his shoulder.

"A record of people to whom he owes money." Anthony turned a few more pages. "Evidently he routinely gets into debt and then somehow manages to pay off his creditors."

"He must win occasionally, in that case."

"This record goes back nearly three years. A few of the debts are quite large. Several thousand pounds in some instances."

Anthony returned the notebook to the desk drawer.

She trailed after him through the remaining rooms on the ground floor. Nothing appeared out of place. It was as if Thurlow had walked out the door only moments before they arrived.

When they returned to the front hall, Anthony started up the stairs. Louisa hurried after him. The oppressive sensation seemed to grow heavier.

At the top, Anthony halted, looking down the short hall to a closed door. Louisa stopped, too, unaccountably chilled.

"What is it?" she asked.

"Wait here," he said quietly. "He may be asleep in bed. Gamblers keep late hours."

She ignored the order, but she was careful to keep a respectful distance behind him. The last thing she wanted to do was walk into the room of a sleeping man.

Anthony seemed unaware of her presence. Everything about him was concentrated on the closed door at the end of the hall. He knocked once. When there was no response, he turned the knob. The door opened with a long, mourning sigh of the hinges. He stood in the opening, looking into the heavily draped and shadowed room. He did not move.

Dread tightened Louisa's nerves. She did not want to go any closer, but she forced herself to move to the doorway. The unmistakable miasma of blood and death flowed from the room.

"You do not want to come any farther," Anthony warned in a flat, cold voice.

She took a handkerchief out of her muff and held it to her nose. Then she looked past him into the room.

A man lay face up on the bed, blankets and sheets tumbled around his waist. There was something terribly wrong with his head. The white linen pillow case was saturated with blood.

A hellish vision seemed to shimmer in the air in front of her. *Lord Gavin had looked just like this when he lay dead on the floor of her bedroom.*

"Louisa?" Anthony's voice was sharp and brutal. "Are you going to faint?"

"No." She pulled herself together with an effort. "I won't faint."

The dead man's arm was crooked at the elbow, she noticed, the hand not far from his head. The lifeless fingers were wrapped around the handle of a revolver.

"Dear God," she whispered. "He took his own life."

Anthony walked across the room to stand looking down at the body.

"Now this is interesting," he said.

Louisa was shocked by the stunning absence of emotion in his voice. Anthony sounded as if he were making an observation on the weather. But his face, she saw, had gone very hard, his eyes stone cold.

"What do you mean?" she managed.

"I wonder what the odds are of two of Hastings's employees committing suicide within the span of a little more than two weeks," he said.

19

He watched Louisa avert her eyes from the gory scene. “Are you certain you’re not going to faint?”

“I told you, I will be fine.”

“Go back downstairs,” he said quietly. “There is no need for you to remain in this room.”

She did not respond to that suggestion. “He certainly fits the descriptions the young ladies gave in their journals. He was, indeed, an exceedingly handsome man. And he appears to have been in his late twenties.”

Anthony turned back to examine the scene more closely. The bullet had inflicted considerable damage to Thurlow’s head, saturating his blond hair with blood, but his face was still mostly unmarred. He had, indeed, possessed the sort of features that drew the eyes of women.

He turned back to Louisa. Her attention was fixed on a piece of paper on top of a waist-high chest of drawers.

"Did Mr. Grantley leave a note?" she asked softly.

"Yes, according to Fowler."

He crossed to the desk, picked up the paper and read the suicide note aloud.

" 'I cannot endure the shame that awaits. My apologies to my family.' "

"What shame?" Louisa looked at him. "Do you suppose he meant his gambling debts?"

"He does not appear to have been overly concerned about them in the past. Why would he suddenly feel the need to kill himself now?"

She nodded. "That is a very good question."

"This is no suicide," Anthony said, looking around the room.

"I'm inclined to agree."

"I wonder if Hastings got rid of both of his employees for some reason," Anthony said. "Perhaps he thought he had cause to fear them. Maybe he believed that they were plotting against him. That would certainly explain why he hired those two guards."

"Yes."

She looked at him with stark, somber eyes. "What shall we do now?"

"I will send word to Fowler immediately. He will want to know about this new development as soon as possible."

She clenched her black muff with both hands. "Yes, of course."

"But first," he said, "I am going to send you home in the cab. There is no necessity for you to remain here until Fowler arrives. I can tell him everything he needs to know."

A flicker of relief crossed her face before she composed herself. "Are you certain?"

"Yes."

She gave him a shuttered look. "Do you intend to mention my name to him?"

"I see no need to do so."

"I am only concerned about protecting my identity as I. M. Phantom," she said smoothly.

"I understand."

He put the note down on the chest of drawers and moved back across the room to take her arm. "Come, we must get you away from this place."

He guided her back downstairs. In the

parlor he paused at the desk to write a short note.

"Are you certain you will be safe here?" she asked. "What if the killer returns?"

The anxiety in the question caught him off guard. She was genuinely concerned, he realized, perhaps even frightened for him.

"The killer may or may not be Hastings." He folded the note. "Regardless, I don't think that he will risk coming back to the scene of his crime. At least not until after the body has been discovered and the gossip has spread."

"How can you be sure of that?"

"Whoever he is, he took a great chance when he came here to commit the murder. He won't take another one if he can avoid it. He will be thinking only of his own safety now."

"You will be careful, won't you, Mr. Stalbridge?" she said, suddenly looking very anxious.

"Yes," he promised, oddly touched. "The cab will take you directly home. I will come for you at eight this evening."

She stiffened. "Why?"

"We both have invitations to the Lorrington reception, remember?"

She shuddered. "I had forgotten. Forgive

me, sir, but I am in no mood to attend any social engagements tonight."

"I'm sorry, Louisa, but I think it would be best if we were seen together in public this evening. It is vital that we act as if nothing out of the ordinary has occurred."

She hesitated and then nodded reluctantly. "I suppose you are right. Dear heaven. Do you think Hastings will be there, too?"

"I don't know. But there will be a large crowd. If he is present, I'm sure we can avoid him."

"If I go home now, I will be able to write a report of the death for Mr. Spraggett. There is still time to get it into tomorrow's edition of the *Flying Intelligencer*."

He considered that briefly. "An excellent notion. If nothing else, it will rattle the killer's nerves when he reads that the police are considering the possibility of foul play."

"Except that they aren't considering that possibility," she pointed out very dryly. "The police don't even know that Mr. Thurlow is dead yet."

"Since when did small details like that stop an intrepid member of the press from reporting the facts?"

She smiled wryly. "Quite right. I shall make

certain to put in some dark hints of possible murder." She hesitated. "You really do think that Hastings killed Mr. Thurlow, don't you?"

"I think it is possible," he corrected evenly. "We need more information."

"That seems to be the chief problem with this investigation: a fearful lack of information."

He lowered the net veil so that it concealed her face.

"I won't argue with you on that account," he said gently.

He escorted her outside and put her into the carriage. When she was seated, he closed the door and handed the note he had written to the driver.

"After you have delivered the lady to her door, please go to Scotland Yard and see that this message is delivered to Detective Fowler."

"Aye, sir." The coachman took the note.

"It is to go *only* to Fowler," Anthony emphasized softly. He gave the coachman some money. "Is that clear? If you must wait for him, then do so."

The coachman checked the coins and

nodded eagerly. “No need to worry, sir. I’ll see to it yer note gets to this Fowler.”

“Thank you.”

The driver slapped the leathers against the rump of his horse. The cab rumbled forward and almost immediately disappeared into the fog.

Anthony went back inside Thurlow’s lodgings and climbed the stairs to the upper floor. The higher he climbed, the more he had to force himself to keep moving. The atmosphere of death was as thick as the fog outside in the street.

Inside the bedroom he went first to the wardrobe. The coats and trousers were all in the latest fashion. The hand-tailored shirts were freshly laundered and crisply ironed.

There was a leather jewelry case on the chest of drawers. Inside were several pairs of expensive cuff links, a handsomely engraved gold pocket watch, and a pearl-tipped tie pin. A silver-backed brush and comb and a jar of pomade were arranged near the jewelry case. Thurlow had taken great care with his personal appearance.

Anthony walked toward the bed and studied the body again. Forcing himself to look past the blood and gore, he noted the details. The portions of Thurlow's hair and mustache not drenched in blood appeared to be trimmed in the latest style. The nightshirt was embroidered.

He began a more thorough, methodical search of the room, looking in places where a man might stash his secrets. He found the strongbox beneath a false panel of wood in the wardrobe. The lock was excellent, crafted by one of the best manufacturers in Willenhall, but it was no Apollo. It took him less than fifteen seconds to crack it.

The only thing inside was a notebook. It contained a record of what, at first glance, appeared to be large sums of money won at gambling. There were only five entries, however. The dates went back nearly three years. There were initials next to each of the amounts. The initials matched those of the five young ladies who had been compromised. He realized that he was looking at a record of the payments Thurlow had received in exchange for delivering the blackmail victims into Hastings's clutches.

He tucked the notebook into a pocket and stood quietly, looking around the room one last time. Something seemed slightly off. He contemplated the items on the dresser for a long moment, trying to understand what it was that was out of place. Vague smudges in the thin layer of dust on the dresser and a few carelessly folded handkerchiefs in a wardrobe drawer were all that stood out. When he could not come to a conclusion, he went back downstairs.

On a hunch, he decided to search the desk again, this time more thoroughly. Opening the folder of unpaid bills, he suddenly knew what was wrong: The bills were out of order. Everything else in Thurlow's lodgings was neatly arranged, but the bills had been dumped into the file in a random fashion. It was as though someone had gone through them in a great hurry and then tossed them back into the drawer.

With that observation in mind, he continued his search. When he was finished, he was certain of his conclusion.

A short time later a carriage clattered to a halt outside in the street. He went to the window and eased the curtain aside in time to see the bearish form of Harold Fowler descend from a hansom.

He opened the door before Fowler could knock.

"I got your message, Mr. Stalbridge."

Fowler came into the hall. He removed his hat and looked around with the stoic curiosity of a man who was accustomed to being summoned for unpleasant reasons. "What is this about?"

"The occupant of these lodgings, Benjamin Thurlow, is dead in the upstairs bedroom. It appears that, in despair over his gambling debts, he put a pistol to his head. There is a suicide note. The words are all neatly printed."

"Printed, you say?" Fowler's bushy whiskers twitched. His sad eyes sharpened. "Like Grantley's note."

"Yes." He handed the note to Fowler. "The printing makes it impossible to compare the handwriting, but I suspect that Thurlow did not write this."

Fowler took the note in his broad paw and scrutinized it for a few seconds. When he looked up, his expression was grim. "I agree with you, sir. But we'll never be able to prove that the killer wrote this note."

"Another thing," Anthony said. "There is no way to prove it, either, but I would swear that someone searched these rooms before I arrived."

"I see." Fowler squinted slightly. "What

sort of information was it that brought you here today?"

"I got word that Thurlow, like Grantley, was employed by Hastings. It appears that Hastings paid him a great deal of money at various times in the past. I wanted to talk to him."

"You think that Hastings killed him, don't you?"

"I think it likely, yes. But that doesn't bring me any closer to finding a motive for Fiona Risby's murder. And now someone else who might have been able to answer my questions is dead."

Fowler's bleak face softened. "I've warned you, Mr. Stalbridge, the odds of learning anything new after all this time are dismal, indeed. My advice is to leave the poor dead girl to rest in peace."

"You don't understand," Anthony said. "I am the one who cannot rest, Detective. I must find out why she was killed."

"In my experience there are only a small number of reasons for murder. Greed, revenge, the need to conceal a secret, and madness."

20

"Are you all right?" Anthony asked quietly.

Louisa looked out over the moonlit gardens. It was nearly midnight. Here and there decorative lanterns bobbed. Off to the right the fanciful shape of a large iron-and-glass conservatory loomed. Behind them the crowded ballroom sparkled and glittered. Laughter and music poured through the open French doors.

"Yes, of course," she said, suppressing another shiver.

But the strain of pretending to enjoy herself for the past two hours was starting to take its toll. Her smile felt frozen. She wanted to go back to Arden Square and drink a very large glass of brandy. "Can we go home now?"

"Soon," Anthony promised. He took her elbow. "Let's walk."

"Well, at least we now know for certain what sort of service Mr. Thurlow provided for Elwin Hastings," she said after a while. "He compromised the victims and then stole their journals and letters to give to Hastings."

"He was a chronic gambler. That meant he was always in need of large sums of cash to meet his debts. Hastings was willing to pay well for the blackmail items. Grantley no doubt handled the collection of the extortion payments. I cannot envision Hastings doing that sort of work."

They went down the terrace steps and followed a gravel path that wound through the elaborately landscaped garden. They were not the only couple who had taken a respite from the heat and energy of the ballroom, Louisa noticed. She heard low voices from the shadows. A man laughed softly. The pale skirts of a woman's gown gleamed briefly in the moonlight before vanishing around a hedge.

The last thing she had wanted to do

tonight was attend the ball, but she understood Anthony's reasoning. They must carry on as if nothing out of the ordinary had occurred that afternoon. Anthony seemed to be having very little difficulty, but she had been fighting a disturbing anxiety all afternoon and evening. The truth was that the discovery of Thurlow's body that morning had unsettled her nerves far more than she had realized at the time.

The murder scene had brought back the horror and fear of that dreadful night a little over a year ago. She had been unable to get the image of Gavin's body out of her head. She knew that no matter how late she stayed up tonight or how much brandy she drank when she got home, she was unlikely to sleep. That was not necessarily a bad thing, she thought. If she did manage to fall asleep, there would no doubt be nightmares.

Anthony brought her to a halt near the entrance to the large conservatory. The glass walls were opaque in the silver moonlight.

"We can be private here," Anthony said quietly.

She sank down onto a marble bench. The skirts of her gown spilled around her ankles.

She looked into the night and shivered again.

"Are you cold?" Anthony asked.

"A little." She could not tell him how much the murder scene had shaken her. He would conclude that she lacked the nerve required to continue the investigation. "What are we going to do now? With Victoria Hastings, Thurlow, and Grantley all conveniently dead we have no more clues to follow. There appears to be no one left who knows Elwin Hastings's secrets."

Anthony braced one foot on the bench beside her and rested his forearm on his thigh. "The only thing we can do is to continue asking questions."

She tried to concentrate on the problem. "It occurs to me that there is a place where some of Hastings's secrets may be known."

He looked down at her. "Where is that?"

"The brothel where he keeps his weekly appointments."

"Phoenix House?" He was silent for a few seconds. Then he nodded slowly. "That is an interesting notion."

She wrinkled her nose. "I hope you are not going to tell me that you intend to book an appointment there yourself in an effort to research your theory."

He smiled faintly. "I doubt that would do any good. I am unlikely to convince any of the women who work there to confide in me on such short notice. But you seem to have won the trust of someone who knows a few of those women."

"You mean Roberta Woods in Swanton Lane."

"Yes."

"I will ask her to make a few more discreet inquiries."

"Excellent. Meanwhile, I can only hope that I will eventually hear something from Clement Corvus. He obviously knows a great deal about Hastings's business affairs."

"I cannot imagine that a crime lord would want to reveal his illegal activities to us," she said.

"We shall see."

She raised her brows. "You really do think he will contact you?"

"It's possible."

"Why would he do that?"

Anthony smiled faintly. "In spite of his business activities, or perhaps because of them, he is said to abide by a stern code of honor. Among other things I am told that he always pays his debts."

"Who told you so much about Corvus?"

"Detective Fowler. Corvus and Scotland Yard have a long-standing relationship."

Fowler again. She suppressed another shudder. "You think Mr. Corvus will conclude that he owes you for whatever was in those papers you asked Miranda to give to him?"

"Either that or he will want more information from me. Nothing is certain in this affair."

She wrapped her arms around herself. "If we are correct in our assumptions, Elwin Hastings has killed not just once but perhaps four times: Fiona Risby, the first Mrs. Hastings, Grantley, and Thurlow. It is difficult to conceive of such evil."

"The business of killing no doubt gets easier after the first time," Anthony said.

She had to fight to keep from leaping to her feet and screaming that he was wrong. No matter how justified, killing was a horrifying experience that haunted one for a lifetime.

Without warning Anthony reached down,

gripped her elbow, and hauled her to her feet.

"Hush," he ordered against her lips.

She opened her mouth to ask him what he thought he was doing, but before she could utter a word she found herself pinned against his chest. His mouth came down on hers, hard and unyielding.

She froze. She had made her decision, she thought. It would be best if there were no more kisses. But even as she repeated that bit of logic to herself, she knew she was in no condition to resist temptation tonight; her nerves were far too overwrought. She longed to be consumed by the fires of passion so that she could forget the scenes of death that drifted through her mind like so many ghastly specters.

She put her arms around his neck and pressed herself against him. Then she heard the faint murmur of voices drifting through the night. A couple was approaching on the conservatory path. Once again Anthony was kissing her in order to create the impression that they were engaged in an illicit affair. Frustration seized her. She wanted him to kiss her in a way that showed he meant it.

A man chuckled. *"It would seem we must find another secluded bower, my dear. This one is already occupied."*

The woman murmured something indistinguishable in response. Louisa realized that the voices were growing softer as the pair moved away into another section of the gardens, but she was no longer paying attention. All she could think about was the feel of Anthony's arms around her. Heat flooded through her. It did not matter that the kiss had never been intended as an act of seduction. The impact was akin to a lightning bolt searing her already sensitive nerves. Everything inside her was ablaze.

"Anthony," she breathed against his mouth.

He gave a soft, husky groan. His arm tightened. His mouth was suddenly rough and demanding. He was kissing her for real now. The same way she was kissing him. There was so much sizzling electricity snapping and crackling between them she was vaguely surprised her hair was not standing on end. His hands moved on her back, closing fiercely around the snug bodice of her gown.

She was inexplicably frantic, shivering with need. Caught up in the maelstrom of a force she could only dimly comprehend, she clutched Anthony's shoulders, hung on for dear life, and kissed him back.

He broke off the kiss and cupped her face between his hands. "Say my name again."

In the shadowy glow of a nearby lantern his expression was not that of a gentle lover. What she saw in his face was a raw, compelling hunger that matched her own.

"Anthony." She shivered but not from nerves this time. Anticipation pulsed through her. *"Anthony."*

He took his hands away from her face and put them around her waist. Then he bent his head and kissed her throat. His mouth was wet and hungry on her skin. She felt his teeth at one point. An exquisite excitement made her catch her breath. This was what she needed. This desperate, intense passion would sear the twin images of Thurlow's and Gavin's bloodied heads from her thoughts, at least for a while.

Anthony scooped her up in his arms and carried her to the door of the conservatory.

"Open it," he muttered.

She reached down, found the knob, and twisted. The door swung open, and a wave of humid warmth flowed over her. She inhaled the scents of greenery and flowers and freshly turned earth, the fragrance of life not death.

Anthony carried her through the opening and set her on her feet near a workbench. He reached back, closed and locked the door. Then he turned to her and pulled her to him again. His hands went to the fastenings of the bodice of her dress.

She was amazed to realize that his fingers, so skilled and sensitive with locks and keys, were actually trembling. She could hear his breathing now. Hot. Urgent. When she touched him she discovered that the muscles of his shoulders beneath his coat were rigid.

Hope spiraled through her. He had loved his dear Fiona, but perhaps there was room in his heart for another woman.

Her bodice came undone. She was intensely grateful for the deep shadows around them. The thin fabric of her chemise was all that veiled her breasts.

He bent his head and kissed her throat.

His thumb grazed a nipple, sending little tremors through her. She clutched at his shoulders, wanting to explore the strength and power she found there, wanting to learn him more intimately, but he gave her no chance.

"*Louisa*, you don't know what you have done to me. I want you now. I need you."

Without warning he lifted her and sat her on the edge of the workbench. Everything was happening so quickly. She could no longer think. On the other hand, thinking was the very last thing she wanted to do.

The next thing she knew his mouth had taken the place of his hand on her breast. He dampened the fabric of the chemise with his tongue.

The sense of need clawed at her. She threaded her fingers through Anthony's hair. When his teeth closed around her nipple she gasped. Immediately he raised his head to silence her with another smoldering kiss.

He caught the skirts of her gown and pushed them up above her knees. His hands closed over her thighs above her stockings, pushing them apart.

Her pulse skittered wildly. She was still adjusting to the stunning intimacy of his touch when he slid his fingers inside the open-crotch seam of her lace-trimmed drawers. The searing heat of his palm on the most private portion of her anatomy was both utterly outrageous and exquisitely thrilling.

"You want me," he whispered hoarsely. "Say it. You want me as badly as I want you."

"Yes." She tightened her hands in his hair. "Oh, *yes*."

Her head was spinning. The world outside the conservatory ceased to matter. This was what it meant to be consumed by passion. She marveled at the exhilarating sensation. The novelists and playwrights were correct. This was why people got involved in illicit love affairs.

"You are so soft," he said, stroking her intimately. "You are driving me mad."

She realized that he was opening the front of his trousers. When she glanced down she caught a glimpse of his hand wrapped around his erection. He removed a square of white linen from another pocket and dropped it on the bench beside her.

Fascinated, she started to reach down to touch him, but he was already pushing himself into the melting core of her body. The pressure felt very, very good. She wanted more. Desperate, she urged him closer.

He gripped her buttocks and pulled her onto his shaft with a single violent thrust, sinking himself to the hilt inside her.

Pain arced across her overwrought senses. Jolted by the abrupt transition from unbearable desire to unpleasant reality, she gasped and went utterly still.

"Damnation." Anthony froze, also. "You're a virgin."

"Well, yes, but I really don't see that as the issue here."

"Why in blazes didn't you tell me that you were a virgin?"

He sounded furious. What right did he have to be angry at her? She was the one who was in pain.

"I did not think it was any of your business," she said, her temper crackling to life.

"How can you say that it is none of my *business*?"

Anger swept through her, dampening some of the physical discomfort. "Really, sir, you would hardly expect me to discuss such intimate details of my life with a gentleman with whom I am barely acquainted."

He looked down at her with a strange expression. "May I remind you that you are in the midst of making love to a gentleman with whom you are barely acquainted?"

"We are not making love," she said gruffly, not wanting to admit to herself, just how much that fact hurt. "We are engaging in an act of illicit passion."

"I see. You are an authority on such matters?"

"Illicit trysts are different. One is under no obligation to confide one's personal affairs to one's lover."

"I cannot believe that I am receiving a lecture from you on the subject of how one conducts an illicit love affair."

She winced. "I think it would be best if you, uh, removed yourself, sir. As you can tell we are not a good match."

"How would you know?" he said, making no move to retreat.

"I would think it is obvious. You are much too big."

"I think we are a perfect fit."

He started to ease out of her. She held her breath.

But he stopped just short of her entrance and pushed slowly, steadily back into her.

She gasped. "I really don't think this is a good idea."

"Allow me to inform you, Mrs. Bryce, that you are no expert."

He kissed her deeply, silencing her before she could argue further.

He repeated the movement, withdrawing almost entirely and then stroking deeply back into her. The sensation was not painful this time, but neither was it pleasurable. She was stretched so tight she could scarcely breathe. Still, it wasn't a bad feeling.

Perhaps predictably, her lamentable curiosity unfurled, suppressing disappointment.

"Very well, if you insist," she said, wriggling a little in an effort to get more comfortable. "But please be quick about it."

Anthony stilled again, buried inside her.

She opened her eyes and saw that he was looking down at her with an unreadable expression. Chagrined, she put her hands on each side of his face.

"Oh, dear, I didn't mean to hurt your feelings," she said anxiously. "Feel free to carry on. I won't say another word."

"Do I have your promise on that?"

"Absolutely, sir. As long as we have gone this far, we may as well finish the business."

"Have a care, my sweet. Such romantic talk will make me swoon."

She was mortified. She was also furious. The mixture proved highly combustible. She caught his shoulders and pulled him closer.

"Damnation, Anthony. Get on with it."

He said something under his breath that she could not make out, but he finally began to move in quick, tight strokes. Her body seemed to have adjusted itself to his now. If the sensations she was experiencing were not the thrilling ones she had anticipated, neither were they altogether unpleasant.

If Anthony found pleasure in this, she could tolerate the exercise.

"Damn it to hell." He sounded as though he was having difficulty breathing. "This is your fault. You have played havoc with my self-control tonight."

"What is my fault? What do you intend to blame on me? How dare you—"

"You promised not to talk," he said, teeth clenched. *"Damn."*

Worried by the low, savage groan that underlay the oath, she opened her eyes. "Are you all right?"

He did not respond. Instead he suddenly jerked free of her body and grabbed the handkerchief. He wrapped it around the head of his erection.

In the dim light she could see that his eyes were squeezed shut. His lips were parted and drawn back in a silent groan. His teeth flashed dangerously in the darkness. And then it was over. He propped himself against the workbench, breathing heavily. He did not open his eyes.

"Damn," he said again, very softly this time.

21

She waited, uncertain of what one did in a situation like this. The authors of sensation novels did not cover this sort of thing in the books that she had read.

Worried, she gently touched his arm.

"Anthony?"

He opened his eyes partway.

She shivered uneasily when she saw the way he was looking at her.

"Are you ill?" she asked.

"An interesting question."

He straightened and turned away from her, swiftly adjusting his trousers. She hopped down off the workbench. That proved to be a mistake. Her thighs were so wobbly she had to grab hold of the bench to steady herself. She arranged her skirts with awkward hands, aware of a distinctly uncomfortable sensation between her legs.

"My apologies, sir," she said brusquely.

He turned around again, alarmingly cool and back in control. "For allowing me to believe that you were a woman of the world?"

"No, for encouraging you a few minutes ago. Although, in my own defense, I must admit that I expected a somewhat different result."

"What, exactly, did you expect, Louisa?"

She waved a hand, glad that the shadows hid her blush. "I'm sure you understand. One hears so much about the thrill of illicit passion, doesn't one?"

"I couldn't say."

"You probably don't read a lot of novels."

"No."

"But you must have seen your sister's marvelous plays."

"In her plays illicit love affairs always come to a bad end."

"That's not the point." She groped for the right words. "The thing is, based on what I have read and seen on the stage, I anticipated a more, shall we say, *transcendent* experience."

"Transcendent," he repeated neutrally.

"That is the way forbidden passion is portrayed, you see." She sighed. "I should have realized that there is a reason why every woman in England is not running around indulging in illicit love affairs."

"It was your first time, Louisa. First times are always awkward."

A thought struck her. *"Hmm."*

He caught her chin on the edge of his hand and raised her face so that she had to meet his eyes. "What is that supposed to mean?"

"Nothing," she said hastily.

"Given what I have just gone through, I think I deserve an answer."

"Very well, if you insist. It occurred to me that the problem here may have been you, not me."

"You're blaming your failure to achieve transcendence on me?"

"No, no, of course not. Not entirely." She cleared her throat. "It is certainly not your fault that nature chose to overly endow certain portions of your anatomy." She paused, considering the subject more closely. "Perhaps a smaller man—"

He leaned very close.

"Do not," he said, his voice ominously soft, "even think about it."

She stepped back quickly and came up hard against the workbench. "Calm yourself, sir. You are a trifle agitated at the moment. We both are. It has been a very difficult day."

He closed the space between them and planted his hands on the table behind her, caging her between his arms.

"Let me make something very plain," he said in that same dangerously soft tone. "This is your fault, not mine. You misled me with your guise as a widow. You played the part far too well. You should have told me the truth."

"Rubbish. If I'd done that, you never would have kissed me in the first place, let alone ravished me."

"You wanted to be ravished?"

"Yes, I did." Anger and frustration leaped within her again. "I was in a mood to be ravished tonight."

His eyes narrowed. "Was this some whimsical decision you made on the spur of the moment this evening?"

"Not at all." She raised her chin. "As it

happens, I have been thinking about that sort of thing a lot of late."

"What a coincidence," he said. "So have I."

She ignored that. "Until tonight I have been in complete control of my emotions, of course."

"Of course."

"However, I regret to say that the events at Thurlow's lodgings left me feeling rather unsettled."

"In what way?"

"I can't explain it. I was agitated and on edge all afternoon. My heart seemed to beat faster than usual. I could not seem to calm my nerves."

He searched her face in the shadows. "I think I understand."

"When you kissed me a few minutes ago it was as if a storm had broken. I was suddenly swept up in a vortex of intense sensation."

"Carried along by the hot winds of passion?" he offered helpfully.

"Yes, precisely."

"Tossed about by a tempest of raging desire?"

He *did* comprehend. She felt somewhat cheered.

"That is exactly the feeling I am attempting to describe." She paused expectantly. "Was it the same for you?"

"It certainly was." He leaned a little closer. "Until the damn snow started to fall."

"Yes, well, it was obviously all a ghastly mistake. I would like very much to go home, if you don't mind. I feel in the need of a large glass of brandy."

"So do I."

"You are annoyed. I don't blame you." An appalling thought occurred to her. "You won't allow this unfortunate incident to alter our arrangement regarding the investigation, will you?"

To her chagrin, he did not answer immediately.

"No," he said finally. "Our arrangement stands, if that is your wish."

"It is," she assured him.

"There is one thing you should consider before you insist upon continuing our partnership, however."

"What is that?" she asked, wary now.

"If we continue to work together, there will

probably be more fiery storms such as the one that just took place."

In spite of everything that had happened, she felt her pulse leap again. A hot little thrill chased its way down her spine. She suppressed it with an effort, pulled herself together, and straightened her shoulders.

"We are both strong-willed people, sir," she said firmly. "I'm certain we will be able to control ourselves."

"Speak for yourself, Louisa."

He escorted her out of the conservatory and back through the gardens. Louisa looked at the lights of the glittering ballroom. Panic shot through her.

"Must we go back inside?" she asked anxiously.

Anthony was grimly amused. "One of the tricks to handling an illicit affair, my sweet, is the ability to face the world and act as if nothing at all out of the ordinary is going on."

He was right. She raised her chin and straightened her already very straight shoulders.

"Excellent," Anthony murmured into her ear.

Mercifully, no one seemed overly interested in them. They passed through the crowded room with only a few casual nods and a handful of speculative glances.

When they reached the front hall Anthony called for his carriage. They went down the steps together. A footman opened the door of the vehicle. Escape was at hand, Louisa thought. She allowed herself a cautious breath of relief.

At that moment another vehicle arrived, halting directly behind Anthony's. The door opened. A man dressed in formal black and white jumped down onto the pavement. He staggered a little and had to grab hold of the edge of the door frame to catch his balance.

He spotted Anthony. Instantly his handsome face contorted with anger.

"If it isn't Stalbridge," he said, slurring the *s*. "I presume this is the little widow from Arden Square I've heard so much about lately. Aren't you going to introduce me to the lady?"

"No," Anthony said. He kept moving, putting himself between her and the stranger.

Louisa was so shocked by the cold rebuff that she tripped on the last step. She would have gone down if Anthony had not steadied her. He handed her up into the cab.

"Julian Easton's the name, Mrs. Bryce." Easton whipped off his hat in a mockery of good manners. "I'm delighted to make your acquaintance. I'd heard the rumor that Stalbridge was amusing himself with a rather unusual female, but this is the first chance I've had an opportunity to see the little country mouse."

Anthony walked toward him. "That's enough, Easton. You're drunk, and you're embarrassing yourself."

Easton ignored him. He looked at Louisa through the window of the carriage. "You do realize that he's using you, Mrs. Bryce. You're not at all his type, you see. The word in the clubs is that he's fucking some other man's wife and concealing the fact by hiding behind your skirts."

Anthony kept walking toward him. At the last instant Easton seemed to realize that he was in danger, but it was too late. Anthony moved with a speed that took everyone, including Easton, by surprise. He caught

Easton by the sleeve of his coat. At the same time he put out one foot. It was over in a heartbeat. Easton went down very suddenly, landing hard on his rear. He sat on the pavement, looking dazed.

"Arden Square," Anthony said to the driver as he vaulted up into the cab.

The vehicle rolled forward immediately. Louisa looked back toward the steps of the Lorrington mansion. Julian Easton was still sitting on the pavement. Fury had replaced the confusion and surprise in his face.

She turned around to face Anthony. "Who is Mr. Easton?"

"We belong to the same club." Anthony's voice was disturbingly neutral.

"Obviously you are not friends."

"No," Anthony said. "We are not friends."

She could almost hear the door slamming shut on that avenue of inquiry. She decided to try another.

"What was it you did back there that took his feet out from under him in such a sudden manner?" she asked.

"It is a trick I learned in my travels abroad. I find it useful on occasion."

He turned his attention to the night scene

outside the window. He did not say another word until he bid her good night at her door.

"I regret that you were forced to endure that scene with Easton," he said.

He sounded grim and strangely weary. Sympathy welled up inside her. She touched the side of his face with her gloved fingers.

"There is no need to apologize," she said gently. "Easton was the one at fault. You have endured a great deal in the months since Fiona died. I hope that we will be able to find the answers you seek, Anthony."

She turned and went into the house.

22

She came awake with a start, hating the familiar too-rapid beat of her pulse and the breathless sensation that always accompanied the dream. She pushed aside the covers and sat up, needing to walk, to move, anything to work off the unwholesome energy that always followed in the wake of the nightmarish images.

She stood, wincing a little when she felt the tenderness between her legs. Memories of the tryst in the conservatory flooded through her, mercifully pushing aside the worst fragments from the nightmare but bringing with them a new set of fears.

She pulled on her dressing gown, shoved her feet into her slippers, and began to pace. What had she done tonight? How had she managed to become involved in an intimate liaison with the one man who could destroy her? A man who was friends with the Scotland Yard detective who had investigated the murder of Lord Gavin? What on earth had she been thinking?

She stopped, all too well aware of the answer to that question. She had begun to fall in love with Anthony from that very first moment at the Hammond ball when he had looked at her as if he knew her deepest secrets. She was going to lose her heart to him. She knew that as surely as she knew her real name. Perhaps it was already too late.

Do not think about the future. Your love is doomed. You can never tell him the truth about yourself, and you will never be able to marry a man unless you reveal your secret to him. It would not be right.

No gentleman of Anthony's rank in Society would marry a murderess. If nothing else, he had his family's good name to consider.

Not that he was likely ever to fall in love with her. He had given his heart to Fiona Risby. He would certainly marry someday—in his position it was expected—but when the time came he would look much higher than a woman with no background or fortune.

Live for the here and now; it is all you will ever have with Anthony.

She halted in the middle of the bedroom, contemplating another glass of brandy. The one she had taken after Anthony had brought her home from the Lorrington house had proved surprisingly effective. She had not expected to sleep tonight, but evidently the dramatic events of the day and evening had exhausted her more than she realized. Another glass might allow her a few more hours of slumber.

She went to the window and stood looking out into the night. The scene was dimly lit by the streetlamps and a pale moon. Directly across from the front door of Number Twelve stood a cloaked figure, her face obscured by a black net veil. She looked like a wraith that had drifted out of the mist-shrouded trees.

The poor, desperate widow who had been forced to turn to prostitution had returned. Louisa was surprised to see her back. Evidently the woman had not yet learned that customers looking to buy what she was selling did not frequent this part of town. Or perhaps she was too frightened to go into the rougher neighborhoods. She was no doubt new to the streetwalking profession.

On impulse Louisa whirled around and let herself out into the hall. She tiptoed downstairs and went into the study. Turning up a lamp, she unlocked a desk drawer and took out the small amount of money that she and Emma kept there for household incidentals. She stuffed the coins and some banknotes into an envelope. Picking up a pen, she jotted an address on the back of the envelope.

In the front hall she pulled on a cloak, opened the front door, and peered out.

The woman in the black cloak and veil was still there, standing in the shadows cast by a tree. She went very still when she saw Louisa walk out onto the front step and pause in the lamplight.

"Good evening," Louisa said quietly.

The woman reacted as if she had been addressed by a ghost. She started violently, took a step back, turned, and began to walk quickly away.

"Wait, please." Louisa hurried after her. "I am not going to summon a constable. I just wanted to give you some money and an address."

Evidently concluding that she was not going to be left alone, the woman halted and turned around, a cornered creature at bay.

Louisa stopped a few steps away and held out the envelope.

"There is enough money in this to see you through the month if you are careful with it. There is an address on the back of the envelope. If you go there and ask for help, you will receive it with no questions asked. It is an establishment run by a woman whose only goal is to assist other women like you."

"Other women like me?" The woman stiffened.

"Women who have been forced onto the streets."

"How dare you imply that I am a common streetwalker? Who do you think you are?"

The words were low and charged with a seething fury. The voice was that of an educated woman who had been reared in respectable circles.

"I'm sorry," Louisa said, chagrined. "I meant no offense."

Without another word the woman walked off swiftly into the night, the folds of the black velvet cloak sweeping out around her ankles.

Louisa watched her until she disappeared. When the widow was gone, she went back into the town house, closed and locked the door.

She tossed the envelope onto the hall table and went up the stairs, the woman's words ringing in her ears. *Who do you think you are?*

It was not that the widow had used the same words that Lord Gavin had employed that fateful night last year. The phrase was common enough, after all. *Who do you think you are?* People said it all the time. What sparked the chill down her spine was the rage that had vibrated in the woman's voice. *It was as though she hated me. But how can that be? I'm sure I have never met her before in my life.*

23

Louisa Bryce had mistaken her for a street whore. Rage, hot as steam, scalded her senses. She longed to go back to Arden Square and kill the stupid woman, but gradually common sense prevailed. She began to breathe more deeply. The white-hot fury receded. She would deal with Louisa Bryce in her own good time.

She walked swiftly, making her way toward a street where she could find a carriage. Night always brought back memories.

The effects of the chloroform were wearing off, leaving her disoriented and slightly queasy. She was vaguely aware of a sense of motion. At first she did not comprehend. Then it dawned on her that she was being carried in a man's arms. She lacked the strength to struggle. Perhaps it was for the best. Some murky instinct told her it would be safer to remain limp and lifeless.

Nevertheless, she could not resist opening her eyes partway. It did no good. She could not see anything. Her face was covered by a heavy cloth. A tarp, she decided. She was suddenly aware that the constricting canvas swathed her entire body. She could not move, even if she wanted to.

Despite the cloth covering her face, however, she could smell the dampness of fog and the river. Panic surged through her.

The man carrying her grunted with effort. She wanted to scream, but she could not summon her voice.

The next instant she was falling, plunging straight down. Striking the water was like striking a stone wall, the protection of the tarp notwithstanding.

She was aware of the deep, bone-chill-

ing cold as she sank beneath the surface. The shroud in which she had been wrapped had evidently not been well secured. She felt the canvas drift free . . .

It was only much later that she realized why Elwin had not bound her hands and feet before throwing her off the bridge. He wanted everyone to believe that she had committed suicide. Such a charade would not have worked if her wrists and ankles were tied when she was pulled from the river.

Luck had been with her that night. Unbeknownst to Elwin, who had fled the scene as soon as he had rid himself of his victim, there had been a witness to his work. A lunatic who made his home in a rickety hovel on the edge of the river had watched the bulky bundle plunge into the water. Curious, he had rowed his boat out to see if anything of value could be salvaged.

She had managed to claw her way to the surface, grateful that in her youth she had learned how to swim. It was a rare skill among women. Even given that ability, she knew she likely would have drowned had she not been dressed in her nightgown. She had been asleep when he had come for her with the chloroform. If she had been wearing one of her fashionable gowns when she tumbled into the water the weight of her skirts and corset would have pulled her under.

The first thing she saw when she surfaced was the outline of a small rowboat. Someone stretched out an oar. She seized it with both hands.

The other bit of good fortune was the fact that her savior had been a madman who claimed to hear voices in his head. People avoided him, and he, in turn, rarely spoke to anyone. The result was that no one knew he had pulled her out of the river that night.

The lunatic, convinced that she was some sort of magical creature given into his keeping, had treated her with reverence. He had cared for her in secret until she had recovered from the ordeal. She had stayed with him for a few weeks, letting him provide her with food and shelter while she contemplated her future and made her plans.

To be safe she had taken care to poison the old fool with arsenic before she left his care. She could not afford to take chances, after all. There was too much at stake. Nothing could be allowed to destroy her grand scheme of vengeance . . .

She pulled her thoughts away from the past. There was an empty hansom in the street. She got into it and gave the driver her address. Ladies who cared about their reputations took care not to be seen in hansoms; the vehicles were fast and the women who rode in them were considered to be the same. In her widow's gown and veil, however, she was anonymous. No one who had known her when she was Elwin Hastings's wife would ever recognize her.

She sat back, gloved hands clenched fiercely together. How dare Louisa Bryce assume that she was a cheap street whore?

24

The hansom was parked in the shadows at the end of the dark street. Anthony sat in the cab. He had been watching the door of the gentlemen's club for nearly an hour, waiting for Hastings to appear. It was three in the morning. The early rumors of Thurlow's death would no doubt have begun to circulate by now. Gossip flowed first through the clubs. He wanted to see how Hastings reacted to the news.

Although he was here to keep an eye on his quarry, his thoughts were on Louisa. She had expected a *transcendent* experience. He'd blundered badly, and he had no one to blame but himself. On the other hand, she had deliberately misled him with her mysterious widow charade. Nevertheless, if he'd exercised even a modicum of control he would have realized that he was kissing an inexperienced woman.

But self-control had not been at the forefront of his thoughts tonight, at least not after he'd initiated that kiss in the Lorrington gardens. At the time he told himself that the embrace had started out as a means of both keeping Louisa quiet and promoting the impression that they were engaged in an affair. But the truth was, he'd been hungering for her since the first moment he'd met her.

Louisa's searing response had pushed him to the edge of his self-control, overwhelming rational thought. The realization that she wanted him had created a sudden, indescribably exhilarating euphoria. In those first tumultuous moments the only thing he had been able to concentrate on was finding a secluded place where they could be together.

In hindsight, however, he had to admit that a gardener's workbench was probably not the most romantic location he could have chosen, and there was no question but that he had rushed things. Even an experienced woman of the world would have had some legitimate complaints under the circumstances. An inexperienced lady whose only knowledge of passion came from romantic novels and plays had every right to be disappointed.

The door of the club opened, just as it had several times during the past forty-five minutes. This time Hastings appeared. A familiar-looking figure in a long overcoat and a low-crowned hat straightened away from the railing he had been lounging against, tossed aside his cigarette, and stepped forward.

"Are you ready to leave?" Quinby asked.

"Get me a hansom," Hastings rasped. "I have just received a message. We must be off at once."

Anthony rapped softly on the back of the cab in which he was seated. "Are you awake up there?"

"Aye, sir," the driver muttered through the opening. "Just resting my eyes for a bit, is all."

Quinby whistled for a hansom. One rolled forward and stopped at the front steps of the club. The two men climbed in quickly.

"I want you to follow that cab at a discreet distance," Anthony said to the driver. "I do not want the occupants to know that we are behind them, but neither do I want to lose them. There will be a good tip in it for you if you can manage to keep up with the vehicle."

"That won't be a problem, sir. They'll never notice us in this traffic."

The driver slapped the reins lightly against the horse's rump. A four-wheeled carriage would have had great difficulty pursuing another cab in the busy streets, but the fast, highly maneuverable, two-wheeled hansom easily threaded a path through the traffic.

After several twists and turns, the cab in which Hastings was traveling entered an older neighborhood, where the streets were cramped and poorly lit, and many of the windows in the buildings were dark. The only bright spot was a small tavern aglow with a sinister yellow glare.

What would make a man like Hastings risk a journey into one of the more dangerous sections of the city?

Hastings's cab halted in front of the tavern. The driver of Anthony's hansom stopped some distance away.

Hastings and Quinby got out of the cab, taking no notice of Anthony's vehicle. Quinby put a hand inside the pocket of his coat and left it there. He carries that gun with him everywhere, Anthony thought.

"The message said he would meet with me at the end of this passage." Hastings halted at the opening of a dark, narrow service walk that separated the tavern from the neighboring building. "Strike a light. You will go first."

Quinby said nothing, but he struck a light, as ordered. The flame illuminated his hard face. Anthony watched him look around, assessing the scene with flat, streetwise eyes. He glanced at the second hansom. Anthony knew there was no way Quinby could see him in the dense shadows of the cab, but the scrutiny raised the hair on the nape of his neck, nevertheless.

Evidently concluding that Anthony's hansom presented no immediate threat, Quinby drew his revolver and led Hastings into the unlit passage.

Anthony dug some coins out of his pocket and handed them to the driver through the opening in the back of the hansom.

"That is the tip I promised you," he said. "There will be another if you are here when I return."

The driver made the coins disappear with a smooth, practiced gesture. "I'll be here."

Anthony got out of the cab and went toward the entrance of the walk where Hastings and his companion had vanished. When he reached it he could see the faint, yellowish glow of the guard's light at the far end. Three figures were illuminated, Quinby, Hastings, and a third man. Voices rumbled faintly, but it was impossible to make out what was being said.

A moment later the guard's light went out. Footsteps sounded on stone. Hastings and Quinby were returning, moving swiftly.

Anthony flattened himself into the heavy shadows of a doorway. Hastings burst out of the passage almost running, followed by Quinby, who, unlike his employer, did not appear to be agitated.

Hastings climbed into the cab in which they had arrived. Quinby got in after him. The driver set off at a brisk pace.

Anthony waited a moment longer. Then he took the revolver he had brought with him out of his pocket and cautiously entered the narrow passage.

At the far end a lantern flared to life, throwing the silhouette of a man against the wall. The figure moved quickly toward the opposite end of the passage. Anthony followed, trying not to make any noise on the stone path, but the man must have heard something or perhaps he was simply nervous. He swung around abruptly and yanked a cigarette out of his mouth.

"Who goes there?" he demanded. He held the lantern high, peering into the shadows. "Is that you again, Mr. Hastings? What do ye want now? I told you everything I know, I swear it."

"Then you can tell me," Anthony said, moving into the light so that the man could see the gun. "I assure you, I will pay as well or better than Hastings."

The man's face contorted with fear. "Here, now, ye've no cause to shoot me."

"I have no intention of doing so. The gun is merely a precaution. I have the impression that this is not the best of neighborhoods. What's your name?"

There was a short pause.

"Did you mean what you said about paying as well as Hastings?" the man asked warily.

"Yes." Anthony reached into his pocket and took out some coins. He tossed them down onto the stones. They bounced, spun, and gleamed in the lantern light. "There's more where that came from if you answer my questions."

The man looked at the coins with a speculative expression. "What do ye want to know?"

"Your name first."

"They call me Slip."

"How did you earn that title?"

Slip grinned, displaying several gaps in his teeth. "I'm good at slipping around without being noticed."

"Is that what Hastings hired you to do?"

"Aye, sir. I'm a professional, if I do say so, and my work is admired in certain quarters. Hastings put out the word that he wanted to employ a person with my skills. The price was right, so we came to an agreement."

"What sort of slipping around did Hastings request of you?" he asked.

"Nothing complicated," Slip said. "I was to keep an eye on a certain gentleman. See where he went. Make a note of his visitors, that sort of thing."

"What was the address of the gentleman?"

"Halsey Street. But ye can save yourself

the bother of calling on him. They carried his body away late this afternoon. Seems he put a pistol to his head. Rumor has it he couldn't pay his gambling debts."

"Did Hastings appear disturbed by that turn of events?"

"He already knew about Mr. Thurlow's death before he came here tonight. Said he'd heard the rumors at his club. He seemed disturbed, right enough. Probably suffers from weak nerves."

"You sent Hastings a message at his club tonight."

"Aye, that I did. I arranged for a meeting so that I could give him my final report on Mr. Thurlow's affairs and collect my fee."

"What information did you give Hastings?" Anthony asked.

"Weren't much to tell. Last night Mr. Thurlow spent the evening in the hells, as was his custom. He went back to his lodgings at dawn, drunk as a lord. I watched him go inside. Then I went home. I didn't return to Halsey Street until two o'clock this afternoon. Figured Mr. Thurlow wouldn't get out of bed until at least noon or later, so I had plenty of time."

Slip had arrived after he and Louisa had

both left Thurlow's lodgings, Anthony reflected. That was good news. It meant Slip had not seen Louisa.

"What of the housekeeper?" Anthony asked. "Did she leave while you were watching Thurlow's door?"

"No. She wasn't there at all. This was her day off."

"What did you do after you got to Halsey Street this afternoon?"

"I could see a constable at the front door and a lot of people standing around in the street. Someone said there was a man from Scotland Yard there, too, so I took myself off straightaway. I make it a policy not to linger in the vicinity of policemen. No good ever comes of it."

"Do you think Thurlow killed himself because of his gambling debts?"

"Doesn't seem likely," Slip said. "He won last night and was in a grand mood when he went home. Must have had some other reason for taking his own life."

"How long did you watch him for Hastings?"

"No more than a day or two."

"Did he have any visitors during that time?"

"If he did, they didn't come through the front door."

"What do you mean?"

"Simple logic, sir," Slip said. "I kept an eye on Thurlow's lodgings from across the street. Can't see the back door from there, now can I?"

The killer had come through the rear door, Anthony thought. Perhaps he had followed Thurlow home last night or maybe he had been acquainted with Thurlow's routine and knew that his quarry would return to his lodgings quite drunk.

Thurlow had gone to bed, dead to the world because of the spirits he had imbibed. He had probably never awakened, never known that the killer was inside his bedroom.

The murderer had put the pistol to Thurlow's head and pulled the trigger. Then he had arranged the suicide scene and conducted a very thorough search of the premises before leaving the note and exiting through the back door.

But if Hastings had hired Slip to watch Thurlow, Anthony thought, there was now a gaping hole in his theory that Hastings had murdered the gambler.

25

"Obviously, she was utterly humiliated when you offered assistance," Emma said. "Judging by your description of her, she was once a gently bred, respectable woman. It was no doubt the remnants of her tattered pride that caused her to refuse your kindness and generosity."

"I suppose you are right," Louisa said, thinking about the encounter with the prostitute during the night. "She did seem gravely offended."

They were seated in the library, drinking tea. The morning had dawned clear, but the fog had crept back early in the afternoon, slinking into the streets of Arden Square and pooling in the small park.

"It is a sad and all-too-common story." Emma picked up the teapot. "One reads about it frequently in the sensation press. There are so many ways a respectable woman can find herself forced to walk the streets. The death or illness of a husband, bankruptcy, debts, divorce, lack of family—any or all of them can render a woman penniless overnight."

"I know," Louisa said quietly.

"Of course you do, my dear." Emma raised her brows. "But do not forget that although you found yourself in desperate straits on two separate occasions, you managed to land on your feet each time without resorting to streetwalking."

"Sheer luck."

"No," Emma said firmly. "It was not luck at all. You are an extremely resourceful woman, my dear. After your father died and the creditors took everything but his books, you saved yourself by going into trade. Following the horrible situation with Lord Gavin, you came about yet again by changing your name, creating a fictitious character reference for yourself and applying to an agency. It was your own ingenuity and determination that kept you off the streets, Louisa, not luck. Never forget that."

Louisa smiled wanly. "You are always good for my spirits, Emma."

Emma looked at her curiously. "What is it that bothers you about the woman you saw in the park last night?"

"I'm not certain, to be honest. I do not believe that she's been in her present dire circumstances for long. Her cloak appeared to be of good quality and quite fashionable, as were the veil and gloves. If she knew she was going to be facing poverty after the death of her husband, why did she spend so much money on stylish mourning apparel?"

"Perhaps she did not find out the extent of her disaster until sometime after the funeral. That is often the way it is for women. Their husbands never discuss their financial affairs with them. The widows do not learn of their true circumstances until it is too late."

"Yes. Well, there is nothing more to be done in that quarter." Louisa set aside her teacup and opened her little notebook. "If you don't mind, I would like to ask you a few more questions about Victoria Hastings."

"Certainly." Emma's head tilted slightly in inquiry. "Why does she interest you?"

"Mr. Stalbridge suspects that Hastings murdered her as well as Fiona Risby. It occurs to me that since we are having very little luck coming up with a motive for Fiona's death, it might make sense to try to reason out why Hastings killed his wife. It seems to me that there must be some sort of link between the two murders."

26

That afternoon she took her customary path across a large park to Digby's Bookshop. The fog had thickened into a seemingly impenetrable sea, but she knew her way very well.

She had the park to herself. This was not the sort of day that brought out kite-flying children and nannies with their charges.

When she reached the far side of the park she found the traffic in the street only moderately heavy. Carriages and omnibuses moved slowly through the mist like a fleet of clattering ghost ships. There were very few pedestrians about.

She hurried across the street and entered the bookshop, bracing herself for the pang of melancholy and the small, icy chill she always experienced when she walked into Digby's. The sight of the shelves crammed with books and the smell of the leather bindings never failed to stir old memories and more recent fears.

Albert Digby, small, stooped, and balding, put down the day's edition of the *Flying Intelligencer* that he had been perusing and peered owlishly at Louisa over the rims of his spectacles. As usual, he was visibly annoyed by the intrusion of a customer.

"Oh, it's you, Mrs. Bryce."

She gave her business to Digby for two reasons. The first was that he was an extremely knowledgeable bookseller with a wide array of contacts among collectors. The second reason she had chosen Digby's was because she had never met him personally during the two years when she was the proprietor of Barclay's Books, so there was no way he could recognize her.

"Good afternoon, Mr. Digby." She went to the counter. "I got your message. I'm delighted to hear that you were finally able to secure the copy of Woodson's *Aristotle*."

"Wasn't easy locating the specific copy you wanted. But I did manage to obtain it for you at a good price, if I do say so myself."

"I appreciate your negotiating skills, Mr. Digby."

"Bah, Glenning's heir doesn't know a damn thing about books, nor does he care to learn. He is happy enough to sell off every volume he inherited from his father. His only concern is the money he got when the old man cocked up his toes."

Digby disappeared behind the counter. When he straightened he had a parcel wrapped in brown paper in his hand. He put it down on the battered wooden surface and unwrapped it slowly. The volume that was revealed was bound in red leather.

A thrill of hope swept through her. It certainly looked like the right book. She picked it up, opened it slowly, and began turning the pages, hardly daring to hope.

When she saw the small handwritten notations, she knew for certain. It wasn't just another copy of Woodson's *Aristotle*; it was the very same copy that she had been forced to sell last year, her father's copy. One of the two books she had stuffed into the suitcase on that dreadful night.

She closed the book, trying not to let her

excitement show. "I am very pleased. How did you manage to track it down?"

He looked sly. "Those of us in the book business have our ways, Mrs. Bryce."

"I understand. Now about the Milton—"

"You'd best forget about that one. I've told you before, the new owner made it clear he would only sell if the price was right. Between you and me, Mrs. Bryce, you can't afford the book."

"Yes, well, people's circumstances change as they did when Glenning died and left the *Aristotle* to a son who didn't want it and didn't know its value. I would be extremely grateful if you would occasionally remind the owner of the Milton that you have a client who is interested in the book."

"I'll do as you wish, Mrs. Bryce, but it's a waste of my time."

She gave him a fixed smile. "Thank you." She glanced at the newspaper on the counter. "I see you read the *Flying Intelligencer*."

He followed her glance and grimaced. "Cheap sensation rag, like all the rest. Except for the *Times*, of course. But I buy it whenever there's a report from I. M. Phantom in it."

"I see."

"Fascinating case of a young gentleman's death today. Outward appearances indicate he took his own life. Seems the victim had a pile of gambling debts. But I. M. Phantom says that rumors are circulating to the effect that it may have been murder. Makes you wonder how many other murders go unsolved simply because it looks like the victim committed suicide."

"Yes, it does."

She paid for the book and went back outside. The fog was so heavy now that it was difficult to make out the trees in the vast expanse of the park. She wondered uneasily if there was a risk of becoming disoriented in such dense mist. What was she worrying about? All she had to do was stay on the path, and she would be fine.

She crossed the street and plunged into the sea of vapor.

She judged she was a third of the way through the park when she heard the soft brush of a shoe on gravel behind her. Her hands suddenly felt very cold inside her gloves. A tiny flicker of electricity touched the nape of her neck, lifting every fine hair.

She stopped and turned very quickly,

searching the featureless gray mist. There was nothing to be seen in the fog except the vague, shadowy outlines of some of the nearer trees. She listened intently for a few seconds, but there were no more footsteps.

She started walking again, hurrying more quickly now. She was on the edge of panic, which was ridiculous. What was wrong with her? There was someone else on the path behind her. What of it? It was a public park.

She wondered if this edgy sensation was an indication that her nerves were starting to fail. She had to get control of herself.

The footsteps started in behind her again. In spite of the little lecture on self-mastery, her anxiety redoubled. Every instinct she possessed was urging her to break into a run, but if it was a man who was following her and if he elected to pursue her, running would do no good. Garbed in a gown, even one fashioned according to the most modern principles of dress design, she could not hope to outrun a man in trousers.

It dawned on her that whoever was behind her could not see her any better than she could see him. That thought broke through the rising tide of panic. The intelligent thing to do was to get off the path, hide in the trees, and allow the other person to go past. If it was another innocent pedestrian, there would be no problem. If the person behind her was bent on mischief, he would likely assume that she was still ahead of him and keep walking. Either way, she would be safe.

She left the path and made her way toward the dark shadows that marked a stand of trees, her footsteps muffled by the damp grass. When she reached the shelter of the trees she turned to look back toward the path. The ghostly outline of a figure dressed in a dark cloak, the hood pulled up over her head, appeared in the mist.

The cloaked woman stopped as though listening and, after what seemed an eternity, turned abruptly and walked swiftly back the way she had come. She was swallowed up in the ocean of fog almost immediately.

Louisa stood very still for a long time. Surely it was not the same woman she had seen last night in Arden Square. One black cloak looked very much like any other black cloak. Still, she could not shake the thought that the streetwalking widow had followed her today.

When her pulse had settled back to a

pace that felt relatively normal, she left the sanctuary of the trees, retraced her steps to the path, and started once more toward Arden Square.

She had gone only a few yards when she saw another figure coalescing out of the fog. A man this time, dressed in a dark gray overcoat.

"Lady Ashton said that you would likely be returning along the path through the park," Anthony said, walking toward her. "Thought I'd come ahead and meet you."

A wave of relief washed over her, quickly followed by a sweeping rush of euphoria. He looked so reassuringly strong and solid, and powerful, her elegant wolf. She longed to hurl herself into his arms.

"Good heavens, sir, you gave me a start," she said, reining in her strong emotions.

He halted in front of her, brows lifting. "My apologies. You do look a little flustered. Something wrong?"

"No." She looked back over her shoulder. There was no sign of the cloaked figure. "I saw a woman a moment ago, but she's gone now. Never mind, it's not important."

"Allow me to carry that for you." Anthony took the parcel she had tucked under her arm. "Lady Ashton said that you had gone shopping. I see you purchased a book."

"Yes."

"A sensation novel teeming with illicit trysts and the like?"

"No." Annoyed by his teasing, she glowered. "What are you doing here?"

He took her arm. "A man who does not call upon the lady the morning after cannot call himself a gentleman."

"The morning after what?" she asked, her mind still on the cloaked woman.

His mouth twisted ruefully. "I am crushed, Louisa. Surely you cannot have forgotten our interlude in the Lorrington conservatory so soon?"

Her breath caught in her throat. She could feel the heat flooding her cheeks.

"Oh, that," she said in a half-strangled voice.

"Continue on in that fashion, my sweet, and I will sink straight into the ground under the burden of my humiliation."

"For goodness' sake, sir—"

"Last night you called me Anthony. I rather liked that."

"I think we should change the subject."

"I assure you, if it is your aim to make me feel the full weight of my abject failure last night there is no need to say another word. I am already keenly aware of how badly I blundered. I came here today in part to beg your forgiveness."

"You must not blame yourself, sir," she said briskly. "I have done a great deal of thinking about the incident, and I see now that I must bear the majority of the blame."

"Because you did not warn me that you lacked experience in that particular enterprise?"

She glowered. "No, for expecting too much from the business itself. I fear I placed too much credence in the glowing descriptions of the novelists and the sensation plays. All that lovely nonsense about exquisite rapture and transcendent passion. I should have known that the reality would fall somewhat short."

"In my opinion, you would do well to withhold judgment on the matter until you have conducted a few more experiments."

"Hmm."

He tightened his grip on her arm. "And I must insist that those experiments be conducted with me."

For some reason the ominous tone of his voice elevated her spirits. Was he just a bit jealous?

"Why?" she asked lightly. "Surely it would be more scientific to experiment with a variety of gentlemen."

He halted, forcing Louisa to stop, too.

"You are teasing me," Anthony said evenly.

"Yes, of course I am."

"Don't. Not when it comes to that subject."

"Very well." She smiled a little.

"Correct me if I am wrong, but I was under the impression last night that you did not object to my kisses."

She blushed. "No. That aspect of the business was quite gratifying."

"I am relieved to hear that."

He slid his warm, powerful hand around the nape of her neck, pulled her close very deliberately and kissed her. His mouth was a slow, seductive drug on her senses. Heat and excitement ignited within her. She put her free arm around his neck and abandoned herself to the tantalizing sensations that were igniting her senses. She could easily become addicted to Anthony's kisses.

When he freed her a moment later, she was feeling breathless again, but not from fear this time.

"I must say, the novelists may have got things wrong when it comes to the denouement of the thing," she announced, vastly pleased. "But they are quite correct when they write about the pleasures of illicit kisses."

Anthony gave her his mysterious smile. "I shall take that as a sign of progress." He took her arm and propelled her swiftly along the path. "But future experiments must wait. We have a more pressing problem."

"Our investigation?"

"That, too. I now have a strong reason to believe that Hastings did not murder Thurlow, by the way."

"What?"

"He set a man to watch Thurlow. I don't think he would have done that if he intended to kill him."

"Good heavens. That means that either Thurlow really did take his own life or—"

"Or someone else murdered him. For the

moment, I'm assuming the latter, but first we must deal with an invitation."

She made an impatient little sound. "Another boring society affair?"

"No. I cannot guarantee that you will enjoy this particular event, but I can promise that it will not be dull."

"What on earth are you talking about?"

"My mother has invited you to tea tomorrow afternoon."

She stopped short, utterly aghast. "Your *mother*. She cannot possibly want to meet me."

"It was inevitable. She has heard the gossip about us."

"But we are having an *illicit* affair. Mothers never want to entertain the women with whom their sons are conducting illicit liaisons."

"You don't know my mother."

27

Anthony waited until the only other customer in Digby's Bookshop had left before he put down the novel he had been pretending to examine and went to the counter.

Digby was seated at his desk. He did not look up from a catalog of rare books.

"What do you want?" he growled.

"I wish to purchase a book for a good friend who shops here," Anthony said. "It is to be a surprise for a special occasion. My friend is very knowledgeable about rare volumes, but I lack expertise in the field. I thought perhaps you could assist me in selecting something that she will truly appreciate."

Digby snorted and turned the page. "What's the name of your friend?"

"Mrs. Bryce."

Digby reluctantly put down the catalog and heaved an exasperated sigh. "No offense, sir, but the lady is a bloody nuisance."

"In what way?"

Digby flung a hand wide, taking in the shelves of books. "Nothing in my shop is good enough for her. She only reads sensation novels. I don't carry that sort of thing. I am a dealer in rare volumes."

"I thought she came here specifically to purchase rare books."

"There are only two such books that are important to her. Both exceedingly difficult to obtain," Digby said grimly. "She's very choosy. Very demanding. Not just *any* first editions, but *specific* first editions. Neither one was in my shop."

"I understand you had some luck. She showed me the copy of a book on Aristotle that you located for her."

Digby's whiskers twitched in an irritated manner. "The only reason I was able to persuade the new owner to sell it to me was because he has no interest in rare books. Didn't know the value of what he had. I haven't been so fortunate with the owner of the Milton. Even if he could be convinced to sell, he made it clear the price would be far beyond Mrs. Bryce's reach."

"Perhaps if I spoke with the collector I could convince him to sell it to me," Anthony suggested. "Would you give me his name?"

Digby scowled suspiciously. "Now, see here, Mrs. Bryce is employing me to find that book. Damned if I'll hand the business over to you, sir."

"I would, of course, pay you a commission as a token of my appreciation for your valued assistance."

Digby did not appear enthused. "Even if I did give you the name of the collector, you probably won't be able to talk him into selling."

"I will pay the commission whether or not I am successful in acquiring the book for Mrs. Bryce," Anthony said.

Digby's brows formed a solid line above the rims of his spectacles. "The commission must be paid before I give you his name."

"Of course," Anthony said.

An hour and a half later Anthony was shown into a library that was so cluttered with bookshelves and volumes he could not immediately locate his host. The housekeeper disappeared before he could request directions.

"Lord Pepper?" he said to the seemingly uninhabited room.

"Over here, sir," a gruff voice called out from behind a towering bookcase. "Near the window."

Anthony threaded a path through a maze of books piled on the carpet and walked past several rows of bookcases.

A large, heavily built man lumbered to his feet behind a vast mahogany desk. His clothes were of good quality but sadly out of style. It had clearly been some time since he'd had his graying hair and whiskers trimmed. He smiled widely, displaying a gold tooth.

"Mr. Stalbridge, a pleasure to meet you, sir." He motioned to a chair piled high with leather-bound tomes. "Sit down, sit down. With any luck my housekeeper will bring us some tea."

"Thank you for seeing me on such short notice, sir." Anthony picked up the stack of books on the chair and looked at his host. "Where shall I put these?"

"Just set them down anywhere on the floor."

Easier said than done, Anthony thought. He eventually located a section of carpet that was not already littered with books and put down his burden, then returned to the chair and sat down.

Lord Pepper resumed his seat. "How is your father, young man?"

"Very well, sir. He sends his regards and asked me to ascertain that you are still satisfied with your Apollo Patented Safe."

Pepper smiled fondly at the massive strongbox that stood next to the desk. "Perfectly satisfied. I have the utmost confidence in the Apollo. I may have to acquire another one soon, however. That one is full."

"My father will be delighted to hear that."

The Apollo was the reason he had got past the front door of Pepper's town house. When he had mentioned the name of the owner of the *Milton* to his father, Marcus had recognized it immediately. *"Known Pepper for years. Very keen on books."*

Pepper laced his thick fingers together on top of the desk. "Now then, what's this about my copy of Milton? Have you become a collector, sir?"

"No," Anthony said. "I wish to acquire it for a very good friend."

"I see." Pepper assumed a sly expression. "Well, I'm not sure I can be of assistance. That book is one of my most valuable possessions. In fact, I keep it in my Apollo."

It was the answer Anthony had expected. He settled into his chair and prepared to go after the information he really wanted.

"I understand, sir," he said. "Obviously I shall have to look elsewhere for a gift for my friend."

"You won't find another copy of a first edition of that particular *Milton* in such excellent condition," Pepper said proudly. He nodded in the direction of the safe. "I spent years trying to obtain that one."

"As a matter of curiosity, would you tell me how it came into your hands?"

Diamond-bright satisfaction gleamed in Pepper's eyes. "I'd heard rumors from time to time that it was in the private collection of a gentleman named George Barclay. I approached him once or twice while he was alive, but he refused to sell."

"What happened?"

"It's a rather sad story, I fear. Barclay took his own life, leaving behind a massive amount of debt. His only living relation was his daughter. She was forced to sell off the house and most of the contents, but she managed to keep Barclay's books. Very few people know it, but the young lady used them to open a small bookshop."

A chill of awareness made Anthony go very still. "She was the proprietor of a bookshop? Barclay's Bookshop, by any chance?"

"Ah, I see you're aware of part of the story. It became quite notorious, of course, after Gavin was murdered there." Pepper lounged back in his chair, shaking his head sadly. "Shocking, really."

"The murder?"

"That, too. But I was referring to Miss Barclay's decline and fall. The Barclays were descended from an old, distinguished family. I've no doubt but that George Barclay would have turned over in his grave at the notion of his daughter lowering herself so far as to go into trade."

"Doesn't sound like he left her much choice," Anthony said evenly. "After paying off his debts she would not have had many alternatives."

"Yes, well, I suppose that's true. Nevertheless, it was a great pity. You'd think a young lady would have had more self-respect."

What was she supposed to do? Anthony

wondered. Walk the streets? Enter a workhouse? Doom herself to a miserable life of genteel poverty as a governess or a paid companion?

He forced himself to suppress his anger. He was here for information, he reminded himself, not a debate. "Continue with your story, sir. I find myself fascinated."

"Let me see. Where was I? Ah, yes, Barclay's Bookshop. It was located in a rather poor part of town, but Miss Barclay knew a great deal about rare books because her father had been an avid collector. She had begun to attract a good clientele and, I believe, must have been turning a profit there at the end. But then, of course, she murdered her lover, Lord Gavin, and committed suicide." Pepper clicked his tongue against his front teeth in a *tsk-tsk*ing manner. "Tragic."

"Were you acquainted with Miss Barclay?"

"No. The Barclays did not go into Society. Never had occasion to meet the girl."

"What of Lord Gavin? Did you know him?"

"Not well. He belonged to one of my clubs, but I rarely encountered him. Had a taste for seventeenth-century volumes, as I recall. Not too particular."

28

Anthony climbed down from a hansom cab, paid the driver, and went up the steps of J. T. Tuttington's Museum of Murder Most Foul. An older, badly faded sign was still visible over the entrance: BARCLAY'S BOOKSHOP.

A bell rang when he opened the glass-fronted door.

The interior was poorly lit. There were still a few volumes on the shelves. Cobwebs draped the higher sections of the bookcases. The sole occupant was a young woman seated behind the counter. She wore a plain dress and a neat white cap. She surveyed Anthony's expensive attire and immediately put down the penny dreadful that she had been perusing.

"J. T. Tuttington?" Anthony said politely.

She giggled. "That's my father, sir. My name is Hannah Tuttington. I look after the museum when he's not here."

He inclined his head. "A pleasure to meet you, Miss Tuttington."

Hannah Tuttington blushed at the polite greeting. "May I be of assistance, sir?"

"I understand that this is the scene of a scandalous murder."

Hannah's eyes widened. "That it is, sir. A most dreadful, bloody event, it was. A woman murdered her lover in cold blood on these very premises. Would you be wanting the full tour, then?"

"Yes, please." Anthony took a coin out of his coat and put it on the counter.

Hannah snatched up the money. "This way, sir. We'll start with the back room. Handsome Lord Gavin used to come around to that door when he called on her late at night."

She hurried around the end of the counter and led the way into the rear of the old bookshop.

Before following her, Anthony glanced at the magazine she had been reading. The cover featured a lurid drawing of a dead woman lying at the foot of a flight of stone steps. The menacing figure of a man stood at the top of the steps, a knife dripping blood in one hand. The title read: *A Complete History of the Dreadful Murder of Frances Hayes, a Prostitute*.

He walked into the back room of the shop, taking his time, absorbing the feel of the place.

"I see you kept some of the previous owner's books," he said, looking at the cartons of old volumes stacked in the small space.

"Only a few left now. Pa sold most of them right after he took over the shop. In the first few days after the murder all sorts of odd people showed up on the doorstep wanting to buy the books."

He looked at her. "What do you mean by odd?"

Hannah made a face. "They told Pa they were collectors. You wouldn't believe the prices they were willing to pay for dusty old books. Who would have guessed that there was a market for that sort of thing? Pa thought we were going to get rich within the month, but after a while that sort stopped coming around."

"And you were left with these volumes?" He motioned toward the cartons.

Hannah regarded them morosely. "Occasionally someone will buy one as a souvenir of the tour, but our customers aren't willing to pay as much as the collectors did. Most of the books go for a few pennies now."

"Do you have a lot of customers for your tour?"

"Not nearly as many as we did in the first few months after the murder." Hannah sighed. "Business has been slow lately, I'm sorry to say. Pa's doing his best to promote the museum, but there's a lot of competition these days. Seems like hardly a week passes without another scandalous murder or suicide in the press. Pa's thinking of going into some other line."

"A wise decision, no doubt. Tell me about the murder."

Hannah cleared her throat and assumed a melodramatic tone. "The name of the murderess was Miss Joanna Barclay. She was very beautiful, with long blond tresses and lovely blue eyes. Her lover's name was Lord Gavin. He was ever so elegant and handsome."

"Where did you get the descriptions?" Anthony said.

Hannah blinked at the interruption. "Why, from the newspapers and penny dreadfuls, of course. I assure you, every detail is based on fact, sir."

"Of course. Please continue."

"On the night of the dreadful event Joanna Barclay heard handsome Lord Gavin knock three times here at the back door."

Hannah made a fist and knocked in what was no doubt meant to be an ominous fashion.

"How do you know that he knocked three times?" Anthony asked.

"It was their secret code."

"If it was a secret code, how did you come to learn it?"

Hannah frowned, thrown off-stride again by the question. "Pa read about the code in one of the penny dreadfuls."

Anthony nodded. "Always a reliable source of information."

Hannah resumed her sepulchral tones. "Miss Barclay came downstairs to greet her handsome lover dressed only in her nightgown, robe, and slippers."

"How do you know what she wore? Did you get that out of the sensation press accounts, too?"

"Pa says the customers like to hear the details," Hannah confided. "So I made up some. Makes the story more interesting that way."

"Very enterprising of you."

"Thank you, sir." Hannah was pleased. "As I was saying, the lovely Joanna Barclay came down the stairs dressed for a night of illicit passion. She unlocked this very door to welcome her elegant lover."

Anthony studied the lock. It was a relatively new model that had not been on the market long. What interested him were the marks in the wood around it. There were several grooves and gouges. He could see the outline of a previous, much larger device.

"Was this lock on the door at the time of the murder?" he asked.

"No, sir." Hannah frowned, obviously bewildered by the question. "Pa had to install a new one when he rented the premises. The one that was on before was broken."

"Any idea how it got broken?"

Hannah shook her head, baffled. "How would I know that, sir?"

"Never mind."

Hannah coughed slightly and once again

took up her tale. "After letting her handsome lover in on that fateful night, Joanna Barclay gave Lord Gavin a most passionate kiss, took him by the hand, and led him up the stairs. Little did he know that he was climbing to his own death."

"No, I doubt that he had any inkling of his fate," Anthony agreed, studying the staircase.

"Come along, sir. I'll show you their secret love nest."

Hannah started up the staircase that led to the rooms above the shop. He followed, listening to the groans and squeaks of the old treads.

She did not go downstairs to open the door for him. She heard him smash the lock, and then she heard his footsteps on the stairs.

At the top of the narrow steps, Hannah swept out a hand to indicate a cozy little sitting room. There was not much in the way of furniture, Anthony noticed. A chair for reading, a table, a lamp, and a heavy trunk. It appeared a lonely little space.

"Furnished just as it was on the night of the murder, sir," Hannah assured him. "As I was saying, Joanna Barclay led her doomed lover into this very room, sat him down, and gave him a glass of wine."

Anthony looked at the table. "I don't see a glass. How do you know she gave him something to drink?"

"Drinking wine is the sort of thing lovers do together."

Anthony nodded. "Should have thought of that."

Hannah's voice lowered to a theatrical whisper. "There was a violent quarrel."

"Did you make up that bit, too?"

"It stands to reason that they argued, sir," Hannah said patiently. "Why else would she have murdered him?"

"An excellent question. Did anyone hear the shouting?"

Hannah sighed. "There was no one living next door at the time."

"What was the quarrel about?"

"According to the reports in the press the quarrel came about because Lord Gavin told Miss Barclay that he was going to cast her aside in favor of another."

"Why?"

"Why?" Hannah was clearly bewildered. "Why, because he was tired of her, I expect. She was his mistress, after all. Gentlemen often get tired of their mistresses. Everyone knows that."

"Please continue."

"Very well." Hannah drew herself up and pointed toward a curtained doorway with a dramatic flourish. "Joanna Barclay invited the elegant Lord Gavin into her bedroom one last time. He went with her little knowing he would never leave it alive."

Anthony went to the doorway and pulled the curtain aside. There was a small dressing table and a wardrobe. The sheets and quilt on the narrow bed were pulled back and rumpled, presumably to indicate energetic lovemaking. There were some old, rusty brown stains on the carpet.

"After their last passionate embrace Lord Gavin fell asleep," Hannah explained. "Joanna Barclay rose from the bed, picked up the poker you see there next to the nightgown, and struck her doomed lover most violently on the head."

A demure white-lawn nightgown edged with dainty lace was draped across the lower portion of the bed.

"Did you replace the bedding?" he asked.

"No, sir. Everything in this room is guaranteed to be exactly as Pa found it when he opened the museum. I shake out the sheets and the nightgown once in a while and dust the furniture, but that's all."

Anthony walked to the bed and looked down. "There are no bloodstains on the sheets. Did you wash them out?"

"No, sir." Hannah frowned. "I don't recall any bloodstains on the bedding."

"Probably because they are on the carpet," Anthony said mildly.

Hannah struggled with that discrepancy for a moment and then brightened. "I expect Lord Gavin woke up just before she hit him and rolled off the bed onto the carpet in a futile attempt to dodge the blow."

"That's certainly one plausible theory."

He opened the wardrobe. Two faded dresses and a pair of shoes were inside.

He walked back into the sitting room and crouched beside the trunk. There was a sturdy lock, but it was open. He raised the lid and looked inside. It was empty.

"What did you find inside the trunk?" he asked Hannah.

She screwed up her face into an expression of deep concentration. "If there was ever anything inside, it was gone before Pa rented the place. Why do you ask?"

"Never mind. It's not important. I was merely curious."

"Well, then," Hannah said, "after Joanna Barclay murdered Lord Gavin in that terrible fashion, her nerves were shattered. She sobbed bitterly."

Joanna Barclay had fitted the trunk with an expensive lock. Whatever had been stored inside must have been of considerable value to her. The lock had not been broken. It had been opened by someone who either possessed the key or knew how to pick a lock.

"They say she committed suicide," Anthony remarked, rising.

"I was getting to that part." Hannah gave a theatrical shudder. "Like I was telling you, after she murdered her handsome lover, Joanna Barclay plunged into a fit of despair. She went to the river, threw herself off a bridge, and drowned. They found a feathered hat caught on a bit of drifting wood."

"But they never found the body."

"No, sir, that's true."

"Thank you, Miss Tuttington. Your tour was very educational."

"I'm glad you enjoyed it, sir."

A short time later he left Tuttington's Museum wondering what had been in the trunk and why a woman who planned to take her own life would have bothered to take the contents with her. It occurred to him that for a little over a year he had been obsessed with the questions that swirled around Fiona's death. Those questions still required answers. But for some reason it was the mystery of another woman that compelled him now.

29

The monthly accounts had balanced nicely, showing a handsome profit again. Madam Phoenix put down her pen and closed the journal. The improvements she had made with the funds provided by the new circle of investors were paying off as she had anticipated.

It was going on midnight. Raucous male laughter could be heard from the grand reception room below. The gentlemen were indulging themselves in the excellent champagne and brandy, lobster canapés, roasted duck, and all the rest of the expensive hors d'oeuvres and spirits that had helped make Phoenix House the most elegant brothel in London.

It was not just the food that had captured the attention of the wealthy, jaded men who came here each night. Madam Phoenix was well aware that the chief attraction was the quality of the women who were available for an hour or two of pleasure.

The females employed in Phoenix House were not common streetwalkers. They were well bred, well educated, and fashionable. Most of them came from the respectable classes, widows and single women who found themselves alone in the world or trying to pay off a husband's debts. All had one thing in common: They had been faced with abject poverty for one reason or another. They had chosen Phoenix House over the streets or the river.

Three brisk knocks sounded on the door.

"Enter," she said, turning around.

The door opened. A pretty young maid, dressed in a tightly corseted gown that displayed her breasts to advantage, bobbed a curtsy.

"The client has arrived and is being escorted to the chamber, Madam."

"Thank you, Betsy. You may go back to our guests."

"Yes, madam." She dropped another curtsy and disappeared.

Madam Phoenix waited until the door closed behind the maid before walking across the room to a bookcase.

She tugged on a hidden lever. The bookcase swung open, revealing a narrow passage that was dimly illuminated by a wall sconce. She moved inside and closed the panel behind her.

The original owner had ordered the concealed passageway built because he did not like to encounter servants on the main stairs or in the formal hallways. The hidden corridors allowed the staff to move unobtrusively throughout the house without being seen by their employer or his guests.

The former proprietor of the brothel had found another use for the secret passageways. After she disposed of her predecessor, Madam Phoenix had continued the tradition. At various points along the way small holes had been cut in the walls, allowing views into the adjoining rooms. The openings were discreetly concealed with paintings on the opposite side of the walls. The occupants of the rooms were unaware that they sometimes provided amusing entertainment for those who paid for the view.

Only the most valued clients were informed that the opportunity to watch others indulging in a variety of sexual acts was available. The fee was exorbitant, of course, but thus far none who had been offered the chance to take advantage of the service had refused to pay it.

Some distance along the corridor she descended a cramped flight of steps. She went a short distance along another corridor and stopped in front of a small hole in the wall.

The room on the other side was lit by a gas lamp that had been turned down very low. The walls and ceiling were covered in black velvet. A bed occupied the center of the room. It was sheathed in ebony silk sheets. Black velvet manacles dangled from each of the four stout posts.

There was a glass-fronted cabinet against one wall. Inside were a variety of devices, including several sizes of whips and some unusual implements.

As she watched, the door of the room opened. One of the pertly dressed maids ushered the client inside.

"Miss Justine gave orders that you are to undress, fold your clothes, and lie down on the bed to await her pleasure," the maid said.

The client nodded eagerly. "I understand."

The maid departed. Metal clanged on metal when she locked the door behind her.

The client undressed with obvious enthusiasm. He folded his clothes neatly and put them on the dresser. He was already fully aroused. He lay facedown on the bed.

The key scraped in the lock again. The door opened to admit a tall woman dressed in a severe, tightly corseted dark gown. She looked like a governess.

"You may stand beside the bed," the woman said in a cool, bored voice.

"Yes, Miss Justine."

The client obediently stood.

"Go to the cabinet of correction equipment and select a whip. The large one this time, I think. I can see that you did not fold your clothes as neatly as you ought to have done. You must be punished."

"Yes, Miss Justine."

The client opened the cabinet and removed the whip.

"Kiss the whip before you give it to me and then put on the blindfold."

"Yes, Miss Justine."

The client dutifully pressed his lips to the hilt of the whip before handing it to her. He walked to a table, picked up a strip of black silk, and wrapped it around his head, covering his eyes.

"Lie on the bed. Facedown."

"Yes, Miss Justine."

The client used his hands to feel his way back down onto the black sheets. When he was in position Miss Justine walked around the bed in a leisurely manner pausing at each post to secure his wrists and ankles. She picked up the whip.

Madam Phoenix turned away from the opening in the wall and started back toward the staircase that led up to her study. There was no pleasure to be had watching Elwin Hastings undergo his punishment. The bastard enjoyed it, after all. He paid dearly for it.

She went back to her private quarters via the concealed hallways.

Things were going very well here at Phoenix House, but a problem loomed. It was clear that something would have to be done about Louisa Bryce. She was asking far too many questions.

She opened the door of her private apartment. He was waiting for her, as she had expected.

"Darling." She smiled and went into his arms.

He kissed her deeply, hungrily. His fingers found the fastenings of her gown. A few minutes later he pulled her down onto the bed.

30

The restaurant was the one they had begun using a little over a year ago when they had wished to meet privately. As was their custom they occupied a booth at the rear of the premises. From that position Anthony and Fowler both had a clear view of the entrance.

The small establishment was owned by a French chef and served a truly remarkable coq au vin. It also boasted an excellent selection of wine. It's chief attraction, however, was that it was tucked away in a tiny, anonymous lane, quite remote from Scotland Yard. Fowler did not have to be concerned about being spotted by any of his colleagues.

"I told you last year that Gavin's murder and Miss Barclay's suicide had no connection to the deaths of Miss Risby and Mrs. Hastings," Fowler said. He forked up a bite of the chicken.

"I'm sure you're right." He had to be careful about this line of questioning, Anthony thought. There was a bond between himself and Fowler because of their mutual interest in learning the truth about Fiona Risby's death, but Fowler was still a detective. "Nevertheless, I find it interesting that so many women chose to cast themselves into the Thames in the space of less than a month. What do you know about Lord Gavin?"

Fowler snorted. "As far as the Yard is concerned, the world is better off without him. I believe his widow is equally pleased to be free of the bastard."

The vehemence in Fowler's tone made Anthony pause. He lowered his fork slowly back down to his plate. "You did not mention your strong feelings on the matter when we discussed Gavin last year."

"No offense, sir, but I didn't know you well at the time." Fowler picked up his wineglass and took a sip. "If you will recall, we had only just met. I told you as much as I thought you needed to know in order to satisfy yourself that there was no link between the Gavin affair and Fiona Risby's death."

"I see. Now, of course, you have made me curious. Why are you pleased that Gavin is no longer among the living?"

Fowler's brows rose. "Were you acquainted with him, sir?"

"Only in passing. Saw him occasionally at the clubs, but we were never friends."

Fowler glanced at the adjoining booths, assuring himself that they were still empty. He lowered his voice. "Lord Gavin was, shall we say, not unknown to those of us involved in murder investigations at the Yard."

Anthony went cold. "I never heard any rumors to that effect."

"Of course not. My superiors were careful to keep it all extremely quiet. There would have been hell to pay if it got out that we had linked his name with an investigation. Gavin would have been furious. Everyone involved at the Yard would have lost his position."

"I understand."

"You must not repeat any of what I am going to tell you in your clubs, sir."

"You have my oath on it."

Fowler nodded once, satisfied. "Very well. A few months before Gavin's death the proprietor of a glove shop, a young widow who had taken over her husband's business, was raped and beaten almost to death. She was found in a state of shock by her shopgirl, who summoned the police."

"Go on."

"The victim named Lord Gavin as her attacker."

Anthony stilled. "I read nothing about that in the press."

"Of course not." Fowler snorted. "It was hushed up immediately. Among other things, the proprietor of the glove shop was not the most credible of witnesses. She was having an affair with a married man at the time and had been overheard quarreling with her lover."

Anthony put down his fork. "So it was assumed that he was the one who had beaten her in a fit of jealous rage and that she had named Lord Gavin as her assailant rather than reveal her lover's name."

"Precisely. In the end the victim suffered an overwhelming attack of nerves and confessed that she had lied about Gavin having assaulted her."

"Surely you are not going to tell me that she plucked Gavin's name out of thin air and gave it to you?"

"No. He was one of her customers. Gavin purchased two pairs of gloves from her in the weeks before she was assaulted."

"Did you speak with Gavin?"

"He refused my request for an interview. With no evidence and my only witness changing her mind about the facts of the case, there was nothing more I could do."

"I sense the tale does not end there."

"No," Fowler said, grim-faced. "It does not. A month later another single woman living alone was found dead in the rooms above her shop. She had been raped, beaten, and stabbed to death."

Anthony pushed his plate aside, his appetite gone. "That murder was in the press. As I recall, there were no arrests."

"Because there was no evidence. The victim was unable to tell us anything because she was dead. However, there were certain similarities to the first assault that bothered me. I eventually found one witness who saw a man of Gavin's description entering the shop on one or two occasions in the days preceding the crime, but that was not enough to act upon."

"What did you do?"

Fowler widened the fingers of one hand. "I wanted to assign a constable to keep an eye on Gavin for a time, but my superiors were afraid that Gavin might notice and complain."

"What happened next?"

"There was a similar death a month later."

Anthony raised a brow. "Another single female shopkeeper?"

"Yes. In that case the victim's neighbor said that in the weeks before the shopkeeper was killed she had confided that one of her gentleman customers was making her nervous. She said he'd made improper advances and seemed angry when she rejected him. After that there were some incidents."

"What sort of incidents?"

"Among other things, the shopkeeper found a crude drawing that had been shoved under her door. It was a picture of a nude woman who had been slashed open with a knife."

"Son of a bitch," Anthony said softly.

"On another occasion the shopkeeper discovered a dead rat in her bed. Its head had been severed. The sheets were soaked with blood."

"I suppose there was no way to link those incidents to Gavin?"

Fowler shook his head. "None."

"Tell me about the scene at Gavin's murder."

"When I received a report that his body had been discovered in the rooms above Barclay's Bookshop I went around at once. I found Miss Barclay's suicide note."

"Anything else?"

"A poker with blood and hair on it."

"Was that all?"

"One more thing," Fowler said slowly. He set his fork down with great precision. "It did not appear in the press because we did not tell the journalists about it. I discovered a knife on the floor beside the bed. Some might say, of course, that Miss Barclay intended to stab Gavin with it after she bashed in his head with the poker just to see to it that he was good and dead."

"I take it you do not believe that was the case."

"No, I do not. I've a hunch the knife fell

from Gavin's hand when Miss Barclay struck him with the poker."

The image of Joanna Barclay fighting for her life against a man armed with a knife iced Anthony's blood. He looked down and noticed that he had made a fist. Very deliberately, he relaxed his fingers.

"He went there to rape her and kill her," he said quietly.

"I'm absolutely certain that was the case. I had a look through Miss Barclay's receipts and journal of accounts. Gavin had purchased three books from her on three separate occasions. That was part of his pattern, you see. He chose single women who were alone in the world. Shopkeepers he thought no one would miss, at least not for long. Women of modest backgrounds whose rank in the social order was much lower than his own."

"Bastard."

"A mentally unstable bastard, I believe," Fowler said. "I've run into his sort before. I think he began by beating his victims, but after a while that was not sufficient to satisfy his unwholesome lust."

"So he started to murder them."

"And would likely have gone on doing so

had Miss Barclay not stopped him," Fowler said. "In my opinion, she did us all a great favor by dispatching Gavin to the Other World. A pity she is no longer with us. I suppose she took her own life because she feared she would be charged with murder."

"Such a fear would not be a fantasy, given her position in the world relative to Gavin's." He held Fowler's eyes across the table. "We both know that if Gavin's family had determined to see Miss Barclay hanged for murder they might well have prevailed."

Fowler's heavy brows rose. "Unfortunately, Miss Barclay had no way of knowing that Gavin's wife had no love for her husband and his family is secretly relieved that he is gone. I suspect they had reason to fear his rages."

"How did you learn that?"

"I talked to the servants, of course. Until his death last year there was a very high turnover in staff in the Gavin household."

31

Anthony emerged from his club shortly after midnight. He paused briefly to consider the wisdom of whistling for a cab and then abandoned the notion. The fog had slowed traffic to a snail's pace. Even the usually quick, agile hansoms were forced to pick their way cautiously through the near-impenetrable mist. Walking would be faster. Besides, he did some of his best thinking while walking, and tonight he needed to think.

He turned up the collar of his overcoat and started down the steps. A hansom halted in the street directly in front of him. A familiar figure descended with unsteady movements. Julian Easton was drunk as usual. Unfortunate timing, Anthony thought.

He should have left the club five minutes earlier.

"Stalbridge." Julian gripped the iron railing on the steps to steady himself. "Leaving so soon? Don't rush off on my account."

"I'm not."

Anthony started down the steps. Julian moved in front of him, blocking his way.

"Off to visit the little widow in Arden Square?" Julian's face twisted in a sneer. "Be sure to give her my regards."

Anthony stopped. "You're in my way, Easton. I would appreciate it if you would move."

"In a hurry to get to her, I see." Julian swayed a little. "I wonder how long it will take for her to comprehend that you are taking advantage of her naïveté."

"Why don't you go inside and have another bottle of claret?"

"Rather unfair of you to use her to cover up your affair with some other man's wife, don't you think?"

"What I think is that you had best keep your speculations to yourself," Anthony said quietly.

"Now why would I do that when there are so many people eager to unravel the mystery?" Julian looked shrewd. "In fact, there are wagers going down in every club in St. James. Amazing how many gentlemen are curious to see which one of their wives you're fucking while you hide behind Mrs. Bryce's very unfashionable skirts."

"Get out of my way, Easton."

Easton's face screwed up into a mask of rage. "Better not try to knock me down again, you bastard. I'm carrying a revolver these days to protect myself from you."

"Have a care. In your present condition you're likely to shoot yourself in the foot. Now I must insist that you get out of my way."

"Damned if I'll move."

Anthony gripped Julian's arm and shoved him to the side. Julian came up hard against the iron railing. He seized it frantically to keep himself from losing his footing. By the time he recovered his balance, Anthony was at the bottom of the steps.

Another carriage halted, disgorging three men in evening clothes. They took in the scene with expressions of amused curiosity.

"Whose wife is she?" Julian shouted, voice rising in fury. "Which one of the gentlemen inside that club are you cuckolding, Stalbridge?"

Anthony did not look back. He kept moving, walking into the fog.

Streetlamps were abundant in this part of town. The glary balls of light in front of each doorway were strung like so many strange, glowing gems in the darkness. But on foggy nights such as this the light did not penetrate far. In the street, private carriages and cabs appeared and disappeared. The slow *clop-clop-clop* of the horses' hooves and the rattle of wheels had a muffled quality. It was as if the fog ate sound the way it did light.

He should warn Louisa about the wagers that were being placed in the club betting books, he thought. He paused at the corner, considering the time. She was very likely in bed, but surely she would want to be awakened with this latest information. She was always reminding him that they were partners, after all.

He thought about how she would look at this hour, garbed in a dressing gown and slippers, her hair tucked into a little white cap or perhaps down around her shoulders.

Smiling, he turned the corner and walked toward Arden Square.

He was not certain when he became aware of the echo of footsteps behind him. There had been a number of other pedestrians on the street in the vicinity of the club. But as he moved into the quieter neighborhoods of town houses and squares there were far fewer people about.

It wasn't just the sound of the footsteps that bothered him; it was the pattern: Too similar to his own, he thought. Whoever was behind him was keeping a certain distance between them. He stopped, testing his theory. The footsteps continued for a few paces and then halted abruptly. He started walking again. The footsteps followed.

He turned another corner and walked into Arden Square. The weak glare of the streetlamps illuminated the doors of the town houses, but the little park in the center was only a dark, shapeless void.

He stopped. The person following him stopped, too. He crossed the street, heading toward the invisible park, the change of direction giving him an opportunity to glance casually to his right. A figure in an overcoat and top hat stood silhouetted on the pavement.

Anthony entered the small park, following the gravel path. There was just enough fog-reflected moonlight to reveal the dark outlines of nearby tree trunks and the massed shapes of bushes.

Hurried footsteps echoed. A moment later gravel crunched behind him.

He removed his coat and hat. When he reached the statue of the wood nymph in the center of the park he draped the coat around the stone shoulders. He balanced the hat on top of the nymph's head.

He moved across the grass into the shadows to examine his handiwork. By day no one would have been fooled, but here in the moonlight and fog the coat and hat bore a reasonable resemblance to a man who had paused to relieve himself.

He waited. The footsteps came more quickly now. There was a certain nervous quality about them, as though the pursuer feared he had lost his quarry.

A figure moved out of the deep shadow cast by a looming tree. The man stopped a few feet away from the draped statue. His arm came up, pointing.

Anthony barely had time to register the dark shape of a gun in the man's hand before he heard the unmistakable cocking of a revolver. A second later the weapon roared. Light sparked. There was a clang as the bullet struck stone. The attacker cocked the gun again and fired another shot. This time when the coat and hat did not fall to the ground, he seemed to lose his nerve. He whirled and fled back along the gravel path.

Anthony lunged out of the shadows. Hearing the pounding footsteps behind him, the man paused, swung around, cocked the gun and fired again, aiming blindly.

Not surprisingly, the shot thudded into a nearby tree trunk. Nevertheless, it occurred to Anthony that pursuit was probably not his most intelligent maneuver. He had his own revolver with him, but he was not prepared to start shooting people he could not identify. Reluctantly, he halted at the edge of the park, watching his quarry disappear into the night. Blood pounded in his veins.

"Bloody hell."

The shots had not gone unnoticed. Shouts of alarm sounded from bedroom windows around the square.

He went back to the nymph to retrieve his

hat and coat. Sticking to the shadows as much as possible to avoid notice by the people peering down from the windows, he made his way through the park and crossed the street.

He should not call on her now, he thought. Nevertheless, he found himself going up the steps of Number Twelve. She would want a report of events. She was a member of the press, after all. And he wanted to see her very badly.

He did not need to bang the knocker. The door was jerked open before he could lift a hand. Louisa stood in the opening, peering anxiously through her spectacles. "Dear heaven, what happened? I heard the shots. I rushed downstairs and looked out the window and saw you coming across the street. Are you all right? What are you doing here? Were you attacked by a footpad?"

The sight of her elevated his mood immediately. He had been right, he thought, oddly pleased. She did look delightfully inviting clad in a robe and slippers. The vital question of the evening was answered. She slept with her hair down.

32

"Dear heaven, he put two bullets right through your coat." Louisa stared, stricken, at the back of the coat. "You could have been killed."

"Except that I wasn't wearing the coat at the time." Anthony crossed the study to the brandy table and picked up the decanter. He watched Louisa hold the coat up to the light, verifying yet again that, yes, one could see straight through the holes in the back. He found her outraged concern deeply touching, but her lack of logic made him smile. "I told you, it was draped over the statue."

"He's right, dear," Emma said gently. "Mr. Stalbridge explained to you that he was not wearing the coat when he, or rather it, was shot."

"That's not the point." Louisa flung the coat across the back of the sofa and whirled back around to face Anthony. "The point is that you should never have taken such a risk. Walking the streets alone at night. Whatever were you thinking, sir?"

He swallowed some of the brandy and lowered the glass. "I was under the impression that this was a respectable neighborhood."

"It is, but that doesn't mean that people should just wander around alone at all hours making inviting targets for every passing footpad."

"It wasn't a footpad who shot my coat," he said quietly.

Louisa and Emma both looked at him.

"What on earth do you mean?" Louisa whispered.

"I'm almost certain it was Hastings." He paused, reflecting. "Although I suppose it could have been Easton." He shook his head. "I believe that Easton was too drunk to follow me in the fog, let alone aim a gun. However, given that I could not be absolutely positive, I held my own fire."

"Dear heaven," exclaimed Louisa, eyes widening. "You're carrying a gun?"

"Bought it when I was in the American

West. Guns are quite common there. In the wake of Thurlow's unanticipated demise, it seemed prudent to keep it on my person." He shrugged. "Not that I would have been likely to hit a running target tonight, not in that fog. One of the things I learned in my travels in the Wild West was that revolvers are notoriously inaccurate except at close range."

"Oh, my," Emma said. "This is a most disturbing development."

"What makes you think it was Hastings?" Louisa demanded.

Anthony reflected briefly. "Right height. Something about the way he moved. I believe he followed me from the club, waiting for an opportunity."

"An opportunity to murder you." Louisa sank down onto a chair, appalled. "Dear heaven. He knows we are investigating him."

"Not necessarily," Anthony said. "I think it is more likely that he has reasoned out that I was the one who took the necklace and the blackmail items from the safe. That's all he knows at this point, but it is more than enough to make him extremely worried. He has no way of knowing what I intend to do with the extortion evidence or the necklace."

Louisa's brows snapped together. "Why

did you come here at such a late hour tonight?"

"I wanted to warn you that there are some unfortunate wagers going down in the club books."

Emma looked up, eyes sharp with concern. "What sort of wagers?"

Anthony tightened his grip on the brandy glass. "The gamblers are betting on the name of the married woman with whom I am supposedly intimately involved."

Emma frowned. "I thought everyone believes that you and Louisa are engaged in a romantic liaison."

"Easton is putting it about that I am using an innocent lady, namely Louisa, to conceal an affair with some other gentleman's wife," he explained quietly.

"Ridiculous," Louisa said briskly. "I am hardly an innocent lady."

Anthony looked at her. So did Emma. Neither spoke.

Louisa raised her chin. "I am a journalist."

Out of the corner of his eye Anthony saw Emma lift her eyes to the ceiling and then take a healthy swallow of brandy. He followed suit.

"If we might return to the more pressing

matter of the shooting?" Louisa said with a quelling glare.

"Indeed." He inclined his head. "I think it is safe to say that it is a good sign."

"A good sign?" Louisa gasped. "Someone just tried to murder you."

"And he failed." Anthony contemplated the logic of the situation. "He took a wild chance and blundered badly. He will be much more cautious the next time because he knows that I am now on my guard."

"The *next* time?" Louisa was beyond horrified now.

"Cheer up, my sweet." He savored the little rush of satisfaction that flashed through him. "I believe we are making progress."

"How can you call nearly getting murdered in the park progress?" she demanded, outraged.

Emma gave Anthony a considering look. "If you are right about Hastings being the one who tried to kill you tonight, I think it is safe to say that you have shaken his nerve. He must be feeling quite anxious, indeed, if he took the risk of attempting to murder a Stalbridge."

He swirled the brandy in his glass. "I certainly hope so. Anxious men make mistakes."

33

"I must tell you that we were all vastly relieved to hear the gossip about you and Anthony," Clarice confided cheerfully.

Louisa tripped over a small stone on the path. She staggered a bit and nearly lost her grip on her parasol before she caught her balance.

"You were *relieved*?" she managed to say, aware that her mouth was probably hanging open in a most unbecoming fashion.

She and Clarice were strolling through the extensive gardens behind the Stalbridges' large house. Anthony had remained inside with his parents.

This was not the first time Louisa had been flummoxed by a statement from one of the Stalbridge clan. It had been like this since Anthony had escorted her into the family's elegant drawing room an hour ago and made introductions.

Nothing had gone quite as she had expected. In spite of Anthony's reassurances to the contrary, she had been braced for grim disapproval. Instead she was welcomed with unsettling enthusiasm. No one seemed the least bit horrified by the gossip that implied that she was having an affair with Anthony. Neither did anyone show any indication of being shocked by her career as a correspondent for the *Flying Intelligencer*. Instead, Mr. and Mrs. Stalbridge and Clarice had been all that was charming and gracious. They seemed fascinated rather than appalled by her.

The discovery that Mrs. Stalbridge and Clarice were both devoted adherents of the rational dress movement had come as another pleasant surprise. Then again, she thought, why had she anticipated that the members of Anthony's family would be any less out of the ordinary than he was? Emma had warned her that the Stalbridges were considered to be eccentrics, one and all.

She remained cautious, of course. Given

her dark past, she could not afford to become too close to anyone. Nevertheless, she had been unable to resist taking an instant liking to Clarice. It had been so long since she'd had a friend who was close to her own age. Navigating the waters of friendship was a treacherous proposition when one carried a terrible secret.

"We are happy to see Anthony taking an interest in you because we have been so worried about him," Clarice explained. "Last year, after his fiancée died, he became absolutely obsessed with the notion that she was murdered. It affected his mood for weeks. We all became quite alarmed, to be honest."

"I see."

Clarice absently twirled her parasol. "We thought he had gotten over it after he was forced to abandon his inquiries last year, but when he suddenly renewed his investigation a couple of weeks ago we realized that he was as committed as ever to his theory that Fiona was murdered. Then we heard the rumors about the two of you. Mama and Papa became extremely hopeful. Indeed, I did, as well."

"Good heavens."

"Now that we have had occasion to see the two of you together, it is obvious that the gossip is true and that is why we are all so delighted to make your acquaintance today."

"I'm not sure I follow your reasoning," Louisa said warily. "My connection to your brother actually is founded upon a business arrangement. As he explained to you, I am assisting him in his investigation. When it is concluded, I plan to write a report for the *Flying Intelligencer*."

"Yes, of course." Clarice gave her a warm smile. "I'm sure that it will be an excellent piece of journalism. But it is also obvious that you and Anthony have formed an intimate connection, and we couldn't be happier. It is good to see him looking at a woman the way he looks at you."

Louisa sighed. "You feared his heart was broken when Fiona died. Now you believe that he is at least willing to allow himself to be distracted by another female, but I really don't think you should leap to any conclusions about the nature of his feelings for me."

"Rubbish." Clarice laughed. "There is no

other obvious explanation for the improvement in his mood."

"Maybe he is more cheerful these days because he feels he is close to solving the mystery of Fiona's death."

"That may be part of it, but I still suspect that you are the main cause of his elevated spirits."

"I really do not think so," Louisa said weakly.

"Come now, Mrs. Bryce. You do not give yourself enough credit. I assure you, my brother would never have brought you here to have tea with Mama and Papa if he was not enamored of you."

Louisa stopped abruptly, horrified. "I assure you, your brother is not in love with me."

"It's all right, Mrs. Bryce. You don't have to pretend around this family. We are not like most of the people who move in Society. In this household, we are all quite straightforward."

"Forgive me, but I fear that all those thrilling plays you write for the Olympia Theater have affected your imagination."

Clarice nodded somewhat wistfully. "I admit that I do find the notion of illicit affairs very intriguing. I insert at least one into every play."

"I have seen several of your plays. While they are marvelously entertaining, I cannot help but note that the illicit affairs always end badly."

Clarice grimaced. "That is only because the audiences and the critics demand such endings. Mind you, they are all quite keen to savor the excitement of illicit affairs on stage, but they feel they can only justify their pleasure if the affairs come to unfortunate conclusions."

"I see." Louisa exhaled deeply and resumed walking slowly along the path. "It is the same way in novels."

"Indeed. Literary conventions and critics can have a very restrictive effect on art," Clarice said with a sage air.

"Do you think that if the conventions and critics did not exist it would be possible to write a play or a novel in which the illicit affair ended happily?"

"Of course," Clarice said.

Louisa stopped again and looked at her.

"Well?" she said eagerly. "How would it conclude?"

Clarice waved a hand. "Why, the lovers would get married, naturally."

"Hmm."

Clarice raised her brows. "You don't like that ending?"

"I believe I see a problem with your logic."

"What is that?"

"If the lovers were to marry, the relationship would no longer be illicit, would it?"

Clarice frowned. "I see what you mean. Still, marriage is the only conceivable happy ending for an illicit liaison, is it not?"

"I suppose so."

And, in her case, an impossible ending, Louisa thought.

Anthony stood at the window, hands clasped behind his back. His mother stood on one side, his father on the other. They all watched Louisa and Clarice stroll through the garden.

"Those two appear to be getting on quite well," Marcus announced. He looked pleased. "I must say, I like your Mrs. Bryce. Fascinating young woman."

"I told you that she was somewhat out of the ordinary," Anthony said.

Marcus chuckled and clapped him on the shoulder. "Indeed you did, and you have seldom been more accurate in your description of a lady."

"Those two do make a pretty picture walking in the sunlight with their parasols unfurled, don't they?" Georgiana observed. She gave Anthony a sidelong glance. "Your Mrs. Bryce was widowed rather young, wasn't she?"

"That does appear to be the case," he said carefully.

"Interesting career she has fashioned for herself," Marcus said. "No wonder she and Clarice hit it off so well. They have a lot in common."

"I wonder what they are talking about out there," Georgiana said. "Whatever it is, they both seem very intent on their subject."

"Gardening, perhaps," Anthony suggested, although he doubted it.

The tension in Louisa's shoulders warned him that the conversation had veered toward the personal.

34

Anthony took her home an hour later. Her silence in the carriage made him uneasy, but his attempts at conversation failed. Louisa seemed lost in her thoughts.

No one opened the door when they went up the steps of the town house. He watched Louisa remove a key from her muff. He took the key from her and opened the door. "Where is everyone?"

"This is the staff's afternoon off." Louisa walked into the front hall, untying her bonnet strings. "Emma is at her Garden Society meeting. No one will be back for hours."

He followed her into the hall. "I see."

She looked at him as though uncertain what to do with him now that he was inside the house.

"Will you come into the study, sir?" she asked.

His spirits rose immediately. "Thank you."

She hung her bonnet on a peg and led the

way down the hall. "I think we should compare notes concerning our investigation. I have been thinking about some information that I acquired early on before you and I became partners."

So much for his hopes. She was not inviting him into the study because she wanted his company. She planned to discuss the damned investigation.

"Of course," he said. He followed her down the hall and into the study. "But first I have a question for you."

"What is that?" she asked, crossing the small room to her desk.

"You and Clarice spent a great deal of time in the garden. What were you talking about?"

"Your sister is very nice." Louisa sat behind the desk. She removed her spectacles and began to polish them with a handkerchief. "I liked her."

"I'm glad." He went to stand in front of the desk looking down at her. "She seemed quite taken with you, too, but that does not answer my question. She pressed you about the nature of our relationship, didn't she?"

"On the contrary, she seems to think she

knows exactly how matters stand between us, sir."

He folded his arms. "My parents have come to a similar conclusion."

She popped the spectacles back onto her nose and regarded him with acute suspicion. "What did you tell them?"

"As we agreed, I insisted that ours was merely a business arrangement."

She made a face. "They didn't believe you, did they?"

"No."

"Your sister didn't believe me, either, when I tried to tell her the same thing. They all think that we are engaged in an illicit affair."

"I did warn you that the members of my family tend to be very forthright. They are also quite intelligent."

"Well, I suppose we must look at the positive side of things," Louisa said, straightening her shoulders. "The fact that the members of your family think that we are engaged in an intimate liaison does indicate that our little charade may be working after all, don't you think?"

He decided not to respond to that because he could feel his temper heating.

She cleared her throat. "My point is that if

your own relatives are convinced that we are romantically involved, Hastings must certainly believe it also, and that is the important thing, is it not?"

He continued to watch her, saying nothing.

She glowered. "Stop looking at me like that."

"Like what?"

"I don't know." She waved her hands. "As if you're about to pounce or something. What are you thinking, sir?"

He unfolded his arms, flattened his hands on the desk, and leaned toward her. "I am thinking," he said evenly, "that my family's conclusion is no more or less than the truth. We *are* having an illicit affair."

She blinked and sat back in her chair. "Not exactly."

"What the devil do you mean by that?"

"You must admit that our relationship is somewhat complicated."

That did it. A man could only be expected to take so much. He straightened, circled the desk, and reached down to haul her up out of the chair.

"I'll grant you that some things about our association are a bit difficult to explain," he said, "but not this particular aspect. We *are* having an affair, Louisa."

"Yes, well, I suppose one could say that in the technical sense of the word—"

"In *every* sense of the word."

She blushed. "Perhaps we should return to the subject of our investigation. As I mentioned to you, I have had a few thoughts that I want to share."

"I've got a better idea."

She blinked again, eyes widening. "What is that?"

"I'll show you."

He swung her up into his arms and started toward the door.

"Good heavens." She clutched at his shoulder. "What do you think you are doing? Where are you taking me?"

"Upstairs." He angled her through the doorway and went down the hall. "Presumably there is a bed up there somewhere."

"Certainly, but what has that got to do with—?" She broke off, comprehension dawning. "Surely you don't mean to—?"

"Make love to you in the comfort of a bed? Yes, that is precisely what I intend to do." He started up the stairs.

"In broad daylight?"

"You said Lady Ashton and the staff would be gone for a few more hours, did you not?"

"Yes, but—"

"Then we must take advantage of their absence."

"You can't be serious, sir."

"Why not? It is the sort of thing illicit lovers do."

"Hardly. Everyone knows they meet in secret by night in moonlit gardens and places of that sort."

"We tried that approach," he said. "It was not entirely successful, if you will recall."

Her mouth opened to respond to that, but evidently she changed her mind. Her brows snapped together in a worried frown.

"You should not be carrying me up the stairs, sir. You might strain yourself."

"Very likely, but it will no doubt serve me right." He kept going. The top of the landing was in sight.

She hesitated. "Am I not a rather heavy object to carry up a flight of stairs?"

"Yes, you are, as a matter of fact." He reached the landing and paused to take a couple of deep breaths. "But I'm certain the exercise will do me good. Which room is yours?"

"The first door on the right."

"I'm in luck. I won't have to carry you all the way to the end of the hall."

"Really, sir, must you complain so much about the business? The lovers in novels and plays never do that."

"I expect the authors leave out those bits. Bad for sales."

The door to her bedroom was ajar. He used his foot to push it open the rest of the way, got his burden inside, and stood her on her feet beside the bed.

Louisa was flushed, her eyes brilliant. Gently he plucked her spectacles from her nose and set them down on the table beside the bed. Everything inside him was clenched with the tension of desire.

"Your eyes are the color of amber," he said softly. "Spectacular."

She was startled. "Thank you," she said very politely. She squinted slightly to study him more closely. "Yours are a very riveting combination of green and gold."

He smiled, and then he began to remove her hairpins one by one. The dark silk tresses tumbled down around her shoulders. By the time he was finished he was rigid. *And I haven't even got her undressed.*

"I have wanted to see you like this ever since I met you," he said.

She looked confused. "Without my spectacles?"

He laughed. "With your hair down."

He peeled off his coat and slung it across a chair. He watched her watching him while he unknotted his tie. Her expression of fascination amused him.

He glanced at the window. It looked out onto the street and the small park in the square. No one could see into this room, he concluded. There was no need to close the curtains. He was free to enjoy the sight of Louisa nude in the warm glow of the late afternoon sun.

He caught her face between his hands and kissed her, slowly this time, intent on seduction, not his own satisfaction.

"Anthony?"

"This is the part you like, remember? The kissing?"

"Oh. Yes. Right." She made a tiny little sound of feminine anticipation and opened her lips for him.

He worked her mouth deliberately for a

time, tasting her but not rushing her. When he felt her shiver and soften against him, he moved his hands down to the fastenings at the front of her gown. Slowly he opened the bodice and slid it off her shoulders, holding her mouth captive the entire time.

A hungry thrill shot through him when he felt her fingers on the front of his shirt. She fumbled for a moment before she succeeded in getting the garment open. Then he felt her hands on his chest, her fingers sliding through the curling hair. The sweet torment threatened to destroy his self-control.

He kissed her throat and then her breast to distract her. When her head fell back against his shoulder and her eyelashes fluttered closed he returned to the task of undressing her. He finally managed to free her entirely from the gown, leaving her in her thin chemise, drawers, stockings, and shoes.

He covered her mouth with his own once more, invading gently. When her tongue touched his in a curious, experimental way, he could not suppress the low, growling sound that welled up inside him. His response seemed to embolden her. She tightened her grip on his shoulders. He deepened the kiss.

When he eventually released her mouth he saw that her lips were wet and swollen. He traced them with the edge of his finger. She swayed a little in response. Her skin was warm and astonishingly soft beneath his hands.

He leaned down and yanked back the quilt. Then he fitted his hands around Louisa's waist, lifted her up out of the circular barricade formed by her fallen gown and settled her on the bed.

The sight of her there, her dark hair fanned out across the white pillow, her lips slightly parted, eyes half-closed with desire was the most stunningly erotic picture he had ever seen. He wondered that he did not climax immediately.

He forced himself to step back long enough to get out of his own clothes. When he was finished he hesitated, seeking some sign of approval.

She levered herself up on her elbow and groped around the nightstand. She found the spectacles, put them on, and looked at him with an amazed expression.

"Oh, my goodness," she said, clearly nonplussed. "I realized the other night that you were considerably larger than the statues of nude males I have seen, but I hadn't realized the enormity of the situation, as it were."

He was not sure how to take that. "I do not believe that I have ever been compared to a statue," he finally said.

She started to giggle. The giggle turned into a laugh. She clapped a hand across her mouth. Her eyes were brilliant.

Another rush of intoxicating need and anticipation swept through him. He removed the freshly washed and ironed linen handkerchief from the pocket of his trousers and walked back to the bed.

He reached down, removed her spectacles for the second time, and set them on the table. Crouching beside the bed, he unfastened first one little high-heeled walking boot and then the other, letting the shoes tumble to the carpet. Slowly he drew a hand down one of her soft, sweetly rounded legs, taking the garter and stocking with it. Then he stripped off the other stocking.

He lowered himself onto the bed beside her. She sucked in a quick, shaky little breath when he tugged her chemise off over her head, but when he bent his head to kiss the taut tips of her breasts she uttered an urgent little moan. Her nails dug into his shoulders, and then she was clawing at his back.

He moved slowly along her body, savoring her, letting her become familiar with his touch. When her legs began to shift restlessly and she twisted, trying to get closer to him, he stripped off the drawers. She flinched as the last barrier to modesty fell away. He looked up and saw that her eyes were very tightly closed, but she did not attempt to retreat.

She moved her hand down between them, encircling him gently. The rush of desire that hit him very nearly did him in then and there.

He threaded his fingers through the triangle of soft curls at the apex of her thighs and found her core with his hand. She was already slick and hot and swollen. He stroked her gently, seeking the sensitive nubbin. When he found it she nearly levitated off the bed.

"Anthony." Her nails bit into the skin of his upper arm.

He teased her until she writhed at his touch and tried to press herself more firmly against the heel of his hand. Then he slid two fingers deep inside, hooking upward.

Louisa gasped and tightened around him. He looked down at her. She was beyond any sense of restraint or hesitation now, caught up in the heat of her own passion. No woman had ever looked more beautiful, he thought.

He slid between her legs. Before she could even begin to realize what he intended to do, he put his mouth on her, giving her the most intimate of kisses.

"What on earth?" she yelped. "Oh, no, you mustn't."

Frantic now, she tried to sit up and scoot backward. He caught her hips, dragged her back into position, and with her anchored there, he resumed stroking her with his tongue. The taste and scent of her body was a drug that he would have killed to obtain.

Her fingers tensed in his hair.

"Anthony?"

He felt the telltale tightening of her body and knew what was about to happen before she did. He inserted his thumbs and stretched her gently.

"Dear heaven," she moaned. "Dear heaven. *Anthony*."

There were no more words. Her release took her away. It very nearly took him with it.

He managed to slide back up her body, easing into her tight, intense heat before the tiny ripples of release had ceased. She clenched around him, destroying the last of his self-control.

His climax exploded through him after only a few strokes. He barely managed to drag himself out of Louisa's snug little channel in time to spend into the handkerchief.

When it was over he collapsed into the pillows, feeling more at peace than he had since the night Fiona died.

35

Louisa floated slowly upward out of the pleasant sea of contentment in which she had been drifting. She stirred, stretched out a hand, and fumbled around on the bedside table. Her fingers finally closed around her spectacles. She put them on and looked down over the side of the bed.

Her chemise lay in a frothy little heap on the carpet. She snatched it up and slipped it on over her head.

Feeling somewhat more modest, she sat up amid the bedclothes and studied Anthony. He was sprawled on his stomach, his head turned toward her on the pillow. His eyes were closed, his dark hair tousled. The contoured muscles of his back looked very sleek and sensual and excitingly powerful. She had loved the feel of his weight on her, crushing her into the bed.

She stretched out a hand and stroked his shoulder gently, not wanting to awaken him.

"I must remember to bring some French letters next time," Anthony said into the pillow.

She jumped, jerking her hand back as though she had touched a hot stove.

"I thought you were asleep," she said.

"Almost." He did not open his eyes. "You exhausted me."

"What are French letters?" she asked, very curious.

He opened his eyes and smiled his slow, inviting smile. "Condoms."

She felt herself turn pink. "I see."

"The technique I have employed thus far is not entirely reliable."

"Oh."

More heat rose in her cheeks. As a woman of the world who was now involved in an illicit affair, she would have to grow accustomed to the casual discussion of such intimate matters, she reminded herself.

"Well?" he asked, watching her intently.

She looked at him, baffled. "Well, what?"

He rolled onto his back and folded his

arms behind his head. "Was that a more satisfactory experience?"

She was blushing so furiously now she was amazed she did not set fire to the sheets.

"Indeed." She cleared her throat. "I now comprehend why illicit affairs are so fashionable."

"Huh."

He did not look nearly as pleased as he had a moment ago.

"Anthony?"

"Yes?"

"There is something I have wanted to ask you. Something very personal. I will understand if you do not wish to answer my question."

He took one arm out from behind his head and used it to drag her down on top of him. "What is it?"

She folded her arms on his chest and rested her chin on her stacked hands. "I have heard the rumors about what happened between you and your fiancée just before she died."

His mouth twisted in a humorless smile. "I'm not surprised. Between the sensation press, the penny dreadfuls, and the gossip in the Polite World, most of London was aware of the rumors."

"Are any of them true? Were you planning to end your engagement to her because you found her in bed with another man?"

He was silent for so long she thought he would not answer at all.

"Yes," he said at last. "I have never told anyone else that, however. I'm not sure how the rumors got started. I can only assume that the man I found her with confided in someone who, in turn, started the gossip."

"Illicit affairs are almost never entirely secret."

"True."

"You must have loved her very much."

He sat up abruptly, swung his legs over the side of the bed, and got to his feet. "My love for Fiona died the day I found her with her lover."

She felt a sharp pang of sympathy. "It must have been dreadful for you."

"In hindsight, I think she intended for me to learn about the affair in that manner." He crossed the room and picked up his underclothes and trousers. "She did not have the courage to tell me the truth straight out, but deep down I believe she wanted me to know that she loved another. In her own way, she was trying to be honest with me before the marriage."

"I don't understand. If she loved someone else, why didn't she just tell you?"

"She couldn't bring herself to do that." He pulled on his trousers and fastened them. "Her family would have been horrified. They were extraordinarily pleased with the marriage. So was mine, for that matter. It was the culmination of years of friendship between our parents."

"In other words, Fiona was under a great deal of pressure to go through with the marriage."

"It is a common enough story." He fastened his shirt with grimly efficient fingers. "In spite of all those novels and plays that you find so inspiring, we both know that the vast majority of marriages are based on money, property, and family connections."

"Yes." Wistful regret drifted through her. "I suppose that is why novels and plays are so thrilling. The ideal of true love is very pleasant to contemplate."

"I wouldn't know," he said coldly. "I am not a great fan of that sort of entertainment."

She smiled and said nothing.

He paused in the act of dressing and

gripped one of the bedposts. He looked down at her with a dangerous expression.

"You find that amusing?" he asked.

"A little." She drew up her knees and wrapped her arms around them. "Say what you like about novels and plays, the truth is you possess the romantic soul of a true hero."

He looked at her as though she had just announced that she could fly.

"What the devil are you talking about?" he asked very softly.

"It is why you are so determined to find justice for Fiona," she explained. "In spite of the fact that she fell in love with someone else, your love for her is steadfast."

He tightened his grip on the bedpost. His eyes narrowed. "Let me make one thing very plain here, Louisa. I am not engaged in this venture because I am brokenhearted over the loss of Fiona."

That stopped her for a few seconds.

"You're not?" she asked cautiously.

"Make no mistake; I cared for her. I knew her since she was in the schoolroom. She was my friend as well as my fiancée. I most certainly feel a responsibility to find her killer, but it was not my undying love for her that launched me on this quest. Do not try to make me out a romantic hero."

She shook her head, utterly bewildered. "Then why did you undertake an investigation into the circumstances of her death?"

"At the start of this business a little over a year ago, I had to find out if she truly did commit suicide because I was about to announce that our engagement was ended." The words sounded as though they had been ground between great stones. "Now do you understand? I needed to know if I was, indeed, the cause of her death, if she really could not abide the humiliation of being jilted."

"Anthony."

"I'm no hero, Louisa. Now that I know that she was, indeed, murdered, I have to find out if it was my fault that she was placed in harm's way."

"How could it possibly be your fault?"

"I don't know. Perhaps my intention to terminate our engagement led her to take some terrible risk that she would not otherwise have taken. She may have become desperate. All I know is that she was my friend and she had been my fiancée. I have to find out what happened that night."

"Stop it. Stop it at once." Appalled, she

uncurled from the bed and scrambled to her feet. She grabbed his arm, holding on to him as though he was about to be swept away by a deep current. "Listen closely to me. It does seem quite likely that Fiona was, indeed, murdered, just as you suspect. But whether that proves to be the case or whether it transpires that she took her own life, *you are not at fault*."

"You don't understand. She was so innocent. She had no experience of the world."

"Innocent or not, if she threw herself into the river because she feared the humiliation of a broken engagement, it was her choice. If she somehow became embroiled in some dangerous affair, it was not through any fault of yours."

"She was under a great deal of pressure, not only from her family and mine but from Society as well." He exhaled a weary sigh that sounded as though it had been dredged up from the depths of his soul. "None of us knew that she was so unhappy. If she had just said something to me—"

"It was her decision to take the risk of falling in love with another man." She paused as a thought struck her. "Which brings up another point. If she was intimately involved with someone else, wouldn't she have planned to marry him after your engagement to her ended?"

"That is one of the things that made me doubt that she committed suicide," he admitted. "All the evidence indicates that her lover did care for her. He was not married, so he would have been free to wed her."

"What happened to him?"

"He blames me for her death and despises me to this day."

"Julian Easton?" she asked quietly.

Anthony's brows rose. "How did you reason that out?"

"It was obvious that he carried some great grudge against you."

"He has never dared to level any outright accusations because he has no proof. Also, I believe he is being cautious because he does not wish to implicate himself in the gossip. Fiona's family would be furious if he besmirched her memory by letting it be known that he'd had an affair with her before her wedding."

She tilted her head slightly, thinking. "I hesitate to suggest this, but do you think that there is any chance that Easton harmed her?"

"No." He ran a hand through his hair. "I

looked into that possibility immediately. His whereabouts that night are well documented by several witnesses. He disappeared from the ballroom for a few minutes, but he returned almost immediately. He later left with friends and went straight to his club. He remained there, playing cards, until dawn. Fiona's body was pulled out of the river at about that time. There simply wasn't time for him to murder her and dispose of the body."

"But Easton is deliberately encouraging everyone to believe the worst of you."

"He believes she did commit suicide, and he blames me for driving her to it. Keeping the gossip alive is his notion of vengeance."

She thought about the scene in the street in front of the Lorrington house. "Actually, I think he may well blame himself."

Anthony frowned. "What do you mean?"

"If he loved her, he may be trying to convince himself and everyone else that you are the culprit because he wants to avoid the guilt he is no doubt feeling for having failed to protect her."

Anthony shrugged and finished fastening his shirt. "All I know is that he hates me."

"He has no right to make you the scapegoat," she announced. "It is not fair. What a tragic muddle it has all become."

His mouth curved derisively. "Easton and Fiona obviously fell victim to the overwhelming power of an illicit love affair. According to you, there is no more thrilling adventure."

"You mistake me, sir," she said sharply. "Illicit passion is obviously a strong force, but we are all equipped with the strength to resist it if we choose to do so."

"So it is a *choice*, now, is it?" His brows lifted. "Not an overwhelming force of nature?"

"Do not mock me. I am very serious about this."

"Yes, I can see that."

"It is one thing to find a person attractive. It is quite another to decide to act on that attraction and to willfully incur the hazards involved. That is the choice that Fiona made. You had nothing to do with that decision, either."

He looked at her with an odd expression, but she never learned what he intended to say because at that moment she heard the sound of a carriage in the street.

"Dear heaven, what time is it?" Panicked, she glanced at the clock. "Five-thirty. Good grief, that will be Emma."

He raised a brow. "Are you certain?"

"Yes. You must leave at once, sir. Emma must not find us together here when I am in this state of undress. Hurry."

He reached for his boots. "You will note that this is one of the great drawbacks to an illicit affair. One must maintain constant vigilance."

She grabbed her robe off a hook. "You can't go out the front door; she will see you. You'll have to use the back stairs and leave through the garden."

He picked up his coat. "I hesitate to mention this, but my hat is still in the front hall."

"Damnation, I forgot all about your hat. We must get it." She rushed toward the door.

He seemed amused by her rough language, but he followed obediently.

She hurried down the stairs, Anthony directly behind her. Out in the street the carriage had come to a halt.

She snatched Anthony's hat off the hall table and tossed it at him.

"Go," she ordered softly.

He caught the hat easily in his left hand. "One question before I leave, Louisa."

"No questions. There is no time." She made desperate, shooing motions. "You must hurry, sir. Emma will be at the door any second."

"I really must have an answer," he warned, but he started down the hall toward the rear door carrying his hat and coat.

"For heaven's sake, keep your voice down," she said, trailing urgently after him.

Anthony opened the back door and halted on the threshold. He turned back.

"My question is, did you experience anything approaching transcendence this afternoon?" he said.

She was horrified by the delay. "For pity's sake, sir, this is no time to talk about that sort of thing."

"I am not leaving until I get an answer."

"Yes, yes, it was all a marvelously transcendent experience. Just as the novelists describe it. Now, leave at once."

He smiled, kissed her once more, very quickly, very possessively on the mouth, and departed.

She thought she heard him whistling in the garden.

She closed the door as quietly as possible and dashed up the cramped rear stairs. Back in her bedroom, she shut the door, and set about straightening the bed.

She would tell Emma that she had taken a nap this afternoon, she decided. That would explain why the bed was rumpled and why she was in her robe.

She glanced in the mirror and was shocked to see how flushed and disheveled she appeared. There was no time to put up her hair.

The door opened downstairs. Louisa grabbed a white cap, plopped it down on her head, and shoved her hair up inside it. Then she threw herself onto the bed.

A short time later Emma came up the stairs and knocked softly on the door. "Are you resting, dear?"

"Yes," Louisa said. "The afternoon was quite exhausting. I'll tell you all about it when I come downstairs shortly."

"I shall look forward to the details of your meeting with the Stalbridges. Take your time. I am going to change my gown." Emma's footsteps receded down the hall to her own room.

With a shudder of relief, Louisa sat up. She was still breathing much too quickly. That had been very close.

She got slowly to her feet and went toward the wardrobe. A strip of dark blue silk dangling over the back of a chair caught her eye: Anthony's tie. Jolted, she picked up the tie, coiled it very carefully, and hid it in a drawer.

Very close, indeed. Thank heavens Emma had not opened the door. Illicit liaisons were quite exciting, but they were proving to be hard on the nerves.

It was the first time he had ever been obliged to sneak out through the back door, Anthony reflected, going up the steps of his town house. Life had certainly become more interesting since meeting Louisa Bryce.

The unusual mode of departure made for a challenging change of pace, but damned if he intended to go on skulking around alleys and gardens indefinitely. Nevertheless, the memory of Louisa's breathless, shivery passion as she climaxed in his arms compensated for a great deal, including his undignified exit.

He was aware of feeling in remarkably good spirits, in spite of the lack of progress in the investigation. It was not only the heated lovemaking that had improved his mood, he thought. It was Louisa's passionate insistence that, regardless of what had happened to Fiona, he was not to blame.

It was one thing to have his family assure him of that; they had always stood with him. Having Louisa defend him so passionately was something else entirely. For a while there in the sun-and-shadows of her bedroom, with the taste of her still on his tongue, he had even allowed himself to believe that she was right.

The door opened just as he reached for his key.

"Welcome home, sir," the housekeeper said. "A message arrived for you a few minutes ago."

"Thank you, Mrs. Taylor." Anthony moved into the hall.

The note rested on a silver platter. Anthony picked it up and tore it open. Satisfaction flashed through him when he saw Miranda Fawcett's signature.

. . . I invite you and Mrs. Bryce to meet my very good friend at ten o'clock this evening.

Clement Corvus had taken the bait.

36

Miranda Fawcett was ensconced on her gold sofa. Louisa thought she appeared even more dramatic than usual in a fashionable gown of pale blue silk and dark blue velvet. Pearls glowed on her fingers, circled her throat, and gleamed in her hair.

"Ah, there you are, Louisa, my dear." She smiled warmly and beckoned with one beringed hand. "Please sit down." She turned to Anthony. "How delightful to see you again, sir. I'm so glad you were free tonight. I realize I gave you very short notice."

Anthony bowed over her hand. "My pleasure. I look forward to meeting your very good friend."

"Mr. Corvus is already here." Miranda

winked. "He is waiting in the wings, as it were. The dear man has spent so much time around me that I fear he has learned the value of making an entrance."

Louisa perched on one of the satin-covered chairs and adjusted her spectacles. "It was very kind of you to arrange this meeting."

Miranda chuckled. "I assure you, Mr. Corvus was eager enough to meet Mr. Stalbridge after he read those papers that you left with me."

A man spoke from the doorway. "Indeed, sir, I was most enthusiastic about making your acquaintance."

Louisa turned her head and saw a surprisingly short, neatly made man. Although he was no taller than herself, there was an unmistakable aura of elegant menace about him. They did not call Clement Corvus The Raven merely because of his name, she thought. A little chill went through her.

His hair had clearly once been jet black. It was now a striking silver. He was clean-shaven and dressed in an exquisitely tailored black suit.

Anthony inclined his head, silently acknowledging Corvus as an equal. "Good evening, sir."

Corvus's eyes crinkled faintly at the corners. Louisa got the impression that he was pleased with Anthony's respectful manner.

"And this is Mrs. Bryce, whom you know very well as I. M. Phantom," Miranda said. "Mrs. Bryce, Mr. Corvus."

Corvus walked to Louisa and bowed formally over her hand. "Mrs. Bryce. It is a privilege to meet you. I am a great admirer of your work."

"Thank you, sir." She smiled. "The pleasure is mine tonight. At last I have an opportunity to tell you how grateful I am for what I strongly suspect has been your behind-the-scenes advice on several occasions."

Corvus smiled indulgently. "Miranda will tell you that I find it vastly entertaining to be of assistance to such an intrepid correspondent."

Miranda laughed. "What Clement really means, of course, is that he is always pleased to help I. M. Phantom rid him of some of his business competitors who happen to move in Society."

Something cold and glittery appeared in Corvus's dark eyes. "It is not the competition that I mind, my dear. I am, after all, a businessman. I enjoy the sport. But I will admit that I take strong exception to certain gentlemen who choose to engage in commercial ventures that cater to the most depraved tastes or those who take advantage of people who do not move in their circles. Those same gentlemen would never dream of lowering themselves to inviting a man of my background into their homes for a glass of brandy, yet they do not hesitate to dirty their hands in businesses that I would not touch."

Anthony's brows rose. "I agree, the hypocrisy is rather blatant in some instances."

"It certainly was in the case of the Bromley scandal and the California Mine Swindle," Corvus said. "May I offer you a glass of brandy, sir? Miranda buys only the best."

"Because I buy it for you, Clement," Miranda murmured.

Corvus smiled. "Thank you, my dear." He did not take his eyes off Anthony.

"A brandy sounds like an excellent notion," Anthony said.

Corvus crossed the room to a small table. He removed the stopper from a cut-crystal bottle and poured two glasses of brandy.

He carried the brandies back across the room, his footsteps hushed by the thick carpet, and gave one of the glasses to Anthony. The two men locked eyes. Two hunters assessing each other, Louisa thought.

"To your good health, sir," Corvus said.

Anthony raised his glass in a small salute. "And to yours, sir."

Louisa watched both men swallow some of the brandy. When Corvus lowered his glass, he appeared to be quietly satisfied. She got the impression that Anthony had just passed another small test.

"Please sit down, sir," Corvus said. He waited until Anthony lowered himself onto one of the chairs, and then he, too, took a seat.

"I take it that the reason you invited us to meet here tonight is because you found those papers instructive," Anthony said.

Corvus inclined his head. "As you obviously knew I would."

Anthony shrugged. "I have had some experience managing my family's investments."

"I am aware of that." Corvus chuckled. "Indeed, it is said that you single-handedly kept the Stalbridges from sliding into bankruptcy."

"As I was the only one in the family who showed no aptitude for creative talent of any kind," Anthony said, "I was more or less stuck with the finances. I know enough to spot an obviously fraudulent arrangement when I see it."

Corvus swirled the brandy in his glass. "I object to fraud on general principle. It is seldom good business in the end. But I find it particularly offensive when I am the intended victim."

Anthony's mouth edged up at one corner. "I understand."

"I am in your debt, sir, as I trust you are well aware. I like to keep the accounts even."

"I have heard that."

Corvus nodded. "I assumed that was the case. I will not embarrass either of us by asking how a gentleman like yourself learned about my personal eccentricities. Let us get down to business. You have done me a great favor. How can I repay you?"

"Mrs. Bryce and I have a few questions about Elwin Hastings," Anthony said. "Would you be willing to answer them?"

"Certainly, if I can." Corvus's mouth tightened with distaste. "Given his intention to cheat me, I no longer owe Hastings the customary loyalty that I generally grant those with whom I do business."

Louisa leaned forward intently. "May I ask why you decided to do business with Mr. Hastings in the first place?"

Corvus sipped his brandy. "A little over a year ago I was invited to participate in one of his investment schemes. It paid off quite handsomely. Naturally, when he approached me with another, similar investment opportunity last month, I was predisposed to consider it with a favorable eye."

Anthony looked intrigued. "You were involved in a business arrangement with Hastings around the time of his wife's death?"

"Yes, although Mrs. Hastings was still alive at the time." Corvus drank some brandy and lowered the glass. "I never met her, of course. Obviously, I did not move in the same social circles. All of my dealings were with Hastings and his man of business, Grantley. Mostly with Grantley, I might add. He was the go-between. I got the impression that Hastings worried about being seen with me."

"You know, of course, that Fiona Risby is reported to have killed herself a few days before Mrs. Hastings and in the same manner," Anthony said.

"I am aware that your former fiancée died that same week, sir. My condolences. Both deaths featured heavily in the sensation press for several days." Corvus paused. "Until they were driven off the front pages by the murder of Lord Gavin, of course."

Louisa sat very still, hardly daring to breathe. No one so much as glanced at her.

"I have reason to believe that Miss Risby did not commit suicide," Anthony said.

Corvus cocked a dark brow. "Indeed?"

"I strongly suspect that she was murdered by Elwin Hastings. If I am right, I think it is safe to assume that he also killed his wife. The coincidence of both women casting themselves into the river in such a short span of time is a bit much."

Cold curiosity lit Corvus's eyes. "That is a very interesting theory. Do you have any proof?"

"Yes," Anthony said. "When I discovered those papers, I also found hard evidence linking Hastings to the death of Miss Risby."

"I see." Corvus looked at Louisa. "Can I

assume that you are involved in this investigation because you intend to write a report for the press about the mysterious deaths of the two ladies?"

"Yes." She pushed her spectacles higher on her nose. "Mr. Stalbridge and I are both pursuing the truth of the matter."

Miranda's eyes widened. "A murder investigation. How thrilling."

"There is a detective at Scotland Yard who also has questions about what happened that night," Anthony said. "His superiors forced him to suspend his inquiries, but he is prepared to take action if irrefutable evidence of Hastings's guilt surfaces."

"Evidence is something I cannot give you, I'm afraid." Corvus reclined in his chair. "I can only tell you what I know. Approximately two weeks ago, Hastings contacted me and requested that I provide him with two armed guards. I obliged him."

"For a large fee, of course," Miranda added as an aside.

Corvus's eyes tightened. "My association with Hastings is based on mutual business interests, not friendship. In any event, he is quite wealthy, and he did not object to paying what I asked for my men. Indeed, he seemed greatly relieved to obtain their services. I got the impression he was decidedly nervous."

"We encountered one of the guards at his home in the course of a ball the other night," Louisa said.

"Yes, I know." Corvus was amused. "Quinby, the guard you met, reported the incident to me along with the fact that certain items were missing from an Apollo Patented Safe. He did not know precisely what had been stolen because Hastings refused to say. Of course, when Miranda gave me those papers, I got an inkling." He looked at Anthony. "Before we proceed, I have a question of my own, if you don't mind."

Anthony inclined his head. "Of course."

"What else vanished from that safe?"

"Items that Hastings had been using to extort money from some wealthy, elderly women," Anthony said.

"Blackmail." Corvus raised his brows again. "I had no notion that Hastings was involved in that particular business." He paused. "May I ask what became of the extortion items?"

"They were returned anonymously to their rightful owners."

A smile came and went around Corvus's mouth. "Yes, of course."

Anthony turned his glass between his palms. "Do you know why Hastings requested the two guards? From what I have seen he never goes anywhere without them these days. He is clearly worried about something."

"He told me that his business manager, Phillip Grantley, died under what he considered suspicious circumstances," Corvus said. "Although according to the press Grantley committed suicide."

Louisa looked at him. "But Hastings did not believe that?"

Corvus considered for a moment. "I got the impression that he hoped the verdict of suicide was true, but for some reason he remained skeptical. Interestingly, when he recently learned that Thurlow had also taken his own life, he became frantic according to Quinby and Royce."

"Both Grantley and Thurlow worked for him," Anthony said. "At first we assumed that Hastings killed both of them. Now, however, that does not appear to be the case."

Corvus nodded. "I agree. I can tell you that Hastings was genuinely alarmed by both deaths. He definitely perceives some threat to himself. That is why he wanted the guards."

"When you consider the matter closely," Louisa said, "Hastings has reason to be afraid. He is a blackmailer, after all. Perhaps he fears that one of his victims tracked down Grantley and Thurlow and will come after him next."

Corvus nodded. "That is a very reasonable bit of logic, Mrs. Bryce. I would not be at all surprised if that is exactly what he is thinking."

"It certainly explains Hastings's fear," Anthony said. "But I don't think the killer was any of the blackmail victims. He chose them shrewdly. They were all elderly women who were trying to protect young, vulnerable members of their families."

Miranda gave him an arch look. "Never underestimate a woman, sir."

"Believe me, I am not inclined to do so," Anthony said with some feeling. "But somehow I cannot see these particular ladies having access to the resources that would have been required to track down Grantley and Thurlow. It is also difficult to imagine one of them obtaining a revolver, learning how to shoot it, and then sneaking into the men's lodgings and killing them."

Louisa looked at him. "I just thought of something. Perhaps one of the elderly women hired someone to murder Grantley and Thurlow."

Corvus looked amused. "Hiring a killer to murder two seemingly respectable men is somewhat more complicated than you appear to think, Mrs. Bryce. Trust me when I tell you that inquiries of that nature would have been brought to my attention."

A little shiver shot down her spine. "I see."

"I'm inclined to agree with Mr. Stalbridge," Corvus said slowly. "I doubt that any of the blackmail victims killed Grantley and Thurlow or paid someone else to murder them. The thing is, intelligent blackmailers usually don't attempt to extort money from victims who might prove dangerous. You must look elsewhere."

"One more question if you don't mind," Anthony said quietly.

Corvus waited politely.

"How many people, aside from you, would have known that both Grantley and Thurlow worked for Hastings?"

Corvus gave that a long moment's deliberation. "I made it my business to learn as much as possible about Hastings before I did business with him. I was aware of Grantley from the start because he handled the details of the investment consortium. But I knew nothing of Thurlow. If you had not asked Miranda about the possibility of Hastings having other employees and provided a rough description, I doubt I would have ever stumbled onto him. As it was, I had to dig quite deeply to discover that there was some connection between Thurlow and Hastings."

"In other words," Anthony said, "the link between Grantley, Thurlow, and Hastings was not common knowledge."

"No," Corvus said with grave assurance. "Not common knowledge at all."

37

A short time later Anthony handed Louisa up into the hired carriage. She sat down, arranged her skirts, and watched him lower himself onto the seat across from her. In the glow of the interior lamp his face was set in forbidding lines.

"What are you thinking?" she asked quietly.

"Whoever murdered Grantley and Thurlow must have known of their connection to Hastings," he said.

"Yes. Obviously Hastings has concluded that as well because he fears that he is in danger." She hesitated. "Perhaps the murderer is someone he cheated in a business deal."

"In which case the killer might well have

known about Grantley, but what are the odds he also knew about Thurlow? Even Corvus wasn't aware of Thurlow's link to Hastings, and he says he thoroughly researched the man at the start of their business dealings."

She sighed. "And why kill them anyway? Wouldn't the person who had been cheated go directly after Hastings?"

"The murder of a gentleman of Hastings's rank would create a huge sensation. It would be in the press for weeks. Even if the killer managed to make it look like another suicide there would be a great deal of attention paid. He might not want to risk that."

"True." She hesitated. "The murders simply make no sense."

"I'm not so sure of that." Anthony folded his arms and stretched out his legs. "It strikes me that by killing Grantley and Thurlow, the killer got rid of the two people who knew the most about Hastings's illicit business arrangements."

"Hmm."

He smiled faintly. "What are you thinking?"

"That if I were to set out to destroy a man and not want to take the risk of murdering him, I might consider getting rid of the people he relied on to handle his business affairs."

"But you would not stop there," Anthony said softly. "Not if you intended to destroy him. If you are right, Hastings is still very much in danger."

"All right. Let's take another approach to this problem," she said crisply. "How many people would know his business affairs quite intimately and also have a reason to want to destroy him?"

"You mean, aside from myself?" he said dryly.

She flushed. "Well, yes. Aside from you, sir. And aside from the elderly blackmail victims."

He considered that for a moment. "As you said, perhaps someone he once cheated is out for revenge."

She should stop right now. If she had any sense she would not say another word, but she could not seem to help herself. Anthony was hungry for answers. She wanted them, too. She had to take the risk.

"Our list of suspects," she said, choosing her words with great care, "would include only those who were both intimately acquainted with Hastings's illicit business affairs and those who would also have a reason to want to murder the two men who aided him in his secret activities."

"Likely a very short list, as you say, but if Clement Corvus could not offer any suggestions for suspects, I doubt that we'll be able to come up with some."

"I can think of one," she said quietly.

"Who?"

"His dead wife."

38

To her amazement, Anthony did not dismiss the notion out of hand. Instead he regarded her, somberly intrigued.

"What makes you think that Victoria Hastings might be involved in this affair?" he asked neutrally.

"I do not know it for certain, of course," Louisa said hastily. "It is a vague hunch that has been gradually forming in my mind. I meant to tell you about it when we returned to Arden Square after tea with your family this afternoon, but we got distracted, if you will recall."

His smile was slow and wicked. "Rest assured, Louisa, I recall every detail of that very delightful distraction."

She blushed and pressed on valiantly. "I am wondering if perhaps we should investigate the possibility that Victoria Hastings is still alive."

"Very well. Let us consider your theory. First, assuming that she is alive, why would she murder Grantley and Thurlow?"

"I do not know." Louisa spread her gloved hands. "But you will admit that she is one of the few people who might have been aware that both men were important to Hastings."

Anthony was silent for a moment. Then he inclined his head. "Go on. I'm listening."

She reached into her muff and took out her small notebook. Opening it to the pages headed VH she ran through the few facts that she had jotted down.

"The thing that caught my attention at the start of this affair was that Victoria's body was never recovered."

"That is sometimes the case with drownings."

"Yes, I know, but you will admit that fact does leave open the possibility that she survived."

"She would have to have been incredibly lucky, and she would have to have known how to swim. Women rarely learn that skill."

Louisa met his eyes. "Victoria Hastings knew how to swim."

Anthony watched her with growing curiosity. "How the devil did you discover that?"

"Emma told me. I had a long talk with her about Victoria. Emma knows how to swim, you see. She mentioned, in passing, that Victoria Hastings was the only other woman she had ever met in Society who also possessed the skill."

"Interesting. Nevertheless, even if Victoria could swim, one would think that the weight of her gown and underclothes would have dragged her under."

"You are assuming that Hastings threw her into the river, but what if she staged her own suicide?"

That gave him pause. "What put that notion into your head?"

She had to be very cautious here. She could hardly tell him that she had come up with the possibility because she herself had faked her own death, and that her inspiration had come from the account of Victoria Hastings's suicide primarily because the body was never recovered.

She made what she hoped was a very casual gesture. "Oh, I suppose it is all those novels and plays about missing wives and husbands who always show up at the end of the story claiming to have miraculously survived a watery grave or some other catastrophe."

"Thereby ruining the possibility of a happy ending for the couple involved in the illicit tryst," Anthony observed.

She flushed and looked down at her notes. "Yes, well, to continue, one of the people I interviewed before I joined forces with you was Victoria's lady's maid. Elwin dismissed her after Victoria disappeared."

"You tracked down the maid? I'm impressed. That was very resourceful of you."

"Thank you." She consulted her notes. "I was only interested in information concerning Mr. Hastings at the time, of course, but I did jot down some of the things the maid said about her former mistress."

"What did she tell you?"

"The maid's name is Sally. After she lost her position in the Hastings mansion she was hired by Lady Mounthaven, who allowed me to speak with her. Sally told me that her last task before leaving Hastings's employ was to pack up Victoria's clothes and possessions and send them to charity.

She mentioned that the only thing missing from Victoria's wardrobe was a nightgown."

"That would seem to work against your theory that she staged her own death. Surely a woman intent on disappearing would be unlikely to go off into the night in only a nightgown."

"But what if she had planned the so-called suicide well in advance? She would have had time to acquire a gown without her maid's knowledge. She could have concealed it until she needed it. When she disappeared, leaving her entire wardrobe behind, her husband would be more likely to believe that she really had suffered a nervous breakdown, wandered down to the river, and jumped."

"You've given this a lot of thought, haven't you?"

She hesitated, once again selecting each word with great care. "You and Emma both agreed that Victoria Hastings did not seem the type to commit suicide."

"True."

"Emma said that Victoria had always struck her as a very determined, very strong-willed woman. She was quite surprised to read in the press that Mrs. Hastings was prone to bouts of weak nerves and melancholia."

"It was no doubt Elwin Hastings who put out that rumor," Anthony said. "What else did the maid tell you?"

"The most interesting piece of information she offered was that Hastings and Victoria talked a great deal about financial matters. She said her former mistress was very clever when it came to that sort of thing and that Mr. Hastings always took her advice."

Anthony went quite still. "You're right. That *is* very curious. None of the rumors I picked up in the clubs suggested that she was intimately involved in arranging his investment consortiums."

"Well, one would hardly expect the gentlemen of the Polite World to consider for even a moment that a lady might possess a talent for financial matters."

"There is no need to remind me that a man can sometimes be quite oblivious to a lady's abilities." Anthony sank deeper into the corner of the seat, looking very thoughtful. "At the time that Hastings and Victoria were married, Hastings was rumored to be facing financial ruin, but within months of the wedding, his finances appeared to have greatly improved. He began putting together his various extremely successful investment consortiums."

A thought struck Louisa. "The blackmail schemes were instituted while Victoria was alive, also."

"But if Victoria was the one who planned those clever financial maneuvers," Anthony said patiently, "why would she disappear and leave everything, including her money, behind? I still say he killed her."

"You may be right," Louisa admitted. "But why would he murder her if she was the source of his new wealth?"

"Perhaps he convinced himself that he no longer needed her. Did you learn anything else from the maid?"

She turned a page in the notebook and glanced at what she had written. "She told me that she and the rest of the staff were given the evening off the night Mrs. Hastings disappeared."

"That was certainly convenient for someone," Anthony said. "Is that all?"

Louisa cleared her throat. "Well, there was one more thing."

"What?"

She took a deep breath and readied herself for the next revelation.

"Sally indicated that Mr. and Mrs. Hastings had what she termed a most *vigorous* private life," she said, trying to sound businesslike and worldly.

Anthony's brows rose. "Vigorous?"

Louisa closed her notebook with a snap. "It is difficult to conceive of this, but evidently a whip was involved."

"I see." Anthony's tone was suspiciously even.

She looked up quickly and found him watching her with an amused expression. Heat rose in her cheeks. "According to the information I received from Roberta Woods, Elwin Hastings has not lost his taste for the whip. Indeed, that is the service he requests on his weekly visits to Phoenix House."

"I think," Anthony said, "that we need more information on Phoenix House."

"Yes."

Anthony fell silent again, watching her from the shadows.

"What are you thinking?" she asked after a moment.

He smiled slowly, eyes darkly brilliant. "That you really are the most amazing woman."

"Oh." She was not sure how to take that. "Well, you are rather amazing, too, sir."

"We make a good match, don't you think?"

Her spirits rose. "Our partnership is certainly working out quite well."

There was another silence. She peered at him uneasily.

"What are you thinking now, sir?" she asked when she could stand the suspense no longer.

"I am thinking that I purchased some French letters on my way home from Arden Square this afternoon."

She blushed furiously. "I see." Curiosity got the better of her. "Uh, where does one buy that sort of thing?"

"The same place one buys books." His smile widened. "In a shop."

"I see." She frowned, amazed. "There are actually shops that specialize in such items?"

"Yes. This particular shop advertised devices guaranteed to satisfy gentlemen of intrigue concerned with discretion."

"How very interesting."

"I'm surprised that you are not jotting down that bit of information in your little notebook."

"An excellent notion, sir. Thank you for reminding me." She started to reach into her muff.

He laughed softly, reached across the seat and pulled her onto his lap.

"Before you do that, I suggest we try out one of my new purchases," he said against her mouth. "Just to ensure that it works in a satisfactory manner, of course."

A rush of excitement swept through her. She touched the side of his face with one gloved hand.

"In a carriage, sir?" she whispered.

"Why not? I have it on good authority that carriages are very popular with illicit lovers."

He pulled the blinds down across the windows. A warm, inviting darkness enveloped them. His mouth closed over hers, seductive, urgent, and demanding.

She stripped off her gloves and then she unfastened his shirt.

The French letters worked as advertised.

"Only think of the time that will be saved laundering and ironing your handkerchiefs," Louisa said some time later.

39

"Sorry to bother you with another message, Mrs. Bryce." Roberta Woods poured tea into a thick mug. "But you did say that you wanted to be kept informed of anything of interest having to do with Mr. Hastings and his visits to Phoenix House."

"That's right, Roberta, please don't apologize. I was delighted to get your message." Louisa took the notepad and pencil out of her muff and put them down on the table. "What have you learned?"

They were sitting in the tiny upstairs parlor of the little house on Swanton Lane. It was midafternoon, and things were relatively quiet at the moment. The women of the streets seldom showed up until after dark.

The muffled clang of pots and pans echoed from the kitchen, where the cook and her assistant were busy with preparations for the evening meal.

Roberta was a strong, vital woman who seemed animated from head to toe with the zealous energy and determination of a dedicated social reformer. She set the mugs on the table and sat down across from Louisa.

"A woman who claimed her name was Daisy showed up here just before dawn this morning," she said. "The poor thing looked quite dreadful. She works at Phoenix House. A few days ago one of the customers beat her within an inch of her life."

"Good heavens. Did she need a doctor?"

"She refused to see one. Said she couldn't afford it. I told her that this establishment would pay the doctor's fee, but she still refused. I could tell that she was badly frightened."

"Of the man who beat her?"

"No, that is the interesting part." Roberta's eyes narrowed. "She was afraid of the proprietor of the brothel."

"Madam Phoenix?"

"Yes."

"Did she say why?"

"It seems that Daisy was more or less sold to the proprietor by one of her dead husband's creditors."

Louisa's fingers tightened around the pencil. "Not the first time we've heard that sad story from a woman who works at Phoenix House, is it?"

"No," Roberta agreed in steely tones. "It isn't. In any event, Daisy was sure the proprietor would be furious if she discovered that one of her girls had run off before she had earned back her purchase price, so to speak."

"Go on."

Roberta drank some tea and put down the mug. "Daisy fled Phoenix House for good this morning. She had a little suitcase with her. She came here to ask for help. She said she'd heard rumors that someone at this establishment was willing to pay for information on one of the clients at Phoenix House. Elwin Hastings."

"Did you give her some money?"

"Yes. Then I sent her to The Agency. She will be safe there, at least for now. They will conceal her identity."

"What did Daisy tell you about Hastings?"

"Not a great deal, but you might find it

interesting. Because of the beating, Daisy has been unable to earn her keep for the past few days. She was assigned to work as a maid until she healed, and she was told to keep out of sight of the customers. One of her tasks has been to scrub Madam Phoenix's private bath every day."

"Yes?"

"Well, yesterday, while she was going about her duties she overheard a conversation between Madam Phoenix and her lover."

Louisa looked up. "The proprietor of the brothel has a lover?"

"Evidently. Daisy was in the bath, cleaning, at the time. She didn't hear everything, but she did catch Elwin Hastings's name."

"What was said about him?"

"Daisy only caught snatches of the conversation, but she said that it was obvious that Madam Phoenix and her lover were arguing about Hastings. Madam Phoenix wanted to wait a little longer to do something. Her lover told her she should do it immediately."

"Do what?"

Roberta moved one hand in a frustrated gesture. "That's just it, Daisy didn't know.

All she could tell me was that Madam Phoenix and her lover disagreed about when something should be done about Hastings. She said the quarrel was quite intense."

Louisa made another note and then sat back, pondering the possibilities. "Did she say who won the argument?"

Roberta made a face. "Madam Phoenix, of course. Daisy says she's very strong willed. No one goes against her, not even her lover. According to Daisy he does whatever Madam Phoenix tells him to do."

Louisa picked up the mug and drank some tea. "Did Daisy know the name of the lover?"

"She said no one knows his name. He comes and goes through the kitchen door, not the main entrance, and he always uses the servant's stairs. The staff is instructed to allow him into the house whenever he shows up."

"How often does he visit?"

"That was one of the interesting things Daisy told me," Roberta said quietly. "It seems that the lover often meets Madam Phoenix in her private rooms at the same time that Hastings is getting his treatment."

Louisa tapped the tip of the pencil against the table. “How did she describe him?”

“Said he was handsome enough, if you liked the hard-eyed type. Daisy does not like that sort, by the way. Dark-haired. Always wears an overcoat when he comes to visit.”

“That could describe a thousand men. Anything else?”

“One more thing,” Roberta said. “Daisy said he wore a very fine ring. Onyx and gold.”

Louisa caught her breath. Then she wrote the name very carefully in her notebook.

Quinby.

40

She hurried back to Arden Square, trying to make sense of what she had learned. It might mean nothing aside from the obvious, of course. What did it signify if Quinby was having an affair with Madam Phoenix? According to Daisy he had started visiting Phoenix House a couple of months ago. The implication was that he had met Madam Phoenix before he had become one of Hastings's guards.

What was so odd about a liaison between Quinby and the brothel proprietor? Quinby was a handsome man, after all, if you didn't mind those reptilian eyes. Madam Phoenix had every reason to be attracted to him and vice versa. They were probably two of a kind.

The door of Number Twelve opened before she could dig out her key.

"Welcome home, Mrs. Bryce." Mrs. Galt stepped back. "There's another message for you. It was delivered a few minutes ago. I put it on your desk."

"Thank you, Mrs. Galt."

Louisa untied the strings of her bonnet and hung it on a hook. She went down the hall to her study, stripping off her gloves.

The white envelope sat on the blotter. She picked it up, tore it open, and read the brief note written in a neat hand.

I have obtained the Milton at a reasonable price. However, another client is quite eager to purchase it and will likely pay more. I will give you until five o'clock this afternoon to come for the book. If I do not hear from you, I shall send word to the other customer.

Yrs.
Digby

Damn Digby. He would have to turn up the Milton this afternoon when she had other matters to deal with. She glanced at the tall clock in the corner. It was four-thirty. If she left immediately she could get to Digby's Bookshop by five, pick up the book, and be home around five-thirty. There would be time enough to send word to Anthony about her recent discoveries after she returned from the shop.

She went back out into the hall, tugging on her gloves. "Mrs. Galt?"

The housekeeper appeared from the kitchen, wiping her hands on her apron. "What is it, ma'am?"

"I must go out again." Louisa went into the front hall and plucked the straw bonnet off the hook. "The message was from Digby. He has found a book that I am anxious to buy. I will be back by five-thirty at the latest."

"Very well, ma'am. Best take your cloak. You don't want to catch a chill."

"You're right." Louisa took down the cloak and pulled it around her shoulders. "I'm expecting Mr. Stalbridge to call. If he shows up, please ask him to wait."

She snatched up her muff and flew out the door.

41

She opened the door of Digby's Bookshop and walked into the gloomy interior. There were no customers. Digby was not at his desk behind the counter.

"Mr. Digby?"

There was no response. The door to the back room was closed.

She waited a moment. When no one appeared, she went around behind the counter and knocked on the inner door.

"Mr. Digby? Are you in there? I've come for the Milton. It is not yet five. If you have already sold the book to another client I will be most annoyed."

There was no sound from the other side of the door.

She wrapped her gloved hand around the knob and twisted gently. The door swung inward, revealing a shadowy, unlit, very cluttered back room. Books were piled high on a workbench. Crates and boxes were stacked everywhere. There was a large roll of brown paper and a pair of scissors on a table.

A faint, rather sweet odor made her wrinkle her nose. She was trying to identify it when she noticed the sturdy shoes sticking out from behind an open carton. The shoes extended from the ends of the legs of a pair of brown trousers.

"*Mr. Digby*. What on earth?"

She rushed into the room and around the carton. Digby lay sprawled face up on the floor. His eyes were closed. There was no sign of blood anywhere. Perhaps he had suffered a heart attack or stroke.

She crouched beside him, took off a glove, and felt for the pulse at Digby's throat. Relief swept through her when she discovered that he was still breathing, albeit lightly, and that his pulse was steady, if somewhat slow. She started to loosen his tie.

A floorboard creaked behind her. It was all the warning she got before a powerful masculine arm clamped around her and hauled her upright. She opened her mouth to scream. A large crumpled square of fabric—a gentleman's handkerchief or a napkin—was shoved against her nose and mouth, forcing her to breathe through the fabric. The sweet odor of chloroform was inescapable now, its fumes choking her nostrils and filling her lungs. A wave of dizziness threatened to swamp her senses. She struggled frantically, only to discover that her forearms were pinned to her sides.

She kicked out furiously, her foot colliding with one of the cartons, overturning it. She tried again. This time there was a satisfying thud followed by an angry oath when the heel of one of her walking boots made contact with her assailant's shin.

"Damn bitch," Quinby muttered. He tightened his grip on her. "You're more trouble than you're worth. If I had my way, I'd slit your throat and be done with it."

The dizziness was getting worse. She felt warm all over. Her stomach twisted. She had heard somewhere that chloroform was generally effective within a couple of minutes, often less; too much could kill. There was very little time.

She stopped clawing at Quinby's arms and abruptly went limp, hoping he would assume that the drug had done its job, but her captor was clearly not about to take chances. He kept the dreadful cloth tight across her mouth and nose.

She could barely think at all now. Everything was muddled. She was vaguely aware that there was something she had to do before she passed out.

Quinby dragged her across the room, evidently eager to get her out of the shop. She felt the weight of her muff dangling from the thin strip of velvet that secured it to her left wrist. She wriggled her hand weakly, hoping that, if Quinby noticed, he would assume the motion was merely an indication that her struggles were almost over.

The last thing she heard was the sound of a door being opened. She shook her hand slightly. It seemed to her blurry senses that the weight of the muff fell away, but she could not be certain. Darkness and the terrifying perfume of the chloroform claimed her.

42

"What do you mean, she hasn't returned?" Anthony removed his gold watch from a pocket and verified the time. "It's nearly six-thirty. She's an hour late."

"Yes, Mr. Stalbridge, I'm aware of that." Mrs. Galt's mouth pursed in a disapproving manner. "It has been my experience that Mrs. Bryce keeps unpredictable hours. In addition, she is very much inclined to go out without giving anyone a clear notion of her destination or an idea of when she will return. At least this time she did mention that she was visiting Digby's Bookshop."

Interrogating Mrs. Galt was useless. He surveyed the front hall. Louisa's bonnet and cloak were gone. That told him only that she was not home. He already knew that much.

"You say she asked me to wait?" he said.

"Yes, sir. When she came home from her visit to Swanton Lane, she said something about wanting to speak with you as soon as possible."

That caught his attention. "She went to Swanton Lane this afternoon?"

"Yes, sir." Mrs. Galt snorted. "I don't know why she insists upon going there so often. It's all very well to give money to those engaged in charitable work, but there's no need for a proper lady to become personally involved with that sort of thing."

"Thank you, Mrs. Galt. You've been very helpful. I am going out to look for Mrs. Bryce."

"Good luck is all I can say, sir." Mrs. Galt opened the door.

He went down the steps, thinking about his next move. Night was coming on swiftly. He did not like knowing that Louisa was out there, somewhere, on her own.

He would start with Digby's. Perhaps the bookseller would have some idea of where she had gone after she left his shop.

43

Louisa awakened to a vague headache and the odor of damp that is generally associated with basements and other below-ground spaces. She was lying on a hard, cold surface. Panic slammed through her.

I'm in a morgue. Dear heaven, I'm dead.

No, that wasn't right. Surely if she were dead she would not be so uncomfortable. Unless, of course, she had gone straight to hell for the sin of being a murderess.

She opened her eyes. Close, deep shadows enveloped her, but there were bars of light on one wall. The bands of light were quite distinct, not fuzzy. Good. She was still wearing her glasses. It was another clue indicating that she was still in the realm of the living.

She tried to summon up some coherent memories that would explain her present situation. An image of Digby's inert body sprawled on the floor floated through her mind. She suddenly recalled the terrifying sensation of being pinned in a grip of steel while she kicked and struggled.

"Damn bitch." Quinby's voice. After that, everything went blank.

She sat up cautiously and pushed her glasses more firmly onto her nose. Mercifully the headache did not worsen. Her stomach felt unsettled, however. She took some slow, deep breaths. That seemed to help.

How much time had passed? She staggered to her feet and turned slowly on her heel, trying to make out the details of her surroundings. The dim, glary light of a lamp filtered through three iron bars in the opening in a heavy wooden door. She was in a small space with a low, vaulted ceiling. There were no windows. An ancient storage chamber, she decided, or a nun's cell. Judging by the stones and the masonry, it dated from medieval times.

She went to the door without much hope and tried the knob. It did not turn. When she felt the cold iron under her fingers, she realized she had lost one glove. She had a dim recollection of having removed the glove to check Digby's pulse.

The opening in the door was at eye level. She peered between the bars and found herself looking into another ancient, low-ceilinged stone room. The lamp that was the only source of light sat on a low table in the middle of the outer chamber. It cast just enough illumination to reveal a closed door in one wall and the darkened entrance to a narrow flight of worn stone steps cut into the opposite wall.

She was about to turn away to explore her cell when she heard the faint echo of shoe leather on stone. A new wave of fear flooded through her. Someone was descending the staircase. She saw the skirts of a stylish black gown and a pair of fashionable black walking boots first.

The woman arrived at the bottom step and moved into the main chamber. The last element of her wardrobe, a small black hat, was perched atop a wealth of golden hair. A heavy black lace veil concealed her features.

Louisa took a deep breath. "Victoria Hastings, I presume? Or should I call you Madam Phoenix?"

The woman paused slightly, startled that she had been recognized. Then she glided slowly across the stone floor to the door of the cell. Coolly she reached up with one black-gloved hand and crumpled the veil onto the brim of her hat. Victoria possessed the face of an angel, Louisa decided, but the unwholesome, pitiless glint in her blue eyes was nothing short of demonic.

"I regret the necessity of having you kidnapped," Victoria said, "but you have only yourself to blame. You were, indeed, getting much too close to the truth, Mrs. Bryce. Or should I call you I. M. Phantom?"

44

The closed sign dangled in the window of Digby's shop. Anthony ignored it and tried the door. It was locked. He took out the lock picks that he always carried in his boot and went to work. He was inside the darkened shop in ten seconds.

A bell chimed when he opened the door.

"Who's there?" an anxious voice called from the rooms above the ground floor. "Go away. The shop is closed for the day."

Anthony walked across the shop and halted at the foot of the stairs.

Digby looked down. He seemed nervous.

"Sorry to intrude," Anthony said. "I'm Stalbridge. I trust you remember me. I was here about the Milton."

Digby peered at him. "I remember you well enough. What are you doing here?"

"I'm looking for Mrs. Bryce. Have you seen her?"

"Not today, thank the Lord. I've had enough trouble."

"You sent her a message earlier this afternoon."

"I did no such thing."

"Are you certain of that, sir?"

"Of course, I'm certain." Digby scowled. "I had no reason to send her a message."

"Are you sure that she didn't arrive around five o'clock today?"

"I just told you, she wasn't here. Now please leave, sir. I'm not feeling quite myself."

"Are you ill?"

"Not now." Digby put a hand to his brow, looking worried. "At least I don't think so. Had a bit of a spell earlier. Don't know what happened. Must have fainted. Came to on the floor of my back room. Decided it would be best to take to my bed."

"You were unconscious for a period of time?"

"Yes. Half an hour or so at most. What of it?"

"What time did you return to your senses?"

"See here, I wasn't looking at a clock." Digby gestured in an irritated manner. "I suppose it must have been shortly after five."

"May I take a look around your back room, Mr. Digby?"

"Why?" Digby's expression darkened with deep suspicion.

"I am concerned for Mrs. Bryce's safety."

"Then you must look elsewhere. I told you, she wasn't here today."

"I'll just be a moment," Anthony assured him.

He walked into the back room of the shop and turned up a lamp.

"See here, sir," Digby yelped from the top of the stairs. "You can't just barge in there and rummage around."

Anthony ignored him, studying the cluttered back room with a growing sense of impending disaster. A carton of books lay on its side. It looked as if it had been kicked over. He went closer to the carton, pausing when he saw a glove on the floor. An icy chill tightened his insides. He picked up the glove.

"What have you got there?" Digby demanded from the doorway. “It looks like a lady’s glove.”

“It is a lady’s glove.”

“How did that get there?” Digby looked both annoyed and baffled. “I’m the only one who goes into this room.”

“An excellent question.” Anthony prowled through the cartons and spotted a crumpled handkerchief. “Is this yours, Digby?”

Digby reluctantly came closer to get a better look. “No. I don’t carry fancy embroidered handkerchiefs. That’s a gentleman’s style.”

A faint, sweet scent drifted up from the handkerchief. Not perfume, Anthony thought. It took him a second to place the odor. When he did, a wave of dread threatened to consume him.

“I believe I know what caused your fainting spell this afternoon, Digby,” he said. “Someone used chloroform on you.”

“Devil take it, are you certain?”

Anthony was about to respond when he noticed the muff. It was on the floor near the alley door.

The ice inside him expanded, chilling the blood in his veins. He scooped up the muff.

The notebook and pencil that Louisa carried everywhere were still inside.

He thought about Mrs. Galt's comments regarding Louisa's visit to Swanton Lane. He reached into the muff, took out the notebook and opened it to the most recent entry.

The first thing he saw was the name *Quinby*. Next to it was a small arrow that pointed to another name: *Madam Phoenix*.

Twenty minutes later he knocked on the back door of the little house on Swanton Lane.

A stern-featured woman looked at him through an iron grate.

"Gentlemen are not allowed on the premises," she said.

"My name is Stalbridge. Anthony Stalbridge. I'm a close friend of Mrs. Bryce. I believe she is in grave danger. I need your help."

45

Louisa took two steps back, moving out of the light that came through the opening in the door and deeper into the shadows of the cell. She could be mysterious, too, she thought.

"I assume you have some purpose in bringing me here," she said.

Victoria stepped closer to the door, peering through the bars. "I'm afraid there is going to be yet another unfortunate suicide in the Thames. This time the victim will be Lady Ashton's unprepossessing and extremely distant relation from the country. Very sad."

"You have made a grave mistake in kidnapping me," Louisa said. "Mr. Stalbridge will not be pleased."

"By the time Stalbridge figures out what

has happened it will be too late for him to do anything about the situation. In any event, I doubt that he will trouble himself overmuch with your demise, even if he does suspect the truth."

"You seem very sure of that."

Victoria's smile was all that was arrogant and certain. "I am sure of it because, unlike you, I understand him. Once you comprehend a man, once you know what he wants most, he is yours to control."

"How can you say that you know Mr. Stalbridge? According to him, the two of you met only in passing at occasional social affairs."

Victoria gripped one of the iron bars embedded in the door. "I said I know what he wants. He is obsessed with obtaining revenge for his beloved Fiona. He suspected from the beginning that her death was not a suicide, you see."

"He is right, isn't he?"

Victoria smiled coldly. "Yes. And soon I am going to give him what he seeks most. Fiona's killer. Rest assured, Stalbridge's concern for your safety is based entirely upon your usefulness to him in the pursuit of his quest. Once you are dead and he has his answers, you will cease to have any value to him."

"Hastings murdered Fiona, didn't he?"

"With my assistance." Victoria's shoulder moved in an elegant little shrug. "We had no choice. She accidentally came upon us that night in the gardens at the ball. I do not know what drew her outside. Perhaps a desire for some fresh air. Whatever the case, she overheard an argument between Hastings and me. The quarrel involved the details of the blackmail scheme I had arranged. It was working nicely, but Elwin wanted to expand it."

"Blackmailing those elderly ladies was your idea?"

"Of course. All of the plans that Hastings profited from so handsomely were conceived by me." Victoria's face tightened with anger. "But the fool convinced himself that he was the brilliant mind behind each venture. My mistake was in allowing him to deceive himself. He actually came to the conclusion that he no longer needed me."

"What did you do to Fiona?"

"When I heard a faint sound from the other side of the hedge I knew at once that someone was there and that she had no doubt heard enough to ruin us. We could not afford to let her live. I went around the corner of the hedge and spoke politely to her, as though nothing was amiss. Hastings came up behind her and struck her on the back of her head with his walking stick."

"Dear heaven," Louisa whispered.

"Once she was unconscious we carried her out through the garden gate and left her in the alley, bound and gagged with items of her own clothing. Leaving her there was a risk, but we could not think of anything else to do. We went back into the ballroom, summoned a cab, and departed as though nothing had happened."

"And then went back to take her to the river?"

"Elwin handled that part. He took one of my cloaks and returned to the alley for Miss Risby. She was still unconscious but not yet dead. He wrapped her in the cloak."

"How did he get her out of the alley and to the river?"

"You will have noticed that Hastings is a large man. Miss Risby was a small woman. Elwin simply put her over his shoulder and hauled her out of the alley as though she were a sack of coal. When he reached a side street he summoned another cab."

"How did he explain his burden to the driver?"

Victoria smiled. "That was simple enough. He explained that the woman with him was a whore who had entertained him and then passed out from too much gin. Out of the goodness of his heart he wanted to see the woman safely back to her lodgings near the river. The driver asked no questions."

Louisa shuddered. "But Hastings made a mistake. He could not resist the temptation of the necklace Fiona wore that night. He removed it before he threw her into the river."

Victoria laughed. "You must not blame Elwin for taking the necklace. I removed it from Miss Risby when we left her in the alley. One could hardly allow such a valuable piece of jewelry to go into the river. I had planned to have the stones reset in the modern style, of course."

"I understand why you and Hastings murdered Fiona Risby, but why did you arrange to disappear and come back as the proprietor of a brothel? Bit of a comedown, wasn't it?"

In less time than it takes for a viper to

strike, Victoria's beautiful features were transformed into a mask of rage.

"Are you mad?" she rasped. "Do you think I *wanted* this? I *loved* him. Do you hear me? Elwin was the one man on earth I trusted. I thought we were two of a kind, meant for each other. I taught him everything he knows about manipulating money and the greed that consumes most people. *Everything*."

Louisa realized she was holding her breath. Victoria was on the brink of some inner precipice.

"What happened?" she asked gently.

"That was when the bastard concluded that he no longer needed me. I think that killing Fiona Risby gave him a sense of power. Having murdered once, he found it easy to do it again. He came for me a few days later when I was asleep. He used chloroform. I woke up too late to do more than put up a weak struggle. He held me down while he finished the job."

"But you lived."

"It was luck and fate that saved me that night. I was partially awake when I went into the water. I knew how to swim, and I was wearing a nightgown, not a dress and corset.

I was pulled from the river by some deranged man who had a hovel near the water's edge."

"What did you do?"

Victoria's mouth thinned, and her eyes tightened. "I survived. It is something I am very good at, Mrs. Bryce."

"Yes, I can see that."

"The man thought I was some sort of fey being that had been sent to him. He took excellent care of me. When I recovered, I made my plans."

"Why didn't you simply come forward and tell the authorities what had happened?"

Victoria gave a scornful laugh. "Surely you are not that naïve, Mrs. Bryce. I had no proof that Elwin had tried to kill me. You know as well as I do that the authorities are very quick to leap to the conclusion that any woman, wife or not, who lodges charges against a gentleman of Hastings's background is suffering from hysteria."

Memories of Lord Gavin's relentless assault on her nerves before the final attack sent another shiver through Louisa. She had known then that if she had gone to the authorities they would have considered her to be suffering from female hysteria.

"Yes," she said. "I know."

"At best I would have found myself locked away in an asylum. The other, far more likely possibility, of course, is that Elwin would have had another go at killing me."

"So you remained in hiding."

"And I formulated my vengeance."

"I'm surprised you didn't simply murder Hastings."

"I thought about it many times, but that would have been far too easy. I wanted him to suffer. I yearned for him to roast over a long fire. I needed him to see his destruction bearing down upon him slowly, inevitably."

"You murdered the former owner of Phoenix House, didn't you?"

Victoria's twisted features relaxed back into their customary beautiful alignment. "It was not difficult to get rid of her and assume control of this place."

"Where does a lady who moved in some of the best circles of the Polite World learn to operate a brothel?"

Victoria was coldly amused. "Why, Mrs. Bryce, can't you guess? I know the business because I was raised in it."

Louisa stared at her. "You were a prostitute?"

"My stepfather sold me to a brothel when I was twelve years old. I learned the business very well, indeed. By the time I was eighteen, I was running the place. I met Elwin Hastings when I was twenty-two. He was a client. We were married eight months later when I convinced him that I could make him rich. I kept my promise, but the bastard didn't keep his."

"You've been following me, spying on me for the past few days," Louisa said.

"I heard rumors that someone was making inquiries about Phoenix House among the women who go to Mrs. Woods's establishment in Swanton Lane. I thought it best to find out what was going on. Imagine my surprise when I discovered that you were a correspondent for the *Flying Intelligencer*."

Louisa did not know what to say. "You are an amazing woman, Victoria." She raised her eyes to the vaulted ceiling. "Where am I now? Inside your new brothel?"

"Yes. Welcome to Phoenix House. Let me assure you that the profits have increased quite dramatically since I took charge."

"I can't believe that you willingly returned to this world."

Victoria made a derisive little sound. "And I would have credited you with a more worldly view of the matter, Mrs. Bryce. The reality of the situation was that I required money in order to exact my revenge. In case it has escaped your notice, it is virtually impossible for a woman who lacks family connections or a wealthy husband to make her fortune in our so-called modern age."

"Was it difficult to lure Hastings to this place?"

"Not at all." Victoria smiled again. "I know his tastes better than anyone, after all. I told you, once you comprehend those things that a man desires above all else, you have him in your power."

"You're going to kill him, I assume?"

"Yes. Tonight, in fact. I hadn't planned to do it so soon. I wanted Elwin to suffer financially first. I have been working on my plans for months. The investment scheme he is so proud of is doomed, I'm afraid. He would have lost everything. Then he would have committed suicide, of course. After which I would have reappeared as the grieving widow. With the profits I have made from Phoenix House I would have been able to resume my rightful place in Society."

"You concocted the scheme?"

"Of course. I used Grantley to handle the details and to lead Elwin to it."

"When you no longer needed Grantley, you killed him."

Victoria shrugged. "I thought it best."

"What of Thurlow? Why did you murder him?"

"He discovered my identity here at Phoenix House. It turned out that one of the girls was servicing him on the side. He became suspicious from something she said and managed to get inside by coming here as a client. He snuck upstairs and spied on me. He caught a glimpse of me without my veil and recognized me instantly."

"What did he do?"

"The fool tried to blackmail me. He threatened to let Elwin know that I was alive."

"So you went to his lodgings, waited for him to come home one night, and shot him."

"Thurlow was exceedingly handsome, but I'm afraid he was not very bright."

"How will you kill Elwin Hastings?" Louisa asked.

"As I said, you and Stalbridge have forced me to move more quickly than I had intended." Victoria was clearly annoyed by that turn of events. "So tonight Elwin will suffer a heart attack while undergoing his weekly treatment here at Phoenix House."

"How do you plan to simulate a heart attack?"

"It is no great secret that a sufficient quantity of chloroform will cause the heart to fail."

"And then I go into the river, is that it?"

"I'm afraid so. You will leave a sorrowful note behind stating that you lost your heart to Mr. Stalbridge and that you recognized that the affair was doomed because of the difference in your stations. Women are always throwing themselves off bridges because of illicit love affairs. Amazing, isn't it?" Victoria shook her head. "I have never understood why anyone would die for love, but there you have it."

"Mr. Stalbridge will not believe it."

"My dear Mrs. Bryce. You really do not comprehend the nature of men. I told you, Stalbridge is only interested in you because he thinks you can help him bring down Hastings. Trust me, once he learns that Hastings is dead, he will be satisfied that his hunt is concluded. There is no reason why he would feel compelled to investigate your death. You are simply not important to him."

"I think you are the one who is in danger of misjudging Mr. Stalbridge. I agree that he is not in love with me, but I assure you he will nevertheless feel an obligation to question my sudden demise."

"You are deluded, Mrs. Bryce." Victoria paused. "Do you know, I regret the necessity of killing you."

"Do you really expect me to believe that?"

"It's true. Aside from your appallingly naïve views on the subject of Anthony Stalbridge, you are an interesting woman. I admire your accomplishments as a journalist. Under other circumstances, I would have enjoyed a closer acquaintanceship with you. I'm sure we would have much to discuss."

"I doubt it."

Victoria paid no attention. "Unfortunately, due to your journalistic endeavors, you have become a problem for me. It became clear that your inquiries were bringing you closer and closer to the truth. It was only a matter of time before you realized my true identity. Sadly, you are in the same situation as Fiona Risby. I'm afraid you know too much, Mrs. Bryce. I can hardly resume my place in Society after Hastings is gone and create new investment opportunities for the gentlemen of the Polite World if a correspondent for the *Flying Intelligencer* is aware that the grieving widow was a former brothel madam."

46

Marcus planted his hands on his hips and squinted upward, surveying the illuminated windows on the highest floor of Phoenix House.

"Are you certain she's in there?" he asked.

"No," Anthony said, "but it seems the most likely possibility. The truth is, I don't know where else to look."

They were standing in the alley behind the brothel. He and his father were dressed in sturdy, working-class clothing that had been purchased hastily from a shop in Oxford Street. Low-crowned hats were pulled down over their eyes. Behind them was a horse and cart. Night shrouded the scene.

He knew all too well that his plan, such as

it was, could only be called desperate, but he had been unable to think of any other approach to the problem and his intuition warned him that time was running out. He could not allow himself to dwell on the possibility that Louisa might already be dead; that way lay madness.

"Odds are they would not keep a prisoner on the ground floor," he said. "It would be too obvious. Roberta Woods told me that the brothel was built on the foundation of an ancient monastery and that there are some old basement rooms underground. Once the commotion begins, I'll start there."

"I'll work from the top floor down," Marcus said.

"We will meet in the kitchens."

Marcus looked at him. "What are we going to do if we don't find her?"

"I do not intend to come out empty-handed," Anthony said evenly. "At the very least I will bring Madam Phoenix or Quinby with me. I suspect that either one of them can tell me the truth."

Marcus raised his bushy brows. "Provided he or she will talk to you."

Anthony flexed the fingers of his left hand. "One of them will talk."

Marcus scrutinized him for a moment and then exhaled deeply. "Very well. I am ready to do my part whenever you give the word."

"Now," Anthony said.

Marcus reached into the back of the cart and rummaged around under the tarp. He withdrew a basket that contained four bottles bearing the labels of a very expensive brandy. Without another word, he started toward the tradesmen's entrance of the brothel.

Anthony watched the door open. A harried-looking woman appeared.

"I've got the brandy Madam Phoenix ordered for her special guests tonight," Marcus said, doing a rather good job of assuming a working-class accent.

The woman frowned. "No one told me anything about a brandy delivery."

Marcus shrugged. "If ye don't want the brandy, it's none of my affair. My employer said he'd bill Madam Phoenix for these bottles at the end of the month. Maybe she won't even notice that she paid for brandy she never received."

The woman hesitated and then widened the door. "Very well. Take the brandy into the reception room. Beth will likely know what to do with it." Marcus disappeared inside the house.

Anthony looked at his watch. He did not have long to wait for the first signs of smoke to come, drifting from a partially open window on the top floor. Screams and shouts of alarm went up almost immediately.

"Fire." The cry came from somewhere inside the brothel.

Although the smoke was difficult to make out in the darkness, Anthony knew that it would soon fill the hallways inside the house, creating panic.

A short time later people began pouring out of the kitchen door into the alley, cooks and their apron-draped assistants appearing first. They were followed by three maids in skimpy uniforms. They all milled about, talking loudly and gazing up at the plumes of smoke now billowing from the top-floor windows.

"Someone should send for the fire brigade," the cook declared.

"Madam Phoenix won't want her guests embarrassed," a buxom maid said urgently. "There are some very important gentlemen inside."

"I doubt if she wants the house to burn

down around her ears either," someone snapped.

"I'm sure she'll be out herself soon enough," the maid said. "We should let her decide what to do."

Smoke appeared at another window. More screams echoed in the night.

Anthony went toward the tradesmen's entrance. No one looked at him or questioned him when he entered the building.

Roberta Woods had drawn a rough floor plan of the establishment based on a description given by a woman known only as Daisy. He had studied it earlier, trying to think the way a kidnapper would think.

The most obvious place to conceal a prisoner was the ancient basement. According to the young woman who had recently left her position in the brothel, Madam Phoenix had forbidden the staff to go down into the basement unless specifically ordered to do so.

He went along a hall, searching for the door that opened onto the basement stairs. A familiar-looking, middle-aged man rushed past him, red-faced and nervous. His open shirt and unknotted tie flapping wildly. Anthony ducked his head and angled his face toward the wall, but there was no need to be concerned that the Earl of Pembray would recognize him. Pembray was clearly intent only on escape.

From what Anthony had heard about the formidable Lady Pembray, that seemed wise. That grand dame would be extremely displeased if a mention of her husband's name in conjunction with a fire in a notorious brothel appeared in the papers.

Two more partially clad men and three women in filmy, near-transparent gowns fled past Anthony. None of them paid him any attention.

He found the door to the basement precisely where Daisy had indicated. It was locked, as she had warned. He took out his set of lock picks and went to work.

47

Faint, muffled shouts of alarm brought Louisa to her feet. She went to the door of the cell and gripped the iron bars. Boots sounded on the stone stairs.

Quinby, wearing his overcoat, came out of the darkness of the stairwell. In the flaring lantern light she could see that his features were set in grim, determined lines.

He had a large, old-fashioned iron key ring in one hand. In his other hand he gripped a revolver.

"What is it?" she asked. "What's happening?"

"A fire has broken out somewhere upstairs. We can't risk having the fire brigade find your body here. There would be too many questions. You're coming with me.

You're going into the river now instead of later."

He shoved the key into the lock of the cell and twisted. The ancient door opened reluctantly, grating and grinding on its hinges.

A glimmer of anticipation sparked to life within Louisa. A fire meant chaos and confusion. Perhaps she would have an opportunity to attract attention or even escape.

The door swung open. Quinby shoved the gun into the pocket of his coat and reached into the cell. His hand closed around Louisa's upper arm.

"Hurry," he ordered, yanking her arm. "There is no time to waste."

"I trust you do not expect me to run in this gown," she said. "It is quite impossible. Everyone knows that if you force a woman to move too quickly, her legs become tangled in her skirts."

"If you go down I will drag you," he vowed. "The choice is yours. Do not even think of screaming. No one will hear you."

So much for her puny threat. The only thing she could do was go with him and wait for an opportunity. She reached down, caught fistfuls of her skirts in both hands and lifted them up to her knees.

Quinby's hand tightened painfully around her arm. He jerked her forward. Her spirits plummeted when she realized he intended to take her out through the door in the wall of the outer chamber, not up the staircase. Her intuition told her that was probably not a good thing.

Quinby yanked her across the outer chamber and shoved one of the iron keys into the old lock that secured the door. The door opened slowly, revealing a stone tunnel. Louisa heard small, skittering sounds. Rats, she thought. A stomach-churning stench wafted out of the darkness.

"Surely you do not intend to go in there without the lantern," she said.

Quinby paused, torn. He uttered a foul oath and tossed the heavy key ring down onto the floor. Maintaining his grip on Louisa's arm, he went back to the table to collect the lantern. He was reaching for it when Anthony's voice rang out from the stairwell.

"Release her, Quinby."

Quinby reacted immediately. He wrapped an arm around Louisa's throat and simultaneously whirled to confront Anthony.

Louisa's back was pressed tightly against

Quinby's chest. He was using her as a human shield. She realized that he had taken out his revolver. The barrel of the gun was not pointed at Anthony. It was aimed at her temple.

She looked at Anthony. He stood at the entrance of the stairwell garbed in heavy boots and rough clothing. He, too, held a gun.

"Stay back," Quinby gritted, "or I'll put a bullet through her head. I swear, I will."

"Let her go, Quinby, and I will not stop you from leaving through that tunnel," Anthony said quietly.

"She comes with me," Quinby said. "Drop the gun now or she's a dead woman."

"You don't need her," Anthony said, moving toward the wooden table. "Whatever you were involved in here is finished. You're free to go."

"Stop right there," Quinby's voice vibrated with an unstable-sounding fury, "or I'll splatter her brains against that wall."

"Very well." Anthony stopped beside the table.

"Drop the gun on the floor and kick it away from you," Quinby ordered.

"She'll only slow you down," Anthony said

gently, "and you need to run for your life, because Clement Corvus knows that you have been serving two masters lately. He is not pleased."

"Damn you, Stalbridge." Quinby's face darkened with rage. "I am my own master."

"Unfortunately for you, Corvus doesn't view it quite that way," Anthony said, "and I doubt that Madam Phoenix does, either. They both see you as a servant, Quinby. Nothing more."

"I'm not anyone's damned servant," Quinby shot back. "My father was a gentleman, you son of a bitch. I may have been born in the gutter, but my bloodlines are better than Clement Corvus's and every bit as good as yours. Just because my father never saw fit to marry my mother doesn't change a damn thing."

"How long have you been Madam Phoenix's lover?"

"Long enough," Quinby said, triumphant. "She's going to marry me."

"Why the devil would you want to marry a whorehouse madam?" Anthony asked, sounding only mildly curious.

"Madam Phoenix is Victoria Hastings," Louisa said.

Anthony raised his brows. "I see."

Quinby smiled coldly. "I'm marrying up, Stalbridge. I know Society will never accept me, but it will accept my children and grandchildren."

"I wouldn't count on Victoria Hastings keeping her promise, if I were you," Louisa cautioned him, "and she certainly doesn't strike me as the maternal type."

Quinby smirked. "She loves me. She needs me. She'll marry me."

"You don't really believe that, do you?" Anthony asked. "If so, then you're a fool."

"They say a gentleman bleeds just as easily as a bastard," Quinby pointed the gun at Anthony. "Let's see if that's true."

Louisa heard the frightening rasp of metal on metal. Quinby had cocked the revolver. He must have realized that Anthony would never fire as long as she was in the way.

Horror crackled through her. It was all happening too fast. She did the only thing she could think of. She lurched backward.

Quinby had been concentrating all of his attention on Anthony. The sudden shift in weight caught him off guard. Reflexively he tightened his grip on Louisa's throat, choking her. At the same time he took a couple of quick steps, struggling to keep his balance and readjust his aim, but Louisa's weight, combined with the voluminous skirts of her gown proved too much. Quinby went down, dragging Louisa with him. Pain smashed through her when her shoulder struck the unyielding stone.

The revolver roared, deafening her. She dimly heard the ring of a bullet on stone.

Anthony moved in swiftly. He lashed out with one booted foot, kicking the gun out of Quinby's hand. The weapon skidded across the floor.

Quinby grunted and released Louisa to seize Anthony's ankle with both hands. He twisted violently. Anthony went down, sprawling on top of Quinby.

Louisa rolled out of the way. She heard dull, sickening thuds as fists smashed into flesh.

She lurched to her feet and started toward the nearest gun. More footsteps echoed from inside the stone stairwell. She realized she was unlikely to reach the gun in time. Even if she somehow managed to get to it she was not at all sure how to fire it.

She altered course, scooped up the iron key ring that Quinby had dropped on the floor, and dashed toward the stairwell. She pressed her back flat against the stone wall on one side.

The skirts of a black gown and the toe of a fashionable black kid boot appeared at the opening of the stairwell. Victoria paused at the foot of the steps and looked at the two men locked in mortal combat. A small derringer glinted in her black gloved hand.

She took in what was happening immediately and just as quickly dismissed Anthony and Quinby. She turned toward the half-open cell door.

"Come out, Mrs. Bryce. The house is on fire. We must leave at once." She cocked the derringer and aimed it at the entrance of the cell. "Did you hear me? Come out at once. Surely you do not wish to roast to death down here."

When there was no response from the interior of the cell, Victoria moved out of the stairwell and started forward.

Louisa came away from the wall in a desperate rush, swinging the heavy key ring with all of her strength.

At the last instant Victoria sensed movement behind her and started to turn, but it was too late. The iron ring struck her head just above her right ear. She fell to one knee, shrieking in pain. Blood flowed down the side of her head, but she did not collapse. Her eyes wild with rage, she started to turn the barrel of the derringer toward Louisa.

Unable to think of anything else to do, Louisa struck her a second time. Victoria sprawled on the stone floor. This time she did not move.

Just like Lord Gavin.

Louisa whirled around. Both men were still fighting furiously. As she watched, Quinby produced a knife. She ran toward the pair, but Anthony, evidently aware of the new danger, broke free and rolled away from Quinby.

Quinby got to his feet and charged, blade raised to strike. Anthony's hand closed around the grip of one of the revolvers. He aimed, cocked the gun, and fired. Quinby jerked violently, spinning backward. He came up hard against the wall. The knife fell to the floor.

"Bastard," Quinby stared at Anthony, raw hatred etched in every line of his face. "You ruined everything. *Everything*."

He gripped his injured shoulder with his

other hand, swung around, and stumbled away into the darkness of the tunnel.

The room went very quiet. Louisa went to Anthony.

"Are you all right?" Anthony asked. The heat of battle still burned in his eyes.

"Yes," she whispered. "You?"

"Yes." He got to his feet and looked at Victoria.

Louisa followed his gaze. Blood matted Victoria's blond hair and pooled on the stone. Again the image of Lord Gavin, bloodied and dead, rose up before her, roiling her stomach. She gasped for breath. She could not be sick, she told herself. Not yet.

"Is she dead?" she managed.

"I don't know."

Anthony crossed the room and crouched beside Victoria.

"She's alive," he announced. "You didn't kill her."

Louisa's stomach calmed miraculously. She breathed deeply. "What about Quinby?"

"He's Clement Corvus's problem now."

Anthony tore a strip of fabric off one of Victoria's petticoats and used it to secure her wrists. He repeated the procedure with her ankles.

Yet another set of footsteps echoed on the stairs, heavy boots this time. Louisa flinched and whirled around to face the opening. Anthony raised the nose of the revolver.

Marcus Stalbridge appeared. He smiled broadly when he saw Louisa. "Ah, I see you found her. Shall we be off, then? The police and the fire brigade will be along soon. It would be best if no one noticed our Mrs. Bryce emerging from a brothel." He winked at Louisa. "Not that we couldn't handle the problem if it arose, of course."

"My cloak," Louisa said. "It's in the cell."

Anthony disappeared into the small chamber. When he emerged he had her cloak in his hand. He secured it around her shoulders, covering her from throat to toe. He adjusted the hood so that it concealed her features.

"Come along, love," he said gently. "It's past time to leave this place. I think there has been enough excitement around here, even for an intrepid journalist such as you."

Love? A figure of speech, she told herself, hurrying up the stairs behind Marcus. There was no time to dwell on the tiny endearment.

When they emerged into an empty hall, Louisa saw a strangely odorless thick white smoke drifting eerily through the air.

"I don't see any flames," she said.

"That's because there aren't any," Marcus chuckled. "The managers of the Olympia Theater don't want real smoke, you see, so I had to go about things somewhat differently."

"I don't understand," Louisa said.

"I'll explain later."

"Take her to the carriage," Anthony said. "I want to look around Madam Phoenix's private rooms before the authorities arrive."

He paused long enough to kiss Louisa hard on the mouth. Before she could question him he disappeared up a staircase.

"Come along, my dear," Marcus said.

He ushered her out through the tradesmen's entrance into a night filled with chaos and shouts. None of the people standing around outside in the alley paid them any heed.

A few minutes later Marcus guided her into a nearby lane. A closed carriage stood waiting. The door of the vehicle flew open. A woman garbed in a cloak leaned out.

"Hurry," Clarice said, her voice bright with excitement. "We must get you away from here, Mrs. Bryce. We do not want to take the chance of you being seen by a member of the press. You know how those correspondents are when it comes to a story of sensation and scandal involving those who move in Society."

Stunned, Louisa got into the vehicle. When she sat down she realized that Clarice was not alone. Georgiana Stalbridge sat on the seat across from her. She, too, was draped head to foot in a concealing cloak.

"Thank goodness you are safe," Georgiana said. "We have been so worried about you. Are you hurt in any way, dear?"

"No," Louisa managed. "I'm fine. Truly."

"That is a relief," Georgiana said. She looked at Marcus as he climbed into the cab. "Where is Anthony?"

"Stayed behind to have a look around before the police arrive," Marcus said. "We'll meet up with him at home."

The carriage rumbled forward.

Louisa looked at Clarice, Georgiana, and Marcus in turn. In the dark confines of the unlit carriage it was difficult to see the expressions on their faces.

"I don't understand," she said to Georgiana. "Why are you and Clarice here? I know Anthony must have felt an obligation to rescue me, and it was very kind of Mr. Stalbridge to assist him, but surely there was no need for you and Clarice to take the risk of being seen this close to Phoenix House."

Georgiana reached out and patted her hand. "Clarice and I refused to remain at home while Anthony's future wife was in peril. In this family we stand together."

Anthony's future wife. Appalled, Louisa stared at her. "I fear there has been some terrible misunderstanding."

"I'm sure that's not the case," Clarice said, relentlessly cheerful. "Now, we will go straight home and relax with a glass of brandy while we wait for Anthony."

48

The door at the end of the hall was closed. All the rest had been flung open by the fleeing staff and clients. Anthony paused on the landing. He had intended to go straight to the top floor where Madam Phoenix's private quarters were located, but the closed door caught his attention.

He went down the hall and stopped. Gripping his revolver, he stood to one side and tried the knob. It turned easily in his hand. He pushed the door open with the toe of his boot, keeping himself out of the line of fire just in case. No shots rang out from inside the room. Instead there was a frantic rustling sound, followed by an urgent moan.

He looked into the room. The walls were

covered in black velvet. A glass-fronted case containing a variety of whips and unusual devices stood in the corner.

Elwin Hastings lay face up on a bed covered in black silk, his wrists and ankles shackled to the bedposts. He was naked. There was a gag in his mouth. When he saw Anthony relief replaced the fear in his eyes. He moaned again.

Anthony walked to the bed and untied the gag.

Elwin sputtered furiously. “Stalbridge. Didn’t recognize you in those clothes. What the devil are you—? Never mind. I thought *she* was coming back to murder me. Untie me. Hurry, man. I heard the shouts. The house is on fire.”

“The house is not on fire,” Anthony said.

“Either way, I’ve got to get out of here. You don’t understand. She intends to kill me.” He paused, finally noticing the revolver in Anthony’s hand. “What’s that for?”

“I met up with your first wife and her lover a short time ago. Things became somewhat complicated.”

Elwin’s eyes widened. “You saw Victoria?”

“Yes. The police will be here soon. There’s a Mr. Fowler from Scotland Yard who will want to talk to you. You remember Fowler, don't you? He was the man who investigated the suicides of both your wife and Fiona Risby. I understand you were not helpful the last time he tried to interview you."

Elwin's eyes widened. "See here, I don't know what you're talking about, Stalbridge, but you have to help me."

"Why should I do that?"

"Bloody hell, man, how can you ask me such a thing? We're both gentlemen. Gentlemen have an obligation to protect each other."

"Oddly enough I feel no such obligation toward you, Hastings. My sole responsibility in this matter is to obtain justice for the murder of Fiona Risby, and that is what I intend to do."

"You're mad if you think you can prove that I killed her."

Anthony reached into the pocket of his rough jacket and withdrew the black velvet pouch. He opened the pouch and let the Risby necklace spill across his palm. The stones sparked with fire in the light of the wall sconce.

Elwin's mouth sagged in shock. "So I was right. You were the thief."

"Let's just say I retrieved it for safekeeping. I have been waiting for the right moment for it to be discovered. Tonight is a good time, I think."

He dropped the necklace back into the pouch and drew the gold cord taut.

"What are you doing?" Elwin shrieked.

Anthony did not answer. He walked across the room to where Elwin's black evening coat hung from a wall hook and dropped the necklace into the pocket.

"That won't work, you bastard," Elwin shrieked. "I'll tell the police you put it there. It will be the word of one gentleman against another. They won't investigate further."

Anthony smiled. "Fortunately we will also have the verdict of the sensation press. Consider how this will look in the newspapers and penny dreadfuls. Your supposedly deceased wife is the operator of one of the most notorious brothels in London, and you were discovered naked on the premises. In addition, you have a financial interest in this house of ill repute."

"Shut your damn mouth."

"I think we can anticipate that when the police arrive, the first Mrs. Hastings will be only too pleased to accuse you of attempting to murder her last year. Add to that the discovery of a dead woman's necklace in your possession and I think we can safely conclude that the weight of public opinion will be on the side of justice."

"Son of a bitch. You can't do this."

"Even if the police do not charge you with murder, you are a ruined man, Hastings. At the very least you will be forced to retire to the country. No club will have you. No hostess in the Polite World will send you an invitation. And now that you're a proven bigamist, your new bride will be free to leave you. I'm told her grandfather is an excellent businessman who took steps to protect his granddaughter's financial interests before the marriage. When Lilly departs, she will take her inheritance with her."

"How dare you threaten me?" Elwin's features contorted. "You should be dead. Do you hear me? You should have died the night I followed you home from your club and very nearly put a bullet in you. If it hadn't been for the fog and that trick you played with your coat—"

Harold Fowler appeared in the doorway, a constable behind him.

"Mr. Crawford, make a note of Mr. Hastings's comments concerning his attempt to murder Mr. Stalbridge," Fowler said.

"Yes, sir." The constable took a pad and pencil out of his pocket.

Anthony looked at Fowler. "I see you got my message."

"Yes. We waited until we saw your father depart the premises with a young woman concealed in a cloak, as you suggested."

Elwin stared at Fowler, desperation in his eyes. "I can explain everything."

"There will be plenty of time for explanations, sir." Fowler looked at Anthony. "I will want to speak with you, also."

"Of course." Anthony inclined his head. "I am at your disposal, Detective. You might also be interested in talking to the late Victoria Hastings. The last time I saw her she was unconscious in the basement. With luck she will still be there."

Fowler's bushy brows jumped. "I see. This affair sounds a bit tangled."

"No," Anthony said. "It is really very simple. You were right, Detective. When it comes to murder, there are only a small number of motives. Greed, revenge, the need to conceal a secret, and madness. In this case, there seems to have been something of all four."

49

Two days later Louisa sat at her desk reading the report in the *Flying Intelligencer*. As usual, Mr. Spraggett had chosen a headline designed to capture attention from a wide assortment of readers. Several headlines, actually. Spraggett was never one to use a single sensational headline when two or three would suffice.

A CASE OF MURDER MOST FOUL IN HIGH SOCIETY. BLOODY EVENTS IN A BROTHEL. MEMBERS OF POLITE WORLD ARRESTED. MISSING WIFE RETURNS FROM A WATERY GRAVE.

by

I. M. Phantom

The Polite World was shocked to learn that Mr. Elwin Hastings was recently arrested for the murder last year of a young lady named Fiona Risby and the attempted murder of his first wife, Victoria Hastings, long presumed a suicide.

The authorities discovered Mr. Hastings in a brothel. A valuable necklace that belonged to the murder victim, Miss Risby, was in his possession at the time. His wife, Victoria Hastings, long believed to be dead, was also on the premises.

Readers will be further astonished to hear that the first Mrs. Hastings is the proprietor of the notorious establishment on Swanton Lane known as Phoenix House. Her husband is an investor in the brothel and a frequent patron.

When found, Mrs. Hastings was dazed and bleeding from a head wound. She was described as suffering from an acute case of shattered nerves. Confronted with the sight of her husband she flew into a violent rage. She accused Mr. Hastings of having attempted to murder her by throwing her into the river. She attributed her survival to the merest chance.

In addition to Mr. and Mrs. Hastings, another man believed to be involved in criminal activities was reported to have been at the scene. He disappeared before the authorities were able to question him. . . .

Someone banged the front door knocker. Louisa put down the paper and listened to Mrs. Galt go toward the front hall. The door opened. She heard Anthony's voice.

"Never mind, Mrs. Galt. I'll show myself into the study."

"I'll just go and put on the kettle," Mrs. Galt said.

Louisa listened to Anthony's footsteps coming toward the study. The familiar little thrill of longing and anticipation tightened her insides. He walked into the cozy room, a package under one arm.

"Good day, my love," he said, crossing to the desk. "I trust I am not interrupting?"

"No," she said quickly. "I was just reading the morning paper."

"The excellent report by I. M. Phantom on recent murderous events in High Society, I presume."

"Yes, as a matter of fact."

"Shocking stuff." He put the package down on the desk, reached down, and hauled her up out of the chair. "Absolutely shocking, but it does make for riveting reading."

He kissed her soundly. She put her arms around his neck and softened against him. When he eventually released her and looked down at her, a familiar, exciting heat in his eyes, she blushed and pushed her spectacles higher on her nose.

"Have you any more news from Mr. Fowler?" she asked, sitting down again very quickly.

He exhaled deeply and lowered himself into one of the reading chairs. "This, it appears, is one of the great difficulties that arises when one engages in an illicit liaison with a member of the press."

She beetled her brows. "What are you talking about?"

He spread his hands. "The latest news, rumors, and gossip always come first."

"Hah. You know very well that is not true. You kissed me before I even had a chance to ask you about your meeting with Fowler."

He raised a finger. "Only because I have learned to move quickly where you are concerned."

She folded her hands on the desk. "Well?"

"I doubt that matters will conclude as neatly as one might hope, but there will, nevertheless, be some justice." Anthony stretched out his legs and relaxed into his chair. "There is no word of Quinby's fate as yet, but Fowler is not overly concerned. He told me in private that he has every expectation that Clement Corvus will take care of Quinby."

She swallowed hard. "Oh, dear."

Anthony's eyes hardened. "Do not trouble yourself with sympathy for Quinby. He kidnapped you without a qualm. He knew full well that Victoria Hastings planned to dump you in the river. In fact, she was going to use him to carry out the deed."

"Yes, I suppose that is true. Still, one cannot help but feel a certain pity for the man. How dreadful it must have been for him to live all his life cut off from the privileges that would have been his if his father had acknowledged him."

"You are entirely too softhearted, my dear. As for Quinby, he should have known better than to cross Clement Corvus."

"What about Mr. and Mrs. Hastings?"

"According to Fowler they are still hurling

accusations and offering proof of the other's guilt. Meanwhile, the second Mrs. Hastings is said to have moved back into the home of her parents and will shortly be filing for divorce on the grounds that her husband is a bigamist. Her grandfather has cut off all funds to Hastings. In order to dampen the scandal, there are rumors that Lilly will soon be wed quietly and quickly to a young man of her choosing. I suspect that he is the very same young man she brought up to her bedroom the night I opened Hastings's safe."

"I'm happy for her. What of Hastings?"

"According to the gossip in the clubs Hastings will soon be destitute. The investment consortium has fallen apart, naturally. Even if he does not hang, he will be utterly destroyed, barred forever from the only world that matters to him."

"Society."

"Yes."

"I wonder what will become of Victoria Hastings."

"Fowler is convinced that Victoria is quite mad and will likely be sent to an asylum."

"Hmm."

Anthony raised his brows. "You doubt that she is insane?"

"I wouldn't put it past her to act the part if she thought it would save her neck."

"I assure you, if she is sane, being locked up in an asylum would prove a fate worse than death."

She shivered. "I do not doubt that."

"There is one more thing to report," Anthony said quietly.

"Yes?"

"I encountered Julian Easton at my club this afternoon."

"Oh, dear. How did it go?"

"He was very subdued. He actually apologized to me. You were right. It seems he blamed himself for Fiona's death. She had gone out into the gardens to meet him the night she died. They had arranged a rendezvous, but she ran afoul of Mr. and Mrs. Hastings before Easton went to join her. When he arrived at the appointed spot, she was not there."

Louisa sighed. "How very tragic."

"That is all I have to report," Anthony said. "I suggest we turn to another, more interesting topic of conversation."

She looked at him curiously. "What is that?"

"You and me, of course."

She blinked, froze, and then hastily removed her glasses. "I have been meaning to speak to you about that very subject." She plucked a handkerchief out of her pocket and hurriedly began to polish an imaginary smudge on one lens. "I fear your family has gained an unfortunate and entirely inaccurate impression of how matters stand between us."

He steepled his fingers. "They think that I am going to marry you."

"Yes, I know." She adjusted her spectacles on her nose and looked at him. "I tried to correct the misunderstanding the other night on the way home from Phoenix House, but no one would listen to me."

He smiled. "In time you will discover that once they have fixed upon a notion, the members of my family tend to be decidedly stubborn. It is, I fear, a family trait."

She sat forward uneasily. "It is really very awkward, Anthony. I do not feel right allowing them to believe a blatant lie."

"Then we must make it a reality."

"What on earth are you talking about?"

He pushed himself up out of the chair, came around the desk, and pulled her to her feet for the second time.

"Anthony, please, you cannot solve this problem by kissing me."

"I love you, Louisa."

She felt as though the ground had fallen away beneath her feet. "What?"

"I love you," he said again, softer this time. "Is that so hard to believe?"

She fought for breath. "But we have been acquainted for such a short period of time, and there are things you do not know that would surely change your opinion of me."

"I sincerely doubt that." He captured her hands and kissed her fingers. "I'll allow you the time you need to fall in love with me. All I ask in return is that you promise me that you will give my offer of marriage serious consideration."

"I don't need time," she said before stopping to think. "I am already in love with you. It is just that marriage is out of the question."

He released her hands, picked up the package on the desk, and handed it to her. Uncertain, not knowing what else to do, she began to untie the string with trembling fingers.

"I know that you are quite taken with the notion of an illicit affair," he said, watching her unwrap the brown paper. "I admit I cannot guarantee that marriage will offer as much in the way of excitement, but in my opinion it would be a far more comfortable proposition."

"No, really, it wouldn't be," she said, fighting back tears. "Not at all."

"Just think, we would be able to share a warm bed every night rather than having to make do with gardening benches and stolen moments. We could have breakfast together every morning while we savor your latest brilliant reports in the *Flying Intelligencer*."

"Anthony, stop. You don't know what you are saying." The package was open now. She stared, dumbfounded, at the leather-bound copy of Milton's *Paradise Lost*. "Oh, *Anthony*."

"Don't worry," he said. "I didn't steal it out of Pepper's safe. He agreed to give it up. It was merely a matter of finding the right price."

She touched the mottled calf binding with her fingertips. Tears burned in her eyes. "I don't know what to say."

"Say that you will marry me, my love. I predict that all of the difficulties you perceive concerning my family will cease to exist."

She felt a great tightness inside, squeezing her heart. The tears escaped and trickled down her cheeks. She jerked off her spectacles, grabbed a handkerchief, and began blotting madly. She had known this moment was coming, she reminded herself. It was just that she had hoped for more time.

"This is the thing with an illicit affair." She lowered the handkerchief and looked at him through her tears. "It cannot end happily."

"There are exceptions to every rule."

"This is not one of the occasions when the rule may be broken."

"Why not?"

"There is a secret in my past that is so dreadful that, if you knew it, you would be horrified. I cannot allow you to bring me into your family. It would not be right."

He looked amused. "I cannot imagine you having a secret of that magnitude."

She should not say a word, she thought. If she had any common sense, any sense of self-preservation, she would keep her mouth closed and send him away. But she loved him. She could not let him leave on a lie.

"Anthony, I am the woman who murdered Lord Gavin."

"Yes, I know," he said very casually. "Now, about my proposal—"

She stared at him, her mouth open. Perhaps she had not heard him correctly, she thought.

"You *know*?" she managed.

"I reasoned it out a few days ago." His eyes gleamed with amused impatience. "Now if we might return to the subject of my proposal?"

"You don't understand." She retreated behind her chair, clutching the back so fiercely that her fingernails bit into the wood. "Anthony, I bashed his head in with a poker. He was a very important gentleman."

"No one seems to miss him very much. I have the impression that, although they have never met you, Gavin's widow and the other members of his family are privately grateful to you. To say nothing of the female shopkeepers who were saved by your action. Gavin was an evil man."

"That is beside the p-point. I am wanted for *murder*. If the police ever find me I will be hanged. Think of the scandal."

"You are not wanted for murder. As far as the police are concerned, you are a suicide, remember."

"But—"

"The case is closed. No one is searching for you, my love."

"What if someday someone recognizes me?"

"Highly unlikely, but in the event that were to happen, my family and I would gladly perjure ourselves on the matter of your identity. When you marry me, you will become a Stalbridge. We protect our own." He smiled his slow, knowing smile. "Trust me when I tell you that no one will even think of contradicting us."

"Quite correct," Emma declared from the doorway. "Louisa, dear, I believe I told you back at the start of this affair that the Stalbridges might choose to ignore Society for the most part, but Society cannot ignore them. The family has the sort of money and connections that make people invulnerable. You will be safe with them."

Louisa looked at her. The tiny, smoldering spark of hope that she had kept locked tightly away deep inside suddenly flared into a bright flame.

"Oh, Emma," she said, "do you really think so?"

Emma chuckled. "I trust that after you are

a married lady, you will find time to help me finish my memoirs, of course. We were just getting to the thrilling bits, if you will recall."

"Of course," Louisa said, smiling mistily.

Smiling, Emma winked and disappeared down the hall.

Louisa turned back to Anthony. "Are you certain this is what you want?"

"It is not merely a question of wanting." He gathered her close. "I need you, my love. You and I are two halves of a whole. I believe we were made for each other."

Joy flooded through her. She wrapped her arms very tightly around his neck.

"Yes," she said simply.

"Welcome to the family."

His mouth closed over hers. She abandoned herself to a love that she knew would carry them both safely into the future.